"Turn the focus of our attention upon Howard Alan Treesong, his wry exploits and the incredible virtuosity of his organizational genius. He is possibly the greatest rogue of all (if, in that perfervid ambience surrounding the Demon Princes, such niceties of comparison carry any shred of conviction). Certainly he is attended by the most extravagant contradictions. His cruelty is wanton and horrid, so that his occasional magnanimities are cast into sharp relief. Judged by the elaborate methodicity of his programs, he would seem passionless, absolutely logical. Against a different perspective, he is seen to be volatile and as frivolous as a circus clown. He is a mystery, and his ultimate purposes cannot even be guessed."

THE
BOOK
OF
DREAMS

Jack Vance

DAW BOOKS, INC.
DONALD A. WOLLHEIM, PUBLISHER
1633 Broadway, New York, N.Y. 10019

The Five Books of the Demon Princes:

STAR KING

THE KILLING MACHINE

THE PALACE OF LOVE

THE FACE

THE BOOK OF DREAMS

FIRST PRINTING, JANUARY 1981

1 2 3 4 5 6 7 8 9

 DAW TRADEMARK REGISTERED
U.S. PAT. OFF. MARCA
REGISTRADA. HECHO EN U.S.A.

PRINTED IN U.S.A.

Chapter 1

From *The Book of Dreams*:

Raise your eyes, stranger, to that age-worn rampart which confronts all else: there stand the paladins, stern, grave, serene. Each is one, each is all.

At the center is Immir of the graces. He controls certain sleights of magic; he is master of ploys and plots and awful surprises. He is Immir the unpredictable and claims no single color.

At Immir's right hand stands Jeha Rais, who is tall in majesty and whose color is black. He is sagacious and always first to notice a far event, for which he construes eventualities. Then he points his finger, to direct the gaze of the other paladins. He is without qualm and advocates decisiveness. Sometimes he is known as "Jeha the Inexorable." He wears a black garment, supple and close as his skin, a black cape and a black morion, fixed at the crest with an orb of crystal in a silver star-blaze.

5

At Immir's left hand stands Loris Hohenger, whose color is the red of new blood. He is the feroce, impulsive and reckless, and ever reluctant to leave the slaying grounds, though of all the paladins he can be most generous. He lusts after fair women and they deny him at great risk to their dignity. Should they make complaint or give chiding, his redress is even more fulsome. When finally he leaves the bed their voices are still and they look longingly after him.

Green Mewness stands beside Loris Hohenger. Expert in skills is Mewness. He can fling a bridge or topple a tower; he is patient, cunning and if the road is closed to right and left, he finds a way between. His memory is exact; he never forgets a face or a name and he knows the ways of a hundred worlds. Soft men of wealth think him ingenuous in his dealings, to their ultimate consternation.

Yellow Spangleway is wry, astonishing and ignores every precedent. He is antic and droll, and able in the acting of roles. All the paladins, save only one, laugh to see his capers; when the time is appropriate all—save only one—dance to his musics, for Spangleway can elicit sweet sounds from a dangling pig, should he so choose to turn his skills. Never think to match Spangleway jape for jape, since his knife is even keener than his wit. In battle, the enemy cries out: "Where is the laggard Spangleway?" or: "Aha! The coward Spangleway takes to his heels!" only to have him on their necks from a new direction, or in some shocking guise.

Beside Jeha Rais stands gentle Rhune Fader the Blue. In battle, though he is dauntless and first to succor a hard-pressed paladin, he is also first to urge mercy and forbearance. He is slim, tall, clear of feature and handsome as the summer sunrise; he is skilled in the arts and graces and sensitive to beauty in all things, especially the beauty of shy maidens upon whom he casts a glamour. Alas, in the battle counsels the voice of Rhune Fader carries little weight.

Beside blue Rhune, and a little apart, stands eerie white Eia Panice, whose hair, eyes, long teeth and skin are white. He wears a full casque of white metal and little of his face can be seen: a high-bridged hooked nose, a harsh chin, gleaming eyes. In the counsels he speaks, for the most part, either "yea" or "nay," but more often than not his word decides the issue, for he seems to know the ways of Destiny. Alone among the paladins he is unmoved by the droll contrivances of Spangleway. Indeed, on those occasions when his grim smile is seen, then is the time for all who can to depart and never look back lest they discover the limpid gaze of Eia Panice fixed into their own.

So then, stranger, go your way. When at last you make your homecoming, wherever it may be among the sparkling worlds, bring report of those who stand brooding yonder.

From *The Demon Princes*—Caril Carphen:

. . . we turn the focus of our attention upon Howard Alan Treesong, his wry exploits and the incredible virtuosity of his organizational genius. At the outset let me, in all candor, confess my awe and perplexity: I do not know where to start. He is possibly the greatest rogue of all (if, in that perfervid ambience surrounding the Demon Princes, such niceties of comparison carry any shred of conviction). Certainly he is attended by the most extravagant contradictions. His cruelty is wanton and horrid, so that his occasional magnanimities are cast into sharp relief. Judged by the elaborate methodicity of his programs, he would seem passionless, absolutely logical. Against a different perspective, he is seen to be volatile and as frivolous as a circus clown. He is a mystery, and his ultimate purposes cannot even be guessed.

Howard Alan Treesong! A name of magic, instilling dread and wonder! What, precisely, is known of him? The few nodes of fact are made ambiguous by a luminous dust of rumor. He is declared to be the most solitary person alive; by other reports he is the ultimate ruler of all criminals. His person is said to be unremarkable: tall, thin, with well-shaped if gaunt features and pale gray eyes of exceptional clarity. His expression is often described as droll and his manner vivacious. He dresses most usually in ordinary garments, without ostentation. By all accounts he enjoys the company of beautiful women, none of whom seems to profit from the association either spiritually or financially. To the contrary, the romances of which anything is known all end tragically, if not worse.

The events which finally brought Howard Alan Treesong to bay ran an erratic course—twisting, forking, making confused halts and unlikely linkages—a consequence of the mystery in which Treesong shrouded himself. According to the few extant descriptions, Treesong stood rather taller than ordinary with a luminous gaze, a broad forehead, a narrow jaw and chin and a foxy rueful mouth. His manner was usually described as gracious with a metallic undertone. Almost every account mentioned a "curious field of suppressed energy," or "unpredictable extravagance," and in one case the word "madness" was used.

Treesong's obsession with mystery extended far. No photographs, representations or likenesses were known to exist, on or off the public record. His origins were unknown; his private life was as secret as the far end of the universe; he regularly disappeared from public notice for years on end.

Treesong's zone of operations encompassed the Oikumene; he rarely ventured Beyond. He was known to have used for himself the title "Lord of the Overmen."[1]

Gersen picked up the track of Howard Alan Treesong essentially by dint of abstract reasoning—pure deduction in the

---

[1] The allusion is perhaps explained in a paragraph from an interview in which Treesong stated: "Men exploit animals to their needs and think nothing of the process. So-called 'criminals' exploit the ordinary ruck to their needs in the same manner, employing equal morality; hence criminals are properly to be known as 'Overmen.'"

classical pattern—using information supplied by one Walter Koedelin, an old-time associate and now a Senior Officer of the IPCC.[1]

The two met in Sailmaker Beach, to the north of Avente, the metropolis of Alphanor, first among Rigel's Concourse of Worlds.

Chancy's Tea House at the top of Sailmaker Beach overlooked a thousand small houses, shops, taverns and a small plaza used by a hundred kinds of people. Each structure was washed a different color: pale blue, pale green, lavender, pink, white, yellow, and each cast a stark black shadow to the crackling Rigel-glare. Far below could be seen a small crescent of beach. Beyond, the Thaumaturge Ocean, soft dark blue, extended to the horizon, where floated pinnacles of white cumulus.

At a table shaded under a dense growth of dark-green mematis sat Kirth Gersen and Walter Koedelin, a sandy-haired, pink-skinned man somewhat more stocky than Gersen, with a short-nosed, big-jawed face. Like Gersen, he wore spaceman's dark blue and gray, the costume for folk who hoped to avoid attention. The two men drank rum punch and discussed Howard Alan Treesong.

In the company of Gersen, Koedelin spoke without restraint. "What is he up to now? That's a real puzzle. Ten years ago he called himself 'Lord of the Overmen.' "

"In effect, 'King of Thieves.' "

"Exactly. He licensed every illicit act from Far Edge to Tangiers Old Socco. One time Howard walked a back street in Bugtown, on Arcturus IV, and a mugger jumped out. Howard asked: "Are you registered with the Organization?'

" 'No, I am not.'

" 'Then you'll not get a cent from me, and I'm also turning you in for a fink.' "

Koedelin drained his goblet of rum punch and looked up at the dark-green foliage from which depended strips of pink blossoms. "Splendid place for microphones. I wonder who is listening to us."

[1] Interworld Police Coordinating Company: originally a small bureau, collecting and collating information for the various police organizations of the Oikumene, gradually expanding, diversifying and undertaking special missions, at last to become the largest and most efficient law-enforcement agency of the human universe.

"No one, according to Chancy."

"It's hard to be certain nowadays. Still, the Organization isn't all that strong around here."

Gersen raised his hand. "Two more of the same . . . So, Treesong is no longer Lord of the Overmen?"

"Hardly that. But he gave up detail work to sub-lords quite some time ago. Howard only looks in from time to time and runs his eye over the books."

"Benign fellow. So what is he up to now?"

Koedelin hesitated, calculating his response, then made a fatalistic gesture and drew himself forward. "There's no harm in telling you, although if the story gets wide circulation we'll be embarrassed. It may not even be true." Koedelin looked right and left. "Don't let it go any farther."

"Certainly not."

"IPCC administration is rather loose—that you know. There is a board of directors and a presiding officer, who is now Artur Sanchero. Five years ago his confidential aide died in an accident. A close friend recommended a man named Jethro Cope for the job, and after the usual background check Cope was hired. Cope proved very efficient, so much so that Sanchero had less and less work to do. And now began a strange process. The directors began to die—by disease, by accidents, by murder and suicide.

"Sanchero, or more accurately Jethro Cope, recommended new directors who were thereupon voted into office. Jethro Cope always handled the vote and counted the ballots. He put seven men into the IPCC Board of Directors and needed only six more to achieve a voting majority. He probably would have gotten them had not one of the new directors, who called himself Bemus Carlisle, encountered an agent who recognized him to be Sean McMurtree of Dublin, Ireland, a high-class blackmailer.

"To make a long story short, McMurtree was quietly expunged, but not before he mentioned a name. Can you guess the name he mentioned?"

"Howard Alan Treesong."

"Quite right. The agents went looking for Jethro Cope, but he was gone and never returned."

"What of the other six new directors?"

"Three were killed. One disappeared. Two are still there. They have no record; they claim innocence, and the other directors won't vote them out."

"Very noble, very corrupt or very frightened."

"Take your choice."

"To be Lord of the Overmen and Chief of the IPCC—both and at the same time—that's like a beautiful dream, no matter which side you're on."

"Alas, indeed. Treesong is a sly devil. I'd still like to carve up his liver."

"What of photographs?"

"Not one to be found."

"So we still don't know what he looks like."

Koedelin gave a grunt of derisive disgust. "People who dealt with Cope remember long blond curls, a bushy blond beard and mustache, an affable manner."

"And since then?"

"Nothing. He's gone invisible. I forgot to mention that three years ago an order went down to the library to void all material pertaining to Howard Alan Treesong, on the grounds of inaccuracy. This was done; now there's very little on tap."

"All successful criminals at some time return to their home towns.[1] Somewhere out there Treesong was born and raised. Dozens of people must know him well. Maybe after three years new material has come in."

Koedelin, leaning back in his chair, ruminated a minute or two. "I'll check over my sources and let you know. Where are you staying?"

"At the Miramonte."

"I'll look in about noon, if that's convenient."

On the following day, at precisely noon, Koedelin joined Gersen in the observation lounge of the Hotel Miramonte, on Avente's esplanade.

"It's as I suspected," said Koedelin. "There's not a clue as to his origin. He first appears on Earth as a young man, robbing banks, swindling, extorting, committing murders, organizing a strike force. He's competent at his trade. Still, it's amazing how little we know of him as a human being."

Declaring himself pressed for time, Koedelin left shortly after. Gersen went out to walk on the esplanade, which for ten miles paralleled Avente's superb white sand beach.

---

[1] Gersen here referred to the book *The Criminal Mentality*, by Michael Diaz.

The harms Treesong had inflicted upon Gersen were now over twenty years old, when Treesong had only just attained his full criminal stature.[1] Since this time his exploits had become ever more grand . . . A wraith of insight flickered through Gersen's mind. He went to lean on the balustrade.

Three years ago Howard Treesong had dropped from sight. This man, who had tried to be, simultaneously, King of Thieves and Chief Director of the IPCC, was certainly not now idle; somewhere he plotted new schemes, more monumental than any before.

Gersen considered a number of possibilities: deeds of cruel magnificence, ingenious abominations, shame visited upon all humanity. None of Gersen's constructions seemed plausible or worth the effort. Evidently, so Gersen told himself, he lacked Treesong's gorgeous, if wild and savage, imagination.

Gersen returned to the hotel and telephoned Koedelin. "Regarding the subject of our conversation, it would seem that something dramatic should be coming to the surface about now. What would answer that description?"

Koedelin could cite nothing definite. "I've been thinking along similar lines—waiting, so to speak, for the other shoe to drop. No matter how hard I listen, I hear only utter silence . . ."

The three populated Vegan worlds were Aloysius, Boniface and Cuthbert. During the first Explosion of Peoples, they had been settled by religious orders, each more fanatic than the next. In the Sixteenth Century of the Space Age the sacerdotal flavor yet lingered, especially in the public buildings, converted from temples during the "Bum's Rush."

Pontefract on Aloysius, a small city notable mainly for its incessant mist, by some trick of fate had become an important publishing and financial center. In the oldest section of town, dominating St. Paidrigh Square, stood the ancient Bramville Tower, now headquarters of *Cosmopolis*, a journal of news, photographs and short essays. The magazine's contents, sometimes profound, often dramatic or even senti-

---

[1] At Mount Pleasant, an agricultural settlement on the world Providence, a consortium of five master criminals—the so-called "Demon Princes"—had dropped out of the sky to enslave the entire population, killing those who resisted. Kirth Gersen and his grandfather escaped and thereafter in Gersen's life there had been room for little but preparation for retaliation and revenge.

mental, were directed to the attention of intelligent middle-class folk across the entire Oikumene.

Kirth Gersen, through the manipulations of his financial adviser, Jehan Addels, had acquired a controlling interest in Cosmopolis; in the guise of Henry Lucas, Special Writer, he used the offices as a convenient headquarters.

Arriving in Pontefract, Gersen went to dine with Jehan Addels at his splendid old mansion in Ballyholt Woods, to the north of Pontefract. During the course of the dinner Gersen mentioned Howard Alan Treesong and his peculiar invisibility.

Addels instantly became tense. "You speak, naturally, only from casual interest."

"Well—not altogether. Treesong is a scoundrel and a criminal. His influence reaches everywhere. Tonight burglars might break into this house and steal your Memlings and Van Tasals, not to mention your Rhodosi rugs. Objects of this quality might go directly to Treesong himself."

Addels nodded somberly. "It is a serious matter. Tomorrow I will submit a memorandum to the IPCC."

"It can do no harm."

Addels glanced suspiciously toward Gersen. "I hope that you take no personal interest in this man?"

"Probably to no great extent."

Addels uttered an angry ejaculation under his breath. "Please do not include me in these investigations, not to the slightest degree!"

"My dear Addels, how can I avoid coming to you for advice?"

"My advice in this case is succinct and definite: let the IPCC do their job!"

"That is excellent advice, and I will assist them in this work as much as possible, and I know that you will do the same."

"Of course, of course," muttered Addels.

At the *Cosmopolis* library Gersen searched for files for references to Howard Alan Treesong. These were voluminous and told Gersen little that he did not know and nothing of the topics which were his chief concern: Treesong's place of origin and his present whereabouts. Treesong's pictorial likeness was conspicuous by its absence.

At the end of a disappointing day, Gersen, for no reason

other than simple persistence, riffled through the contents of a
file labeled: *Miscellaneous: Sort*, discovering nothing to his
immediate interest. A pair of trays marked "File" and "Dis-
card" caught his eye. The "File" basket was empty; the "Dis-
card" basket contained a large photograph, almost a foot
square, depicting a party at a banquet. Five men and two
women were seated; three men stood somewhat to the back.
At the top someone had scrawled: *H. A. Treesong is here.*

With numb fingers and a prickling skin, Gersen stood staring at the photograph. The camera had recorded a full circle,
from the center of a circular table, so that each member of
the group was depicted from the front, though none was
looking directly at the camera and perhaps no one was aware
that the picture was being made.

In front of each place stood a curious little semaphore, displaying three colored flags, and each place had been served a
silver dish containing three purple-brown objects about four
inches high: apparently the first course to the banquet.

Aside from the scrawled notation across the top, the photograph lacked further legend except for a number printed at
the bottom: 972.

The diners were of various age and race. All projected a
confident air, the effluvium of position and wealth. They were
identified by place cards, unfortunately turned away from the
camera.

Gersen looked from face to face. Which might be Howard
Alan Treesong? His description, fitted more or less loosely,
perhaps four of the men . . . A file clerk approached, a
jaunty young man wearing a pink and black striped shirt with
baggy brown trousers in the local style. He gave Gersen a
glance which, while respectful and affable, also contained the
shadow of a sneer. Around the *Cosmopolis* offices Gersen
was regarded as a man of questionable talents. "Rummaging
through the garbage, eh, Mr. Lucas?"

"Everything is grist for the mill," said Gersen. "This photograph which you were about to throw away—where did it
come from?"

"Oh, that affair? It arrived a few days ago from our Starport office. The Watch and Ward Society at its annual glut,
or something similar. Is it useful?"

"Probably not. Still, it's rather quaint. I wonder who H. A.
Treesong might be?"

"One of the local gobboons. The ladies are absolute frumps. Nothing here for our readers, that I assure you."

But Gersen was not to be discouraged. "From our Starport office, you say. Which Starport, incidentally? There must be at least a dozen."

"Starport on New Concept, Marhab Six." Again the flavor, almost undetectable, of condescension. Around *Cosmopolis* no one understood how Henry Lucas had gained his job, and even less how he held it.

Gersen was indifferent to the opinions of his colleagues. "How did the photograph get here?"

"It came in the last mailbag. When you're finished, throw it back in the trash, there's a good fellow."

The clerk went off about his duties. Gersen took the photograph to his private cubicle and called the personnel office. "Who is our representative at Starport, New Concept?"

"Starport is a zone headquarters, Mr. Lucas. The zonal superintendent is Ailett Mayneth."

Gersen discovered upon looking into *Universal Travel Routes* that direct connections between Aloysius and New Concept were nonexistent. If he wished to travel by passenger packet he must expect three stopovers at junction points and three changes of ship, with consequent delay.

Gersen closed *Universal Travel Routes* and replaced it on the shelf. He rode out to the spaceport and boarded his *Fantamic Flitterwing*, a serviceable and competent space cruiser, with a small cargo hatch and accommodations for four: a vessel larger than his *Distis Pharaon* and more comfortable than his *Armintor Starship*.

In the late afternoon of the day on which he had discovered the photograph, Gersen departed Aloysius, with Vega hanging cold in the sky on his port quarter. He gave appropriate coordinates to the automatic pilot and was whisked off toward the middle reaches of Aries.

During the voyage he studied the photograph at length, and slowly the banqueters took on a static two-dimensional life. Of each male face Gersen asked: "Are you Howard Alan Treesong?"

Some answered indignantly in the negative, others held their own counsel and several seemed to return a brooding challenge, as if to say, "Who I am, what I am—interfere at your own peril!" And one of the men Gersen examined ever

more often, with increasing fascination. Glossy chestnut hair
framed a philosopher's forehead; hollow cheeks were joined
to a gaunt jaw by a sheath of corded muscle; the thin tender
mouth was twisted as if in recollection of a mischievous joke.
A face strong and subtle, sensitive but not soft; the face of a
man capable of anything: so thought Gersen.

Ahead glowed Marhab; off to the right wheeled the planet
New Concept and its three moons.

Chapter 2

From *Civilized Ideas and Civilized Worlds,* by
Michael Yeaton:

> As the student reflects upon the development of the
> newly settled worlds he notices an odd and ironic
> circumstance, recurring so often as to seem the rule
> rather than the exception. The ideal program by
> which each new society is shaped, by some as yet
> unenunciated law of conduct, begins to generate its
> own obverse, or opposite, impulse, which in due
> course overcomes the original scheme. Human per-
> versity? The malice of Fate? Who can say? In any
> event, the examples are everywhere. For instance,
> consider the world New Concept . . .

Arriving at New Concept, Gersen located Starport and
landed at the space terminal. A sleek car riding a monorail
shuttled him the five miles between the terminal and Starport;
Gersen was thereby afforded a view of the New Concept
fells, here overgrown with heavy, dark-blue turf. In the
middle-distance the dark blue gave way to maroon, and beyond, purple. A mile from the terminal the monorail skirted

an area of moldering white ruins, originally an intricate almost complex of structures in the Neo-Palladian style: almost
a small city. Now the columns were chipped, broken or toppled; the roofs had partly collapsed; the once-noble entabla-
tures were stained and streaked. At first Gersen thought the
ruins uninhabited; then he noticed movement here and there,
and a moment later saw a pack of gangling animals loping
across a once-grand plaza.

The ruins fell behind; the monorail entered Starport and
came to a halt at a central depot. At an information booth
Gersen learned the location of the local *Cosmopolis* office—a
suite in a ten-story tower a few hundred yards from the
depot—and set out on foot.

Starport seemed a city of no distinction whatever. Except
for the lemon-yellow sunlight and the flavor of the atmosphere[1], Gersen might have fancied himself in an outer
suburb of Avente on Alphanor, or any of a dozen quasi-mod-
ern cities of the Oikumene. The folk wore garments similar
to those of Avente and the cities of Earth. Whatever "new
concept" had originally been intended, was now no longer in
evidence.

Presenting himself at the *Cosmopolis* office, Gersen approached a counter behind which stood an elderly man with
a keen birdlike cast of countenance, bright blue eyes and a
crest of gleaming silver hair. He was thin, taut and carried
himself with a stern and exact posture, somewhat at odds
with his garments, which were casual: a bright blue turtle-
neck shirt of lightweight velour, soft beige trousers and sandals of dark suede. He addressed Gersen in a formally terse
voice: "Sir, your requirements?"

"I am Henry Lucas, from the Pontefract office," said Gersen. "I would like a few moments with Mr. Ailett Mayneth.

"I am he." Mayneth looked Gersen up and down. "Henry
Lucas? I have visited the Pontefract office and I can't remember hearing your name."

"I carry the title 'Special Writer,' " said Gersen. "I am in

---

[1] Experienced space travelers become sensitive to the variations of a
breathable atmosphere, discriminating between inert gases, oxygen levels
and complex organic exudations peculiar to every individual planet. In
the air of New Concept Gersen noted a musty peppery redolence, evidently rising from the blanket of turf which cloaked the fells.

fact a general-purpose roustabout; whenever there's a job too dull or uncomfortable for anyone else I'm assigned to it."

"I see," said Mayneth. "And what is so dull and uncomfortable here at Starport?"

Gersen displayed the photograph. Mayneth's manner changed at once. "Aha! So that is how the wind blows. I wondered what would happen. So you are here to investigate?"

"That is correct."

"Hmm. Perhaps we can make ourselves more comfortable. Shall we go up to my apartments?"

"Whatever you like."

Mayneth conducted Gersen to an elevator, which lifted them high to the top floor. Mayneth slid open his door with easy indifference. Gersen entered what he recognized to be the domicile of a connoisseur of judgment and, so it would seem, wealth. In all directions he saw beautiful objects, of various eras and as many places of origin. Many of the objects Gersen could not precisely identify: for instance, a pair of earthenware lamps glazed a dull gray-brown. Possibly ancient Japan? In regard to the rugs he knew somewhat more, by reason of an episode in his early career. He recognized a pair of Persian rugs, glowing serenely in the sunlight, a Qūli-Qūn, a Mersilin from the Adar Mountains of Copus, several small gypsy rugs probably from the Khajar Realm of Copus. A satinwood case displayed a group of Myrmidense porcelains and casual arrangement of precious old books, bound in shagreen and hornskin.

"Since I have nothing better to do with myself," said Mayneth half-apologetically, "I try to surround myself with beautiful objects . . . I fancy myself as a shrewd trader and I enjoy nothing more than to prowl the country bazaars of some remote little world. This is my so-called study. The books in here are exclusively from Earth. A miscellaneity, I fear. But sit down, if you will." Mayneth touched a gong with his fingers, producing a plangent tone. A servant appeared, a young girl of odd appearance, thin and supple as an eel, with a shock of curly white hair, slate-colored eyes in a small pinched face, a small pointed chin and a thin lavender mouth. She wore a short white smock and moved with a curious lithe sliding gait. She watched the two men attentively, without any trace of self-consciousness. Gersen could not identify her racial stock. He thought that, if she were not feebleminded, her rationality was surely of a most unconventional sort.

Mayneth hissed between his teeth, touched the palm of his hand, held up two fingers; the girl backed away. She returned almost immediately with a tray, two goblets and two squat bottles. Mayneth took the tray; the girl was gone in a whisk of fluttering smock. Mayneth poured. "Our excellent Swallowtail beer." He served Gersen and picked up the photograph which Gersen had placed on the table. "A very strange affair, this." He seated himself, drank a dainty swallow of beer. "A woman came into the office, and I inquired her business. She stated that she had valuable information which she wished to sell, for a substantial sum. I seated her in my office and looked her over. Her age was about thirty, a bit run to seed; just short of blowsy. Still, she seemed respectable, if in a dreadful state of nerves. She was not a local woman; she stated that she had come directly from the space terminal and that she desperately needed money. I looked her over once again, even more carefully, but I could not place her background." Mayneth took a meditative sip of beer. "I noticed one or two small points, still—" he shrugged, as if to dismiss the problem. "She began to work up her proposition. She said she was able to offer an item not only unique, but highly valuable. Not her exact words, of course. She was so nervous as occasionally to be incoherent.

"I tried a bit of whimsy—rather sophomoric, really—'You've brought me the directions to a cache of hidden treasure!'

"She became angry. 'Are you interested in what I have to offer? Mind you, I want a fair price!'

"I told her that I'd have to see to judge. Immediately she became cautious. It was quite a game. Finally I said, 'Madam, show me what you want to sell, otherwise I can't spare any more time.'

"She asked me in a whisper, 'Have you heard the name Howard Alan Treesong?'

" 'Yes, indeed. He is Lord of the Overmen.'

" 'Don't say that! Although it's true . . . I have his photograph. How much will you pay?'

" 'Let's see the picture.'

" 'No, first you must make me a good offer!'

"I'm afraid I became a bit lofty. I asked her, 'How can I buy something until I've seen it? Is it a good likeness?'

" 'Indeed, it's a good likeness. He is about to commit a mass murder.'

"I said nothing and finally she produced her merchandise." Mayneth indicated the photograph. "I examined it carefully, then said, 'This is admittedly an excellent picture, but which is Treesong?'

" 'I don't know.'

" 'Then how do you know he's here?'

" 'I was told so, by someone who knew.'

" 'He might have been joking.'

" 'If so, he was killed for his joke.'

" 'Really?'

" 'Yes, really.'

" 'May I inquire your name?'

" 'Is it important? In any event, I won't give my proper name.'

" 'Where was the picture taken?'

" 'If I told you that, other people would suffer.'

" 'Madam, be practical. Consider the circumstances. You show me a photograph; one of the persons, so you say, is Treesong, but you can't point him out to me.'

" 'That proves I'm honest! I could easily point to anyone in the photograph; that man there, for instance.'

" 'Quite true. As a matter of fact, he's my own choice. All this aside, and conceding your own honesty, how do you know that the picture is authentic? Someone has been killed. Who? Why? Without these details the picture has no particular value.'

"She thought a moment or two. 'Can you guarantee confidentiality?'

" 'Naturally.'

" 'One of Treesong's aides is named Ervin Umps. His brother was a waiter at the restaurant where the picture was taken. He was also my husband. He spoke with Ervin, and discovered that Treesong was at the banquet. The photograph is automatic, for the restaurant's records, and my husband took this copy which he left in my keeping. He told me only that Treesong was in the picture, and that Treesong had murdered everyone else present. The picture, he said, was very valuable. That same night he was killed. I knew that I'd be killed too, whether I gave up the photograph or not, so I left at once, and that's all I can tell you.'

" 'And where is the restaurant?'

" 'I won't tell you. It's not necessary that you know.'

" 'I don't understand. You've told me everything else.'

" 'I have my reasons.'

"That's where the matter rested. We had a long discussion about the price. I explained that I was taking her on trust; that the photograph might not be worth a hollow dinket. She agreed but wouldn't yield an inch. I asked, 'How much do you expect me to pay?'

" 'I want ten thousand SVU!'

" 'That is out of the question.'

" 'What will you offer?'

"I told her I'd risk a hundred SVU of company money and fifty of my own. She started to leave. I decided that I couldn't risk letting the picture get away. I offered another hundred and guaranteed that if *Cosmopolis* used the picture she'd be paid two hundred more.

"She caved in. 'Give me the money. I must leave here at once. The picture is dangerous.' I paid her off. She ran from the office and I saw no more of her." Mayneth filled the goblets with Swallowtail beer.

"What happened next?"

Mayneth cleared his throat. "I inspected the picture with great care. I found few clues. The clothes are diverse, and suggest a variety of backgrounds. They seem to be light-weight, which indicates a warm local climate. Those little semaphores—I can't understand them. Nor can I identify the food."

"You hinted at one or two details in connection with the woman."

"So I did. Her clothes were standard, but she spoke with an accent. Around the stars you'll hear a thousand accents and dialects. It is one of my interests, and my ear is fairly keen. I listened carefully but I could not place her particular speech."

"What else?"

"At the corner of each eye she wore a little blue shell. I've seen these before but I can't connect them with any particular place."

"She never mentioned her name?"

Mayneth pulled on his chin. "Her husband's brother is Ervin Umps. She might or might not use the same name."

"Possible. Not necessarily probable."

"My own feeling. Still, I became curious and decided to

make inquiry at the spaceport, and I did so, although the trail by then was three days cold. I checked passenger lists, asked questions and to make a long story short, I found no 'Umps.' She apparently called herself Lamar Medrano. She transferred aboard the ship at a place called Virgo Junction, out on Spica Six. I checked the place in *Universal Travel Routes*. A dozen different liners touch there. I doubt if she could be traced away from Virgo Junction."

"When did she leave New Concept?"

"Possibly never."

"How so?"

"She booked passage to Altair aboard a Green Star packet, the *Samarthi Tone,* departing three days after her consultation with me. I checked around the hotels and found her at Hotel Diomedes, where she had stayed two nights. They remembered her well, because she skipped without settling the bill."

"Odd."

"Sinister. I made further inquiries at the Diomedes, and learned that she had become acquainted with a certain Emmaus Schahar, a salesman in sports equipment from Krokinole. One morning Schahar paid his account and departed. Lamar Medrano went out the previous night and never returned."

Gersen gave a dour grunt. "As to this Schahar, what of him?"

"A saturnine fellow, soft spoken, with plenty of money."

"He's not now in Starport?"

"He left on the *Gacy Wonder*. One of its way-points is Virgo Junction."

"Interesting."

"Very much so. I don't know whether or not to be reassured."

"You wonder why Mr. Schahar did not call on you?"

"Exactly."

"Schahar might conceivably be an innocent salesman with only ordinary interest in Lamar Medrano."

"Conceivably."

"Assuming that Schahar is not an innocent salesman, Lamar Medrano might have become fearful and fled, so that she is now hiding somewhere on New Concept."

"Possible."

"Thirdly, Lamar might have died before revealing where she had taken the photograph. Perhaps she convinced Schahar that she had put it in the mails."

"Possibly she had two copies of the photograph. Schahar considered his mission accomplished and is now pleased and happy."

Gersen laughed. "When Howard Treesong reads *Cosmopolis*, sometime in the near future, Schahar will not be so pleased and happy." He brought out stylus and paper, wrote a few words, placed five hundred-SVU certificates on top, pushed all over to Mayneth. "Your expenses and a bonus for constructive activity. Please sign the receipt so that I may recover from the Central Bursar."

"Thank you," said Mayneth. "That is indeed generous of you. Perhaps you will take lunch with me?"

"It will be a pleasure."

Mayneth touched the gong; the white-haired girl appeared. Mayneth made signs and sounds; the girl slid off, easy and soft of motion. She returned with beer, paused to watch as Mayneth filled the goblets, peering in fascination at the foam, her lavender-pink tongue darting in and out of her mouth.

"She loves beer," said Mayneth. "I won't allow her any because she becomes agitated. She'll lick all the foam from our empty goblets."

Daringly the girl hooked some foam from Gersen's goblet with her finger and put it into her mouth. Mayneth slapped her hand without any great vehemence, and the girl jumped back like a playful cat. She hissed at Mayneth, who hissed in return and gestured; the girl departed. Passing through the door she bent to arrange a tassel in the fringe of the rug; Gersen noted that under the short white smock she was nude.

Mayneth sighed and swallowed half a goblet of beer. "I'll be leaving New Concept before long. I came originally as a collector. The original settlers created many beautiful things: hand-illuminated books, grotesques, musical instruments. Notice that gong yonder; it sounds to no more than a touch. The best are supposed to sing even before they are touched. Some were exported, but the best were hidden in caves. I've explored a thousand miles of caverns, acquisitiveness conquering my claustrophobia."

Gersen leaned back in his chair and looked out across the fells. The sun stood at its zenith; across a low ridge in the middle distance ran a pack of animals, gamboling and curvetting on long lank legs. They darted into the shadow of a thicket and began to graze on a growth of green sedge.

"This doesn't seem a particularly well-managed world," said Gersen. "I don't see any signs of agriculture."

"It's been tried. The Feeks destroy crops before they get started. There's no keeping them out short of poison, which is prohibited."

"I noticed classical ruins out near the space terminal. Do they represent the 'New Concept'?"

"The original structures were the gift of a mad philanthropist. The 'New Concept' was dietary—vegetarianism, in fact, mixed with stints of meditation. For fifty years the settlers lived in the great Temple of Organic Unity. They ate alfalfa sprouts, collard greens and odd bits of the native vegetation. The human form is wonderfully adaptable. The settlers adapted all too well, and there they are now—" Mayneth pointed to the pack of lank animals grazing under the thicket "—having their lunch . . . Speaking of lunch, we might as well go examine our own."

Mayneth led Gersen to his dining room, where the white-haired girl stood staring in fascination at the table. Sudden illumination came to Gersen. "She is one of the locals?"

Mayneth nodded. "They leave babies lying out on the fells. Simple forgetfulness, I suspect. Sometimes they're brought in and trained, more or less successfully. Catch them early and they'll learn to stay clean and walk on their hind legs. Tiptoe here is a clever one; she serves beer and fluffs pillows and generally behaves herself."

"She's fascinating to look at," said Gersen. "Is she, well, affectionate?"

"It's been tried, with generally poor results," said Mayneth. "Are you curious? Touch her."

"Where?"

"Well, to begin with, on the shoulder."

Gersen approached the girl, who swayed back, blinking her great gray eyes. Gersen reached out his hand; she uttered a quick spitting hiss and sprang back, mouth open to show sharp teeth, hands raised and fingers curled.

Gersen drew back, grinning. "I see what you mean. Her opinions are very definite."

"Some of the local lads use a bait of molasses candy," said Mayneth. "They like it and while they're eating they can't bite . . . Well, here's our lunch. She'll go away now, because she can't tolerate anything but lettuce and occasionally a bit of boiled carrot. Such is the dark side of vegetarianism."

Chapter 3

From *Life*, Volume I, by Unspiek, Baron Bodissey:

. . . I often reflect upon the word "morality," the most troublesome and confusing word of all.

There is no single or supreme morality; there are many, each defining the mode by which a system of entities optimally interacts.

The eminent entomologist Fabre, observing a mantis in the act of devouring its mate, exclaimed: "What an abominable custom!"

The ordinary man, during a day's time, may be obliged to act by the terms of a half-dozen different moralities. Some of these acts, appropriate at one moment, may the next moment be considered obscene or opprobrious in terms of another morality.

The person who, let us say, expects generosity from a bank, efficient flexibility from a government agency, open-mindedness from a religious institution will be disappointed. In each purview the notions represent immorality. The poor fool might as quickly discover love among the mantises.

Gersen, returning to Aloysius, landed at Dunes Spaceport a few miles south of Pontefract. The time was late on a dark purple-gray afternoon. Mist blowing in from Bottleglass Bay almost obscured the terminal buildings. Gersen bowed his head and walked to the depot across a boardway of weathered sea-wood.

He rode first by underground train, then by taxi to the mansion of Jehan Addels, his financial adviser and general business factotum, in Ballyholt Woods.

Addels greeted him with his usual air of sour disapproval, which Gersen believed to be a mask for esteem and possibly even affection, though this might be asking a bit too much from Addels, whose views of man and the universe were filtered through a lifetime of mistrustful cynicism. Addels looked the part, with a gaunt yellowish face, a tall thin forehead, a long thin nose with a tremulous tip. His hair was scanty and yellow-brown; his eyes a bland pale blue.

Gersen went to his usual room, bathed, dressed in garments left on a previous occasion. He dined with Addels and his numerous family in a grand dining room, at a table illuminated by candles. The tableware was antique silver and they ate off ancient Wedgewood.

After dinner the two men returned to Addels's *sampang*-paneled study and sat before a fire with coffee served from a silver coffeepot.

Gersen displayed the photograph, to Addel's consternation. "I had hoped that you were finished with this sort of thing."

"Not quite," said Gersen. "What do you think?"

Addels feigned stupidity. "Regarding what?"

"We want to identify Treesong and discover where he makes his headquarters."

"And then?"

"Perhaps we'll bring him to justice."

"Bah! And perhaps someone will get himself killed by being hung on a hook a mile in the air, which was what happened to poor Newton Flickery."

"A shame, that. Well, we must hope for the best."

"Therefore I hope that you will have nothing to do with this business. Here, let me throw the photograph into the fire."

Gersen ignored him, and for the hundredth time studied the photograph. "Which is Treesong? How can we identify him?"

Addels said crossly, "He's one of ten persons. The others must know him, or at least know themselves. Treesong can be identified by eliminating the others."

"First we must identify the others."

"Why not? Each must have many friends and acquaintances. But let us talk no more of this foolishness."

Gersen wandered the crooked old streets of Pontefract. He sat in small irregular squares, planted with boxwood and wallflowers. He idled along alleys smelling of age and wet stone; he took several meals at a restaurant suspended over Bottleglass Bay on rotten black pilings.

He saw little of Addels except at the stately dinners which Addels considered a basic element of civilized existence. Addels refused to discuss Gersen's preoccupation, and Gersen had only small interest in the highly profitable dealings by which Addels augmented Gersen's wealth.

On the fourth day Gersen settled upon a method to increase the leverage of his single tool to the utmost. For several years the *Cosmopolis* directorship had contemplated a companion magazine, to be known as *Extant*. Much of the preliminary work had been done. The new journal would rely heavily upon *Cosmopolis* production and distribution facilities, with an editorial policy intended to appeal to a livelier and less sedate readership than that of *Cosmopolis*.

Through a linkage of holding companies, Gersen owned *Cosmopolis* outright. Now he ordained the instant existence of *Extant*. Overnight it came into being. Copy long prepared entered printing machines, and *Extant* surged out through the *Cosmopolis* distribution adits to the far edges of the Oikumene.

To increase its impact on the market this first issue would be given away free. It featured a remarkable contest, certain to attract the attention of all its readers. A photograph on the cover depicted ten persons at a banquet. The caption read:

WHO ARE THESE FOLK?
NAME THEM CORRECTLY AND WIN 100,000
SVU!

The inside cover added qualifying details. Only the first three contestants to identify all the depicted faces would win prizes. Should no one name all persons correctly, then those three persons identifying the largest number of faces would receive the prize. Six additional rules stipulated the prizes to those who were first, or among the first, correctly to identify fewer than all the faces. Entries were to be mailed to: *Extant;* Corrib Place, 9-11; Pontefract, Aloysius (Vega VI). Such entries would be adjudicated by members of the *Extant* staff.

Wherever periodicals were sold *Extant* impinged on the eye, the more so for the prominent overprint on its cover: FREE.

At refuges on the frozen salt tundras of Irta; under the lime trees of Duptis Major; at halts along the cableways of the Midor Mountains; at kiosks along the grand boulevards of Paris and Oakland; on Alphanor, Chrysanthe, Olliphane and Krokinole, and every other world of the Rigel Concourse: *Extant.* In spaceports, barber shops, jails, hospitals, monasteries, bordellos, construction camps: *Extant.* Millions of eyes saw the faces, usually with only casual interest. Not a few studied the photograph with care, and even fascination, and took occasion to write letters to Contest Editor, *Extant.* Two persons especially, separated by light-years of space, saw the photograph with startled amazement. The first sat frowning through his window as he pondered the significance of the contest. The second, occasionally sounding a rather harsh chuckle, took pen in hand and addressed a letter to Contest Editor, *Extant.*

Gersen decided to move into town, closer to the *Extant* office. Addels recommended the Penwipers Hotel. "It is convenient to your office, and quite the best address in town, very respectable." His gaze lingered thoughtfully upon Gersen's costume. "In fact . . ."

"In fact what?"

"Nothing whatever. You will be made comfortable at Penwipers. They take good care of their guests. I will call to make arrangements; they seldom accept new clientele without favorable recommendation."

The façade of Penwipers Hotel, six stories of carved brownstone and fluted black iron, surmounted by a Flemish mansard roof of green copper tiles, overlooked Old Tara Square. An inconspicuous portal opened into first a foyer, then a reception hall, with the lounge to one side and the dining room to the other. Gersen registered at a counter of carved brown marble, supported by pilasters and corner columns of glossy black gabbro. The receptionists wore formal morning clothes of old-fashioned cut—how old-fashioned Gersen did not immediately appreciate. The style, in fact, had changed by not so much as a buttonhole since the hotel's opening eleven hundred years before. At the Penwipers, and in Pontefract generally, tradition yielded grudgingly, if at all, to novelty.

Gersen waited while the registration clerk quietly consulted the head porter, the two glancing at Gersen from time to time. The consultation ended; Gersen was conducted to his suite. The chief porter led the way, an assistant carried Gersen's small handbag, a third carried a velvet box. At the door the chief porter opened the box, withdrew a damask cloth scented with lavender, with which he briskly wiped the door handle, which he then twitched with thumb and forefinger. The door opened; Gersen entered a set of high-ceilinged rooms, furnished in a style of austere comfort, something short of luxury.

The porters moved swiftly around the room, adjusting the placement of furniture, wiping surfaces with their scented cloths, then departed, swiftly and quietly as if they had merged into the shadows. The chief porter said: "Sir, the valet will attend you at once to assist with your wardrobe. The water is already drawn for your bath." He bowed and prepared to leave.

"One moment," said Gersen. "Is there a key to the door?"

The chief porter smiled benignly. "Sir, you need not fear intrusion at Penwipers."

"Possibly not. But, for instance, suppose I were a jewel merchant carrying a parcel of gems, and a thief wished to rob me. He need merely saunter to my room, open the door and divest me of my wealth."

The chief porter, still smiling, shook his head. "Sir, such a terrible thing could never happen here. It would simply not be tolerated. Your valuables are quite safe."

"I don't carry any valuables," said Gersen. "I merely suggested a possibility."

"The inconceivable, sir, is rarely possible."

"I am totally reassured," said Gersen. "Thank you."

"Thank you, sir." He drew back as Gersen extended his hand. "The staff is adequately paid, sir. We prefer to accept no gratuities." He inclined his head crisply and departed.

Gersen bathed in a sunken tub carved, like the reception desk, from a block of brown marble. He emerged to find his belongings packed neatly into a bottom drawer of an ancient wardrobe. The valet, deeming his garments unsuitable, had laid out new: sedate dark brown trousers, a lavender and white striped shirt, a cravat of white linen crash, a knee-long coat of black twill, pinched at the shoulders, belled at the hips.

In rueful resignation Gersen dressed in the new garments. If nothing else, Jehan Addels would be pleased.

Gersen descended to the lobby and crossed to the main entrance. The chief porter stepped forward to intercept him. "A moment, sir, I will fetch your klapper." He tendered a large black velvet hat with a wide rolled brim, a coil of dark-green and a small stiff brush of black bristles. Gersen looked askance at the hat, and would have slipped past had not the doorman contrived to position himself between Gersen and the door. "You'll find the air a bit brisk, sir. It is our pleasure to assist you in the use of appropriate attire."

"That is kind of you," said Gersen.

"Thank you, sir. Allow me to arrange the hat. Just so . . . Afternoon wear will be laid out for your use at the stroke of the second gong. The weather portends a drifting wet mist, with showers later in the day."

In the foyer Gersen paused to glance at himself in the mirror. Who was this somber exemplar of Old Pontefract gentility who stared back at him? Never had he worn a disguise more deceptive.

Gersen wandered along the crabbed streets, under tall narrow-fronted buildings, across the ubiquitous small squares, each with its boxed beds of wallflowers, pansies, native bulrastia and St. Olaf's Toe. From time to time the mist parted to allow a shaft of Vega-light down to glisten on wet stone and infuse a sudden gush of color into the flowerbeds. At a public telephone he called Jehan Addels and arranged a meeting at the *Extant* office, at Addels's convenience.

"That will be in one hour's time," said Addels.

"I will be there."

Gersen turned into Corrib Place, a short street somewhat wider than ordinary and paved with slabs of polished granite, dovetailed each to each, and laid down long ago as an act of penance by the Estebanite monks.

Corrib Place occupied the oldest part of Pontefract Old Town. To one side the ancient Estebanite monastery had been converted into commercial suites; the structures opposite, built of age-darkened mace and ganthar wood, bound with brackets of black iron, stood tall and gaunt and compressed, often with upper-story bays overhanging the street.

With time to spare before his appointment with Addels, Gersen sauntered along Corrib Place, looking into shops, which here affected a special *éclat* and offered only goods of distinction and elegance: fancy pastries and imported sweetmeats; rare gems, pearls from the local rorqual, crystals won from dead stars; gloves, cravats, gaiters, kerchiefs; perfumes, philtres, magic Duhamel oil; bibelots, curios, portfolios of antique art: Giotto and Gostwane; William Snyder and William Blake; Mucha, Dulac, Lindsay; Rackham, Nielsen; Dürer, Doré, David Russell. Gersen paused ten minutes to watch a pair of puppets at a game of chess. The puppets were Maholibus and Cascadine, characters from the Comic Masque. Each had captured several pieces; each in turn, after deliberation, made his move. When one captured a piece, the other made gestures of rage and agitation. Maholibus made a move and spoke in a creaking voice; "Checkmate!" Cascadine cried out in anguish. He struck himself on the forehead and toppled backwards off his chair. A moment later he picked himself up; the two arranged the pieces and started a new game . . .

Gersen entered the shop, bought the chess-player puppets and ordered them delivered to Penwipers: one of the rare occasions of his life when he had encumbered himself with a trivial article.

Strolling along Corrib Place, Gersen found himself opposite the offices of Extant Publications. He paused by the window of the Horlogicon, to study a timepiece seemingly fashioned from puffs and swirls of mist, with spots of colored light designating the time. Interesting, but impractical, thought Gersen . . . Jehan Addels turned into Corrib Place and approached, placing his feet carefully one before the other. The time was several minutes early. He stopped beside Gersen to catch his breath and inspect the *Extant* offices. After an incurious sidelong glance, he ignored Gersen and continued peering toward the Extant offices.

Gersen spoke. "Sir, are you expecting someone?"

Addels swung around, stared in bemusement. "My dear fellow, I failed to recognize you!"

Gersen smiled a wintry smile. "The hotel has allowed me the use of these clothes. They feel that my ordinary attire is a bit too ordinary."

Addels spoke in a precise voice. "A person makes a statement about himself with his clothes. A genteel person wears genteel clothes to establish his status, and status, whether we like it or not, is a key factor in human interrelations."

Gersen said, "At the very least I am provided an excellent disguise."

Addels's voice rose a quick tone or two. "Why should you need a disguise."

"We are dealing, you and I, with a remarkable man. He is a ruthless murderer, but at the same time a paragon of gentility who could lodge without qualm at Penwipers Hotel."

Addels gave a glum grimace. "You surely don't expect him here?"

"I don't know what to expect. We are publishing his photograph, which he has been at great pains to conceal."

"Please do not use the word 'we' so loosely. But I agree that the contest will attract his attention."

"That is part of my plan. He will wonder who is interested in him and investigate."

Addels sniffed. "Or he might simply decide to destroy the entire building."

"I think not," said Gersen. "First, he will want to discover the facts."

"He will try to infiltrate your organization. It will be very difficult to forestall him."

"I won't even try. In fact, I'll make it easy."

"Risky business! What good can come of it?"

"His infiltration in effect becomes our infiltration. We will lure him close, then work to arrange a meeting. You will be the intermediary—"

"By no means! Never! Not in a million years!"

"I expect no danger until after he satisfies his curiosity."

Addels refused to be convinced. "That is like telling a staked-out goat that the tiger will not bite until after he sniffs around a bit."

"I wonder if the parallel is quite exact."

"Regardless, I do not intend to participate in this scheme. I have had my fill of scares and frights! My proper work lies elsewhere."

"Just as you say. We will make our plans accordingly."

Addels was not yet reassured. "When do you expect him to act?"

"As soon as he sees the photograph. He will then send someone here to investigate, or possibly he will arrive on the scene himself. We still have a few days to prepare."

"The lull before the storm," muttered Addels.

Gersen laughed. "Don't forget, we are laying the plans, not Treesong. Come along, I'll take you to lunch at Penwipers, if you think they'll allow you in the dining room."

On the door of the *Extant* offices appeared a sign:

NOTICE TO THE PUBLIC
STAFF IS NOW BEING ENGAGED. TEMPORARY HELP IS REQUIRED TO ASSIST WITH PHOTOGRAPH IDENTIFICATION CONTEST. IT IS PREFERRED, BUT NOT ESSENTIAL, THAT APPLICANTS MAKE APPOINTMENTS FOR AN INTERVIEW.

An applicant, upon entering the Extant offices, found himself in an anteroom divided by a counter. To the left was a door with a notice reading:

CONTEST PROCESSING ROOM
AUTHORIZED PERSONNEL ONLY

The door to the right was imprinted:

EDITORIAL OFFICES

At the counter the applicant would be met by Mrs. Millicent Ench, a brisk, dark-haired lady of middle age, who invariably

wore, day after day, a long black skirt, a pale-blue blouse with
a red sash, a cap with a red visor, glossy black shoes which
laced up past the ankles. Mrs. Ench performed a screening
process, turning away those applicants who were patently unsuitable. Others she sent into the adjoining room where they
filled out an application form, under the eye of the personnel
manager. This was Mr. Henry Lucas, who, from the evidence
of his clothes, fancied himself a patrician of the most refined
gentility. His features were good if a trifle harsh; his mouth
was wide, thin and crooked. Black ringlets were arranged
with care across his forehead and down past his sallow-pale
cheeks.

After a casual word or two with the applicants, Henry
Lucas seated them in cubicles, back to the room, and asked
them to respond to a questionnaire. The cubicles and desks
were apparently improvised and roughly constructed for the
occasion. Actually, they concealed and disguised exceptionally sensitive sensors and stress gauges which recorded every
slight tremor of the applicant, each flicker of his eye, every
variation of blood pressure, every alteration of brain-wave
pattern. The findings, when collated, were indicated as
colored lights at Gersen's desk and colored marks upon a facsimile of the questionnaire.

Gersen had composed the questionaire with care, in order
that the responses and their associated reactions should
provide the maximum information, even though the questions
in themselves seemed innocuous.

The first questions were straightforward, in order to establish normal circumstances and to calibrate the equipment.

Name_____ Sex_____ Age_____
Type of Employment Desired_____
Local Address_____
Birthplace _____
Name of Parents:
    Father_____ Address_____
    Mother_____ Address_____
Occupation of Father_____ Mother_____
Birthplace of Father_____ Mother_____

The next group of questions, so Gersen calculated, would
place a rather greater strain on other than a legitimate applicant.

How long at local address_____

Local references (List at least two. These people may or may not be consulted in regard to your character and competence.):

    1. _____
    2. _____
    3. _____

Previous address, if any_____

List at least two persons who have known you at this address. (They may be consulted):

    1. _____
    2. _____
    3. _____

Your address previous to address noted above, if any _____

List at least two persons who knew you at this address:

    1. _____
    2. _____
    3. _____

NOTE: *You will understand that, under the circumstances,* Extant *must diligently ensure the integrity of its personnel.*

The following questions were intended to exert maximum stress upon any person intending deception.

If nonresident, why have you come to Pontefract? (Give specific reasons. Do not generalize.)_____

_____
_____
_____

Contest personnel must necessarily be impartial. Examine the photograph here depicted, which is submitted to the contestants. Do you know or recognize any of the persons herein? Write 'O' in

the boxes of the persons you do NOT know. Fill in
solidly the boxes of the persons you DO know.

1	2	3	4	5	6	7	8	9	10
☐	☐	☐	☐	☐	☐	☐	☐	☐	☐

　　　(Read clockwise from bottom left center.)
What is his/her name, or their names?_____
_____
_____
　　　(List names with corresponding numbers.)
What are the circumstances of your acquaintance?
(Please be specific.)_____
_____
_____
_____

If engaged, when can you start work?_____
_____

In due course applicants for employment presented themselves to the office: students from Saint Griegand's Seminary
and the Celtic Academy, and as many middle-aged women
with time on their hands. Gersen rigorously applied his sensors to each applicant, in order to adjust the mechanism and
to establish the accuracy of his methods. Apart from a few
fluctuations and trivial exceptions, his system of colored im-
prints certified the innocence of each applicant. Of these,
Mrs. Ench, who also supervised the judging procedure, selected a group to process the beginning flood of entries. Each envelope as it entered the office passed through a numerator to
establish the priority of its reception.

Gersen himself opened and examined a number of envelopes, but found a wide disparity of response, lacking all con-
sistency.

On the afternoon of an uncommonly sunny day Gersen returned from lunch to encounter among the applicants a slim,
slight red-haired girl, in whom he took an immediate interest,
for at least two reasons. In the first place, she was very pretty
in a style at the edge of the unconventional. Her face, rather
wide of forehead and cheekbones, slanted across flat cheeks
down to a small chin and a curving pink mouth, which even
when still seemed to express intriguing possibilities. Her
gray-blue eyes, under dark lashes, were clear and direct. She
was perhaps a trifle smaller than average but constructed of
apparently durable material; she was engagingly suntanned,

as if she spent much of her time outdoors. She might have been a student from one of the local institutions, but Gersen thought not. He noticed her first through his window, standing across the street, wearing pale gray trousers, black sash and a pale gray cape, not at all in the local mode . . . She stood a moment with a bleak expression on her face, then squared her shoulders, crossed the street, out of range of Gersen's vision. A moment or two later Mrs. Ench allowed her into Gersen's office.

Gersen gave her a brief stare. The bleak expression had vanished; she now seemed composed, and here was the second reason for Gersen's interest. There was a third rising from his subconscious, and perhaps most important of all.

She spoke in a pleasant husky voice, with the trace of an accent Gersen could not identify. "Sir, you are offering employment?"

"To qualified persons," said Gersen. "I suppose that you are aware of the *Extant* contest?"

"I've heard something about it."

"We need temporary clerks to help with the contest, and we are also hiring permanent personnel."

She considered his remarks. Gersen wondered whether her artlessness was real or most carefully contrived. He took care of accentuate his half-debonair, half-supercilious formality. She offered a polite suggestion. "Perhaps I could start as a contest clerk, and then, if I do well, you might consider me for a permanent job."

"That is certainly possible. I'll ask you to fill in this form, which is self-explanatory. Please answer all questions."

She glanced at the questionnaire and uttered a soft sound under her breath. "So many questions?"

"We consider them necessary."

"Do you investigate all this for everyone you hire?"

Gersen spoke in a flat voice: "A great deal of money is involved in the contest. We must ensure that our personnel is absolutely honest."

"I quite understand." She took the form and went to the booth.

Gersen, pretending to occupy himself with paper work, touched a switch and watched a pair of desk screens, as the red-haired girl filled in the questionnaire. To the left appeared her face, to the right the questionnaire and colored lights to indicate the verdict of the stress detectors.

She had started to write.

> *Name:* Alice Wroke
> *Sex:* Female

The question as to gender and its response, certifying a self-evident condition, calibrated the instruments at base level. Conceivably, as in the case of a man disguised as a woman, the question might generate stress, thus distorting the interpretation of every other reading. In addition to the colored-light indicators, a graph recorded responses in terms of absolute units; anomalous responses might therefore be identified. In practice the color-coded indexes had provided reliable information. Blue lights now signified that Alice Wroke had truthfully declared her name and her gender; although before she wrote her name, the light flickered into pink for a moment, as if she were debating the use of a false name. The warnings from his subconscious were apparently vindicated. Surprising! He had hoped for Treesong to attempt infiltration of *Extant*, but that the infiltrator should be someone like Alice Wroke was quite unexpected. Gersen felt a surge of primitive excitement. The game had begun. With his own pulse accelerated, Gersen watched Alice Wroke write responses to the questions he had framed.

> *Age:* 20[1]

A clear blue light: no dissimulation.

> *Type of Employment desired:*

Here Alice hesitated. The color, wavering from blue into blue-green, indicated indecision rather than stress. She wrote:

> Clerical or journalistic work. I am qualified for either.

As she wrote the final sentence the blue-green verged momentarily into green, as if perhaps she were not as sure of her qualifications as she professed . . . She still hesitated and

---

[1] By general convention, age and almost all other units of duration were reckoned by terrestrial standards.

the green gradually became sharper and more acid. She added to her response:

> However, I am prepared to work in any capacity, and do whatever is required of me.

As she considered the next question, the color shifted back to blue-green, indicating a heightened state of consciousness.

Local address:

The color shifted not an iota. Alice wrote:

St. Diarmid's Inn.

This was a large cosmopolitan hotel at the heart of the city, frequented by tourists and offworld travelers, considerably less prestigious than Penwipers, but not without distinction and certainly not inexpensive. Alice Wroke would seem to be in no immediate need.

Birthplace: Blackford's Landing, Terranova, Denebola V.
Name of Parents:
   Father: Benjamin Wroke
      Address: Wild Isle
      Occupation: Engineer

   Mother: Eileen Sversen Wroke
      Address: Wild Isle
      Occupation: Accountant

These questions were negotiated without stress, except in regard to *Father's Occupation,* where the light glowed yellow-green.

Now commenced those questions which were intended to apply pressure upon a dissembler.

How long at present address?

Alice had defused this question by identifying her residence as a transient hotel. Still, the indicator shifted into the bright green as she wrote:

Two days.
Local references: list at least two:
1. Mahibel Wroke
   The Blawens, Gungold Street
2. Sean Paldester
   Dingle Lane, Tuorna

On this response the indicator glowed placidly blue. The first was evidently a relative, as might be the second who resided at Tuorna, a nearby village.

Your previous address, if any:

The blue brightened to green, flashed momentarily into yellow. Watching Alice's face, Gersen saw her compress her lips, then lean forward with a determined expression; simultaneously the indicator swung back through green toward blue. She wrote:

Wild Isle, Cytherea Tempestre

The references were:

1. Jason Bone
   Wild Isle
2. Jade Channifer
   Wild Isle

To the next question, inquiring as to previous address, she responded without tension:

1012–792nd Avenue, Blackford's Landing, Terranova, Denebola V
As references she cited:

1. Dain Audenave
   1692–753rd Avenue
2. Willow Tarras
   1941–777th Avenue

The following questions were those designed to exert maximum pressure.

If nonresident, why have you come to Pontefract?

As Alice studied the question the indicator glowed yellow and flickered into orange. Her tension diminished . . . The indicator returned to green. She wrote:

To secure employment.

Turning the page, Alice discovered the photograph of the contest, and the question:

Do you know or recognize any of the persons here depicted?

The indicator light glowed yellow, then orange. She deliberated a moment and the color became yellow-green. Presently she filled in all the boxes with O's. At box 6, the light glowed pink. She quickly turned the page, to avoid looking at the photograph, and her tension diminished slowly into green.

What is his or her name, or their names?

The light glowed vermilion. Alice answered the question with a dash.

What are the circumstances of your acquaintance?

The light glowed red. Alice answered with a second dash.

If engaged, when can you start work?

The light cooled quickly into green and greenish blue, as if in relief.

At once.

The questionnaire now was complete. As Alice reread it, Gersen watched her face. This slender red-haired girl was the instrument of Howard Alan Treesong. Conceivably she knew him by another name, and in this case she might or might not know his reputation. In due course the truth would become known . . . Gersen rose to his feet and sauntered across the room. She looked up with an uncertain smile. "I've just finished."

Gersen glanced at the responses. "This looks to be in order . . . You're originally from Terranova, it appears."

"Yes. My family moved out into Virgo five years ago. My father is—well, a consultant at Wild Isle. Have you ever been there?"

"No. I understand it's rather a different environment than here." Gersen contrived to speak in a voice of tired disapproval.

Alice encompassed him with a glance, expressionless save for a flicker of wonder. She responded without intonation. "Yes. It's a kind of dreamland, not altogether real."

"Out of idle curiosity, why did you leave?"

Alice shrugged. "I wanted to travel, and see something of other worlds."

"Do you intend to go back?"

"I hardly know. At the moment I'm only interested in working for *Extant*. I've always wanted to be a journalist."

Gersen paced slowly back and forth, hands behind his back, a figure of pompous elegance. He spoke in a ponderous voice. "Allow me a moment to consult Mrs. Ench. I'll find what positions are open."

"Certainly, sir."

Gersen wandered through the contest room where a dozen clerks processed great stacks of contest envelopes. He checked the computer read-out. Thirteen persons already had identified number seven as John Gray; and ten knew number five as Sabor Vidol: identifications which might well be considered definite. The tall gaunt man with the philosopher's forehead and the foxy jaw was known by a variety of names: Bentley Strange, Fred Framp, Kyril Kyster, Mr. Wharfish, Silas Sparkhammer, Arthur Artleby, Wilton Freebus, a dozen more.

Gersen returned to his office. Alice Wroke had moved to a chair close to his desk. Gersen halted to look at her, admiring the pleasant accord between her orange-red curls and her dusky ivory-tan skin. She smiled. "Why are you inspecting me so?"

Gersen spoke in his most pompous and nasal voice. "If nothing else, Miss Wroke, you are indeed a most decorative bit of work. Though I will ask, should you choose to enter our employment, that you dress a bit more sedately."

"Then I am to be hired?"

"Tonight we will check your references, and I am sure that they will reinforce my favorable opinion of you. I suggest that you report for work tomorrow at the second gong."

"Thank you very much, Mr. Lucas." Alice's smile conveyed no great emotion. If anything, she seemed strained and disheartened. "Where will I be working?"

"At the moment Mrs. Ench is adequately staffed; however, I need an assistant to manage the office when I am out. I believe that you are well-equipped to handle the job."

"Thank you, Mr. Lucas." Alice rose to her feet. She turned Gersen a glance over her shoulder, flirtatious, demure, puzzled, sad and apprehensive, in equal proportions.

She departed the office. Gersen looked after her. Curious, most curious.

Chapter 4

A former colleague recalls Howard Alan Treesong, then about eighteen years old, when they worked at the Philadelphia factory of the Elite Candy Company.

"He was restless and fluid and unpredictable, like a puddle of quicksilver on a table, but I always got along well with him. He seemed mild and rational. Certainly he was clever and amusing, and he had an inclination for wild practical jokes. Sometimes he carried the mischief too far—much too far. One day he brought in a box of dead bugs—cockroaches, bumblebees, beetles—and carefully fixed up a box of chocolate creams, each candy containing a big bug. He put it out for shipment, and said to me with a faraway look on his face: 'I wonder who will receive my little surprise.'

"But that wasn't what got him fired. There was a foolish old lady named Fat Aggie who always wore high-topped black shoes, which she took off when she sat down to work. Howard stole the shoes and filled them to the brim with peanut fondant in one and our Supreme Molasses Taffy Delight in the other, then put them back under Aggie's chair.

"That trick cost Howard his job. I never saw him again."

In the morning Alice Wroke appeared at the *Extant* offices wearing a skirt and jacket of a soft blue stuff which clung lovingly to her slender haunches. A black ribbon confined her orange hair; coming through the old black wood doorway she made an arresting picture. She was intelligent enough to realize as much, so Gersen felt assured. The costume was hardly as conservative as that which he had suggested, but he decided to let the matter rest; he gained nothing by exaggerating his role as a pompous frump. Alice Wroke who seemed not only intelligent but perceptive, might not be deceived.

"Good morning, Mr. Lucas," said Alice in a soft voice. "What do you wish me to do?"

This morning the valet at Penwipers had laid out for Gersen gray trousers with a lavender pinstripe, a black frock coat, pinched at the shoulders, flaring at the hips, with a white high-collared shirt and a black and lavender striped cravat, to which the chief porter had added a black hat with a foppish side-slanting brim and a purple ribbon. In the costume Gersen felt cramped and constricted; he needed only to hunch his shoulders to split the coat down the back. His discomfort and annoyance, together with the need to hold his chin high over the stiff collar, imposed upon him a manner which might easily be interpreted as priggish disdain for the commonalty with whom he was forced to associate. Well, so be it, thought Gersen. He said, in a voice to suit his costume: "Miss Wroke! I have taken counsel with Mrs. Ench and temporarily at least you will be assisting me, in the capacity of private secretary. I am discovering more paper work than I care to handle and, if I may say so, you add a colorful accent to an otherwise drab office."

Alice Wroke gave a small involuntary grimace of annoyance, which amused Gersen. A most peculiar situation. Alice Wroke, were she intimately associated with Howard Alan Treesong, must be a wicked woman indeed. Hard to believe . . . Gersen invented work to keep Alice occupied, and went out to check the tabulations.

Incoming mail now filled a bin. Six clerks opened the entries, examined the contents, entered the information into the rationalizer. Gersen went to the read-out screen at the end of the room, which only he and Mrs. Ench were allowed to use. He touched a button to call up the tabulations to date.

Nineteen persons now had identified number 7 as John Gray, of Four Winds, on Alphanor; his identity might be regarded as certain. The same could be said for number 5, Sabor Vidol, of London, Earth; number 1, Sharrod Yest, of Nova Bactria, and number 9, A. Gieselman, of Long Parade, Espandencia, Algenib IX. Number 6 was known far and wide across the Oilumene by a variety of names: Kyril Kyster, Timothy Trimmons, Bentley Strange, Fred Framp, Silas Sparkhammer, Wilson Wharfish, Oberon. Number 4 was named twice as Ian Bilfred, of the Pallas Technical Institute, at Pallas, Alcyone.

Gersen returned to his office, remembering, as he passed through the door, to reassume the role of Henry Lucas.

During his absence, Alice had reconsidered her tactics. Now, the better to manipulate this overdressed dunderhead, she thought to try to breezy affability, perhaps even a bit of flirtation. Good enough, thought Gersen. Why not?

"I wonder if I have read any of your articles, Mr. Lucas. Your name is very familiar."

"Possibly, Miss Wroke, quite possibly."

"Do you have special subjects you write about?"

"Crime. Vice. Dreadful deeds."

Alice looked at him askance. "Really?"

Gersen realized that for an instant he had let his mask slip. He made an airy gesture. "Someone must write such things. How else is the public to know?"

"But you hardly seem the sort to be interested in such things."

"Oh? What topics would you consider appropriate for me?"

Again Alice turned him a glance of wary speculation. "Civilized things," she said brightly. "The best restaurants, for instance. Or the wines of Earth. Or Lily Milk,[1] or Si Shi Shim dancing."

Gersen gave his head a sad shake. "Those aren't my subjects. What of yourself?"

"Oh, I'm not expert at anything."

---

[1] A precious ceramic ware, produced along the Susimara Islands of Yellow Sun Planet.

"This Si Shi Shim dancing, how does it go?"

"Well—one needs the proper music. Gongs, water flutes, a kurdaitsy—that's a rather repulsive trained beast which squeals when its tail is pulled. The costumes are mostly feather anklets, but neither the dancers nor the audience seem to mind. Actually, I can't do it well, if at all."

"Oh, come, I'm sure you're over-modest. How does it go?"

"Please, Mr. Lucas. Suppose someone looked into the office and saw me gyrating about, what would they think?"

"Quite right," said Gersen. "We must set an example of decorum. At least during working hours. Where are you staying now?"

"I'm still at St. Diarmid's." Alice Wroke's response was guarded and cool.

"You're here alone? That is to say, you have no local friends or relatives?"

"I am quite alone, Mr. Lucas. Why do you ask?"

"Simple curiosity, Miss Wroke. I hope that you are not offended?"

Alice gave a tolerant shrug, returned to the work which Gersen, at some effort, had contrived for her.

At noon a caterer's van arrived at the premises. Lunch was served to Mrs. Ench and her clerks in a small refectory; to Gersen and Alice Wroke in Gersen's office.

Alice expressed surprise at the arrangements. "Why don't we all eat together? I'm curious as to how the contest is going."

Gersen gave his head a magisterial shake. "That is not possible. My superiors have stipulated maximum security, especially in view of the rumor."

"Rumor? What rumor is that?"

"A notorious criminal has interested himself in the contest: that's the rumor. Personally I am skeptical. Still, who knows? We've even arranged sleeping accommodations here for our clerks. They won't leave the premises until after a winner is declared."

"It seems a bit exaggerated," said Alice. "Who is the notorious criminal?"

"It's absolute rubbish," declared Gersen loftily. "I refuse to disseminate such nonsense!"

Alice became haughty. "I'm really not interested." And during the lunch she retreated into herself, from time to time darting opaque glances toward Gersen.

After lunch Gersen invented more work for Alice, then carefully set the slant-brimmed hat on his head. "I'll be gone an hour or so."

"Very well, Mr. Lucas."

Gersen went to the Penwipers Hotel. From his room he called St. Diarmid's Inn. "Miss Alice Wroke, please."

After a pause the receptionist replied: "Miss Wroke is not currently in the hotel, sir."

"I believe she's in room 262?"

"No, sir, it's room 441."

"Is any other member of her party in the room?"

"She's alone, sir. Will you leave a message?"

"No, it's nothing important."

"Thank you, sir."

Gersen assembled various articles of gear, packed them in a case. To forestall difficulty at the front desk, he changed into afternoon wear, then departed the hotel.

At this time of day, afternoon tea break, the dank old streets of Pontefract were crowded with men in flare-bottomed brown and black suits and buxom pink-faced women in voluminous patterned skirts and black capes. Gersen soon arrived at St. Diarmid's Inn. He entered and surveyed the lobby, but saw nothing he could consider consequential.

He approached the registration counter and pretended to make calculations on a sheet of paper. The clerk watched a moment, then approached. "Sir, may I oblige you?"

Gersen wrote several numbers on his paper while the clerk watched in perplexity. "I need a room for several days or a week, during the Numerologists Congress. Mathematical vibrations indicate number 441, and I will engage this room." Gersen placed an SVU on the counter, and the clerk hastened to consult a read-out screen.

"A pity, sir! That room is already engaged."

"Then I must have either 440 or 442."

"I can oblige you with room 442, sir."

"It will serve adequately. I am Aldo Brise."

Established in room 442, Gersen went to the wall and placed a microphone against the paneling. From 441 came no sound.

In the corner he dropped to his knees, drilled a minute hole and inserted a near-invisible audio pickup. He attached a recorder, which then he coupled to the telephone. He placed the recorder in a drawer, opened the circuit, made tests and departed.

Returning to his office he entered, stalked across the room, carefully doffed his hat, placed it on a shelf. Then he favored Alice with a stately nod, to which she returned a demure murmur and a quiet side glance from under her long dark lashes. Gersen settled himself at his desk with a grunt, sat frowning into space for five minutes, as if deep in thought. Then he rose to his feet, went out into the passage and so to the workroom.

The clerks were at the full tide of work. Gersen looked over the current listing at the rationalizer. Identification of all the subjects could now be considered complete, save for number 6, who was known by a variety of names. As yet no one had used the name Howard Alan Treesong.

Gersen went back to his office. Alice looked up from her desk. "How goes the contest?"

"Extremely well, from a promotional standpoint. Response exceeds our projection by seventeen percent."

"But no one has won the grand prize?"

"Not yet."

"Why did you use that particular photograph?"

Gersen went to his desk and seated himself with the gravity of a judge. He spoke in his nasal voice: "I have never thought it appropriate to ask."

Alice pulled in the corners of her mouth but said nothing.

After a moment Gersen put the tips of his fingers together. "I think that I can inform you, in absolute confidence, of course, that all our subjects except one have been correctly identified."

Alice gave an indifferent shrug. "I'm not all that interested, Mr. Lucas."

"Come now," said Gersen, heavily facetious, "let's not have our noses out of joint. I believe you mentioned that your home is Cytherea Tempestre?"

"For several years now, yes."

"I understand that people conduct themselves most informally on Cytherea."

Alice considered. "I'm not sure I know what you mean by 'informally.' "

"Isn't there often—let us say—a bit of excess?"

"Yes, that's occasionally true. Tourists often misbehave

when they're away from home. Some of the worst offenders are from Pontefract."

Gersen laughed. Alice, watching him sidelong, thought: *The idiot is human after all.*

"Have you ever visited the Wild Isle casinos? I'm told people gamble away vast sums of money."

"They can hardly expect to win."

Gersen said with plangent severity: "The money they lose lines the pockets of notorious criminals."

"So I've heard," said Alice. "My father lines his pockets, so to speak, at the casinos, but I don't think that he is a notorious criminal."

"I should hope not. Is he a gambler?"

"To the contrary. He designs gambling machines and adjusts them so that they fleece the gamblers. He finds his work entertaining. I've heard him say that he lacks all sympathy for gamblers. He considers them self-indulgent, foolish and lazy, if not psychotic." Alice inspected Gersen with an innocent expression. "I hope that you're not a gambler, Mr. Lucas. I wouldn't care to hurt your feelings."

"Rest easy, Miss Wroke. I am neither vulnerable to casual deprecation nor a gambler."

"In regard to the contest, which one has not yet been properly identified?"

Gersen said evenly: "Number 6."

"When will the contest be over?"

"I don't know." Gersen looked at his watch. "I have no further work for you today, Miss Wroke. You may leave at any time."

"Thank you, Mr. Lucas." Alice slipped on her jacket and went to the door. She paused and gave Gersen a tentative smile. "Will there be anything more tonight, Mr. Lucas?"

"No, thank you, Miss Wroke. I'll see you in the morning."

Alice departed. Gersen went out into the contest room and stood watching the operatives. Then he returned to his office, removed his coat and subjected walls, windows, floor, ceiling and all the contents of the room to a slow and expert inspection. Had the need arisen, he could have carried detection devices to measure the quiver of energy flux, but the process might well attract attention to his vigilance. High in a corner of the ceiling he noticed a few strands of web, which might have been spun by a spider: something the eye would slide away from, unheeding.

After five minutes of scrutiny he decided that the web indeed was the work of a spider and brushed it away.

He sat in his chair, collar open, cravat loose, and reflected. The time was now late afternoon. Gersen went out into the workroom to find that the evening shift had come on duty. He watched a moment, then, adjusting his garments for the street, departed the office and strolled through cool evening mist to Penwipers.

The doorman acknowledged his arrival with a grave bow; the footman hurried forward to take his hat and to assist him up the stairs, as if he were a centenarian.

Gersen went up to his rooms. He removed his coat and seated himself at the telephone . . . He hesitated, hand in midair. He gave a snort of sour mirth. Eavesdrop devices at Penwipers? Unthinkable!

To make absolutely sure—after all, the doors were innocent of locks—he tested the premises with his detector, the specifications of which he himself laid down.

The room was clean of spy cells.

Gersen went to the telephone and called room 442 at St. Diarmid's Inn.

"Mr. Brise is not in," stated his answering device. "Please leave a message."

Gersen spoke a code word to activate the recorder. A musical tone notified him that material had been recorded and announced the time of the reception: only half an hour previously.

The first sound was Alice's voice. "Mr. Albert Strand, please."

"Thank you, madame." An institutional voice, thought Gersen. A moment later: "Hullo Alice!"

"Hello, Mr. Sparkhammer. I—"

"Tish, Alice! Also tush! Remember, here I am the gentleman Albert Strand of the Wambs County Strands."

"Sorry. Does it make any difference?"

"Who knows?" The voice was airy. "We are dealing with clever people. Not that we can't deal with them, but let us nurture our advantages. Boldness, power, stealth, decision! Let these be our watchwords!"

"Don't forget fear," said Alice in a soft, bitter voice.

"And of course, fear! So then, what have you learned?" This was a rich voice, under exquisite lilting control. Gersen listened with rapt attention.

Alice responded in a voice almost without expression. "This morning, when I arrived at work, Mr. Lucas told me I was to be his private secretary."

"Oh, dear me. I had not reckoned upon that. So then, what of Mr. Lucas?"

"He is careful about security—extremely so. I am not allowed into the contest room. Today I tried twice while he was out, but Mrs. Ench turned me away. I asked Mr. Lucas how the contest was going and he became insufferably pompous. He said that everyone in the picture had been identified except one—number six. No one as yet has come near winning the prize."

"And that is all?"

"I'm afraid so. Mr. Lucas says very little. He's a silly overdressed fool but rather a cunning fool, if you gather my meaning."

"Perfectly. Still, it seems that he is not impervious to your rather remarkable charms."

"Well—I'm not sure."

"Well then, find out! We can't waste time. I have important commitments in the near future."

"I'll do my best, Mr. Strand." Alice hesitated, then said: "Actually, you've never explained exactly what you want me to find out."

"Haven't I, though?" Mr. Strand's voice became briefly acrid and venomous. "Find out why they are using this specific picture! When and where did they get it? There's something going on, something in back of this contest, and I want to know what."

The conversation ended.

On the following day Alice made her second report. "Mr. Strand?"

"I am here, Alice."

"I don't have much to tell you. Today was much like yesterday. I tried to talk about the contest but Mr. Lucas won't answer my questions. He just sits and looks down his nose at me."

"Time is becoming critical, Alice." Mr. Strand spoke in a harsh hissing voice, curiously at odds with his mellifluous tones of the day before. "I want results. You know the circumstances."

Alice's voice became dull. "I'll try again tomorrow."

"You had better try something effective."

"But I can't think of anything. He is totally secretive!"

"Take him to bed. It's hard to be secretive without any clothes on."

"Mr. Sparkhammer—I mean Mr. Strand—I can't behave like that! I wouldn't know how!"

"Tush, Alice, everyone knows how!" Mr. Strand chuckled and his voice lost its menacing rasp, rising in pitch to become gay, quick, and almost brittle in quality. "If you must, you can—and indeed you must!"

"Mr. Strand, really, I don't—"

"Alice, you make such an affair of it all! It's most simple. You smile at him, he takes you to dinner. One thing leads to another, and presently you find yourselves without your clothes. Mr. Lucas is panting like a beached haddock. You start to snivel. 'My dear Alice!' cries Mr. Lucas. 'Why, at this ecstatic moment, all these tears?'

" 'Because, Mr. Lucas, I am sad and afraid. You are only trifling with me, isn't it true?'

" 'Not so, Alice! I am ardent; can't you tell? The thought of your orange curls on that white pillow yonder sets me aquiver! Feel my pulse! Trifling? Never! I am deadly in earnest!'

" 'But you treat me like an outsider! Why can't you truly demonstrate your regard for me?'

" 'I am ready and anxious to do so!'

" 'Not in that fashion. I want your full trust and esteem. For instance, when I show a natural interest in office affairs, such as the contest, you turn away your head. This is why I am sad.'

" 'Hrrumph, harra—I wouldn't want so petty a matter to come between us. Tomorrow at the office—'

" 'No, Henry, you might become cold again. You must tell me now, to prove your faith.'

" 'Well, it's really a simple matter.' And so—out come all the secrets, in a great vulgar belch. In the morning, tired but happy, you communicate what you have learned to me, and all will be well. Otherwise—" here Mr. Strand paused "—otherwise," and his voice dropped half an octave, "I can offer no such assurance."

"I see."

"You can handle the job?"

"I suppose so."

"Remember, time is of the essence, as I have a commitment which cannot be disrupted: a gathering of old school chums, in fact. So please put your best efforts into this project, in the manner which I have outlined. After all, you were brought here to Pontefract for precisely this function."

"I'll do my best, Mr. Strand."

"Your best, I'm sure, will be adequate."

The conversation ended; there was silence in the room.

Chapter 5

From: *Fauna of the Vegan Worlds*, Volume III:
The Fish of Aloysius, by Rapunzel K. Funk:

Gaid, also known as *The Night-train*: this is a splendid fish of a lustrous black color, often reaching a length of twenty feet. The body is exceptionally well-shaped, with an almost round cross section. The head is large and blunt with a single visual bulb, an aural pod and a wide mouth, which when open displays an impressive dentition. Immediately behind the head and almost to the tail grows a row of dorsal spines, to the number of fifty-one, each tipped with a luminifer which at night emits a bright blue light.

By day the gaid swims beneath the surface, where it feeds upon wracken, borse and similar creatures. At sundown the night-train rises to the surface and cruises steadily with all lights aglow.

The pelagic voyages of the night-train remain a mystery; the fish peregrinates on a direct course, as

if to a specified destination. This may be a cape or
an island or perhaps an unmarked station in the
middle of the ocean. Upon reaching its destination,
the night-train halts, floats quietly for half an hour,
as if discharging cargo, or taking on passengers, or
awaiting orders; then it swings about with majestic
and ponderous deliberation. It hears a signal and
sets off once more to its next destination, which
well may be five thousand miles distant.

To come upon this noble fish by night, as it
cleaves the black waters of the Aloysian oceans, is
a stirring experience indeed.

Gersen felt restless, on edge. He went out into the evening
and wandered the crooked streets of Pontefract.

Somewhat to his surprise he found himself at St. Diarmid's
Inn. He halted and looked along what was by Pontefract
standards a garish façade, of pale blue and purple tiles. Gersen moved on, across Mullawney Square into Portee Old
Town, a tawdry district of taverns, odd shops, artists' studios,
fried-fish booths and discreet brothels, each showing an illuminated green-glass globe, in accordance with ancient law.
Presently he arrived at the waterfront.

He stood looking across Bottleglass Bay, to the far lights of
Port Rufus. A breeze brought him the smell of the Aloysian
mud flats. Gersen had stood beside many shores, on many
worlds. No two had smelled alike . . . At the end of a
nearby pier a string of colored lights festooned the front of a
restaurant. Gersen walked out on the pier, looked into the
restaurant, which seemed cheerful and clean, with red-check-
ered cloths on the tables. The name of the restaurant was
Murdock's Bay View Grill.

Gersen entered and dined upon the house specialties,
which were in the main derived from the ocean. Aloysian
cooking tended to blandness; Murdock, however, seemed to
have no fear of sharp herbs and piquant sauces . . . Gersen
sat a long time looking out the windows toward the lights of
Port Rufus and listening to the mutter of slow waves on the
ancient piles below.

It seemed that as time went by Gersen found himself ever
more susceptible to strange moods, to which no name could
be applied. In the early years his emotions focused along a
single axis: hate, grief, revengeful lust. He had been humor-

less, clenched, passionate only in his dedication. Now there were numerous axes, in many directions. Was the intensity thereby diluted? A profitless line of inquiry . . . His strategies, so he reflected, were at least partially effective. Howard Alan Treesong had been lured into tantalizing proximity, conceivably in Pontefract itself. Possibly at this instant he strolled the cramped old streets, or took his ease in one of the formal hotels, where now he sat thinking dire thoughts, contriving plans.

Gersen looked around the restaurant. Somewhere Howard Treesong might be at his evening repast . . . Among the patrons of Murdock's Bay View Grill there was no tall spare man with a philosopher's forehead and a cunning foxy jaw. Treesong was elsewhere.

Gersen went to the telephone, called the Penwipers Hotel. "Henry Lucas here. Has my friend Mr. Strand registered? . . . No? What about Mr. Sparkhammer? . . . No one of that name either? . . . Then do me a service, if you please. With discretion—do not mention my name—try to find where Mr. Strand and Mr. Sparkhammer are staying."

"I'll do my best, sir."

Gersen returned to his table. Small chance of locating Treesong so easily. He must be teased, baited and tricked, and Alice Wroke must necessarily be the intermediary. It would be a fascinating game, mused Gersen, especially since Alice thought him pompous, stuffy, vain, overdressed and silly.

Gersen departed the restaurant and returned to Penwipers. The desk clerk, as expected, had been unable to locate either Mr. Strand or Mr. Sparkhammer. Gersen assured him that the affair was of no consequence and went to his room.

No one had passed through the door since his departure; the telltale he had installed was still in place.

In the morning the valet outdid himself and dressed Gersen in a costume so splendid that even the doorman stared in admiration. Gersen arrived at the *Extant* offices to find Alice Wroke already at her desk. Gersen gave her a civil greeting, to which she replied in kind. Today she wore a knee-length skirt of a dark brown stuff and an ash-beige singlet, which suited her coloring to perfection. The costume showed her slender figure to advantage; her orange hair had been brushed till it shone. Sitting at his desk, Gersen pretended to ignore her presence. Several times, glancing across the room, he found her eyes upon him, pondering, appraising, wondering.

Gersen went out into the contest workroom. Mrs. Ench brought him a letter. "A near-winner, Mr. Lucas! Perhaps even a winner! And how very strange it all is!"

Gersen read the letter:

> Contest Manager, *Extant*
> Pontefract, Aloysius
>
> Sirs:
> I can identify the persons in your photograph. It was my duty to attend them at the terrible event which cost them their lives. This photograph was taken in the Rainflower Room at Wild Isle Inn. They are about to sup on the charnay which unaccountably poisoned them all, save only Mr. Sparkhammer. The names of those at the table are, reading from left to right:
>
> > Sharrod Yest
> > Dianthe de Trembuscule
> > Beatrice Utz
> > Robun Martiletto
> > Sabor Vidol
> > Stanley Sparkhammer
> > John Gray
>
> The men standing are:
>
> > Ian Bilfred
> > A. Gieselman
> > Artemus Gadouth
>
> I know their names from the place cards which I myself prepared. Two other men were present. Neither of whom ate charnay and so both survived. The picture, incidentally is customarily made in order to record the sign of the chef who prepared each serving of charnay. The signs are the little colored signal posts of each place. In this case the wonder persists, as several chefs prepared the char-

nay. Poison was evidently transmitted by a tainted utensil.

I trust that I have satisfied the conditions of your contest and will win the prize.

> Cletus Parsival
> Wild Isle Inn
> Wild Isle, Cyntherea Tempestre

"Most interesting," said Gersen. "The letter is evidently genuine."

"So it seems to me." Mrs. Ench turned Gersen a curious glance. "Did you know what this Parsival fellow tells us—that these men died of poison?"

"I am as surprised as you. But it won't hurt *Extant's* circulation."

"Why would anyone eat this charnay if it is known to be poison? Very strange goings-on!"

"Exactly so, Mrs. Ench."

"Well, this Mr. Parsival seems to have the names correctly," said Mrs. Ench.

"All except number six. Sparkhammer is not his proper name."

"Hmmf," said Mrs. Ench. "That number six is a will-o-the-wisp in the matter of identity."

"Yes, he seems a strange case."

"I'd be inclined to name Mr. Parsival the winner and let be," said Mrs. Ench. "Surely no one has given us so long a list."

"I'm inclined to agree," said Gersen. "But still we'll have to wait out the rest of the contest. How is the mail?"

"About the same. Perhaps slacking a trifle."

"Very well, Mrs. Ench, keep up the good work. And ask your people to be most attentive in regard to mention of number six."

"I will do so, Mr. Lucas." Unlike Alice Wroke, Mrs. Ench considered Gersen a polite and gracious gentleman, "without any side to him," as she put it to her sister.

Gersen returned with the letter to his office.

Alice asked brightly, "Do you have exciting news?"

Gersen ponderously settled himself at his desk. Alice waited, her face frozen in a mask of cheerful expectancy.

Gersen spoke in his most nasal and affected drawl. "As a matter of fact, we have a letter identifying all our faces."

"Correctly?"

"He claims to have inscribed the place names at the banquet."

"Then the names would seem to be correct."

"Not necessarily. There is one very dubious identification."

"Oh? Which one?"

Gersen darted her a stern glance. "I'm not sure that it's proper for me to comment upon these matters, Alice. Not just yet, anyway."

Alice's face fell. She gave a small grimace. Gersen, watching surreptitiously, thought: *now she considers how best to arrange her beguilements.*

Alice jumped to her feet, went to the commode, where she poured two cups of tea. She placed one of these before Gersen, took the other to her own desk, where she poised herself, half-leaning, half-sitting. "Have you always lived here in Pontefract, Mr. Lucas?"

"I have traveled, of course, to many places."

Alice sighed. "Pontefract seems so impersonal, even a bit dreary after five years at Wild Isle."

Gersen proffered no sympathy. "I can't understand why you came here in the first place."

Alice gave a dainty shrug. "A dozen reasons. Wanderlust. Restlessness. Have you ever visited Cytherea?"

"Never. I'm told that it's a most hedonistic environment, and that the residents live very unconventional lives."

Alice laughed and turned Gersen a saucy side glance. "In some cases that's true. But not all. At Wild Isle you'll find every range of life-style. My mother is almost as conventional as you."

Gersen raised his black eyebrows. "What? You consider me conventional?"

"Yes, to some extent."

"Aha." Gersen gave a scornful grunt, as if to imply that Alice's opinions were callow and superficial. "Tell me more about Wild Isle. Is it true that criminals manage the casinos?"

"That is a considerable exaggeration," said Alice. "My father is not a criminal."

"But no one ever wins."

"Naturally not."

"Do you ever go into the casinos?"

"No. It's not at all amusing."

"Wild Isle is a city?"

"It's more like a tourist resort: casinos, hotels, restaurants, yacht harbors, beaches and lots of little villas in the hills. It's no longer wild, of course."

"Have you ever visited a charney restaurant?"

Alice turned him a look of wary perplexity. "No."

"What is charnay like?"

"Well, it's a purple fruit with rough skin. Inside, tubes full of poison run along the husk. The fruit itself is said to be delicious, but I've never tried it. I don't want to die. And it's fearfully expensive."

Gersen leaned back in his chair. "We've received a suggestion that our contest photograph depicts a charnay banquet."

Alice picked up a copy of the photograph and examined it. "Yes . . . That might well be true."

"Very strange! You might have passed some of these people in the street."

Alice's response was cool. "Possible. But not likely. Thousands of transients pass through Wild Isle. And there's no indication when the picture was taken; it might be ten years old."

"It's a recent picture. Everyone has been identified, and we're now into authentication."

"So someone has won the contest?"

"I made no such statement."

Alice asked ingenuously: "How did you come by the picture?"

"I rescued it from the trash can, as a matter of fact. But I mustn't gossip about the contest; all results are not yet in. Why don't you take the rest of the day off, Alice? I'll be busy away from the office."

"Thank you, Mr. Lucas. I don't quite know what to do with myself. I'm acquainted with no one in town but yourself—and you're so remote."

"What nonsense!" declared Gersen. "You can't really think so!"

"But I do! Perhaps you don't think it proper to have social contacts with the staff. Is that company policy?"

"I'm sure there's no such rule."

"Do you think I'm dowdy and plain?"

"To the contrary," said Gersen in all sincerity. "I consider you most engaging. Extraordinarily so. I'm sorry that you find Pontefract so dreary. Perhaps we might have supper together sometime."

Alice's lips trembled. A smile? A grimace? In a demure voice she said, "That would be nice. Why not tonight?"

"Why not indeed? . . . Let me see. Where are you staying?"

"Saint Diarmid's Inn."

"I'll meet you in the lobby, at Median."

"I feel much better already, Mr. Lucas."

Chapter 6

In Praise of Charnay!

> Of all the good things to be had in this bountiful
> universe, there is nothing to exceed a fine ripe char-
> nay, except two or three more of the same.

> —from *Gustations*, by Michael Wiest

If one must die—and this seems to be the general
fate—why perform the act in mean and vulgar
style? Rather, die splendidly, in a manner all will
envy, engorged with charnay.

> —Gillian Seal, chef, musician, and bon vivant.

Believe or disbelieve as you will, but a safe, salubri-
ous and nonpoisonous charnay could easily be developed, grown and harvested. But every effort in
this direction has been thwarted by the Charnay
Growers Association, nor is there any great public
clamor for such a development. It is possible that

the admittedly fine flavor of charnay is enhanced by
the presence of awful danger?

—Leon Wolke, journalist, writing for *Cosmopolis,*
who, two weeks after publication of his article, ate
improperly prepared charnay and died.

St. Diarmid's Inn had passed through the hands of various
owners. Each had contributed original ideas to the decor,
eventually producing an effect of considerable novelty. The
lobby occupied the entire ground floor. Heavy columns, decorated in ancient Cretan style, supported the ceiling, which
was patterned in lavender and pink. Beside each column Rho-
danthus palms, in terra-cotta pots, grew to the ceiling, where
the bare boles terminated in balls of dark-green foliage. By
Vegan standards the decor was garish. The movement of
many folk, in costumes from every corner of the Oikumene,
added life and drama to the hectic and vaguely disheveled atmosphere which characterized St. Diarmid's.

Gersen arrived punctiliously on time, wearing what the
valet had considered appropriate for an informal evening on
the town: skin-tight black trousers, a shirt vertically striped in
black, dark gray and light gray, with a high black neckband
in lieu of a cravat. The black jacket, responsive to the dic-
tates of high Pontefract style, was cut away in front, cramped
at the shoulders and almost bell-shaped around the hips. Gersen had refused a plumed hat, and the valet somewhat sulkily
had allowed him the use of a soft, square black cap. With his
harsh saturnine face, black curls and pallid skin tone, he
made a striking picture, one which, however, brought him
satisfaction other than a kind of mischievous pleasure in playing disguises and befuddling poor Alice Wroke.

Gersen saw her coming along the central aisle, looking dif-
fidently this way and that. Gersen examined her as if he had
never seen her before: the wistful mouth, short delicate nose,
cheeks slanting to a small chin. Tonight her orange hair hung
loosely past her ears, almost to the shoulders of her simple
smoke-gray frock.

She saw Gersen; her expression became charged with a
synthetic enthusiasm. She flipped up her hand in a gay greeting and crossed the room at a half-trot, to halt ten feet from
Gersen. She gave him an admiring head-to-toe inspection. "I

must say, Mr. Lucas, that you turn yourself out most elegantly."

"It's Penwipers all the way," said Gersen. "Give the credit to my valet."

Alice heard him without any great comprehension. Still smiling brightly she said, "Well then, where shall we dine? Here? The Escutcheon Room is pleasant."

"Too loud, too crowded," said Gersen. "I know a place far more exclusive."

"I place myself completely in your hands," said Alice.

"This way then, out into the Vegan night."

They left St. Diarmid's and Alice gingerly took Gersen's arm. "Where are we going?"

"It's a pleasant night," said Gersen. "We can walk, if you like."

"I don't mind."

They crossed Mullawney Square to Beaudry Lane, and so into Partee Old Town. Unreal! muttered Gersen to himself. We walk the streets of Pontefract, she in her masquerade, I in mine.

Alice sensed something of Gersen's mood. "Mr. Lucas, why are you so somber?"

Gersen evaded the question. "You may call me Henry. We are not at the office."

"Thank you, Henry." She looked uneasily over her shoulder. "I haven't been in this part of town before."

"It's not at all like Wild Isle?"

"Not at all."

Presently they arrived at the waterfront and Murdock's Bay View Grill. Alice considered Gersen thoughtfully. Mr. Lucas, so stuffy and meticulous, seemed to have unconventional facets to his character.

They sat in a corner of the restaurant, beside a window. Below them the water heaved in slow swells and sighed through the piles; stars and far lights reflected from the dark surface. Gersen asked, "Can you find your home star?"

"I don't know the patterns from here."

Gersen looked around the sky. "It's already set. But there's old Sol yonder."

Their dinner was served: a soup of native artichokes, a stew of crustaceans, onions and herbs bubbling in brown pots, a salad of fresh greens. Alice nibbled at this and that, and in response to Gersen's question, pleaded lack of appe-

tite. She drank several glasses of wine and achieved a degree
of vivacity.

"And what of the contest?" she asked. "Is it still a mystery? Especially from me?"

"Mystery? No longer. But let's not talk shop. You're the mystery. Tell me about yourself."

Alice frowned out across Bottleglass Bay. "There's nothing much to tell. Life at Wild Isle isn't all that exciting, except for the tourists."

"I'm still baffled about why you came to Pontefract."

"Oh—circumstances."

Dessert was served: fruit tarts and heavy coffee smothered with cream, in accordance with Aloysian taste.

Gersen, who felt that he had lapsed far enough from character, attempted a ponderous analysis of Pontefract politics, of which he knew next to nothing. Alice sat apathetically, looking out the window across the dark water, her own thoughts obviously not focused on Gersen's remarks.

Finally Gersen asked: "Where now? There isn't much entertainment in Pontefract, except at the Mummery, and we're too late for the program. Would you care for a carouse in one of the taverns along the docks?"

"No . . . I suppose we should go back to the hotel."

A top-heavy old cab conveyed them back to St. Diarmid's Inn.

In the lobby Gersen halted and performed a pontifical bow, as if to take his leave. Alice said quickly, "Oh please don't go so soon." Looking off across the lobby she spoke in a carefully offhand voice, "You can come up to my room, if you like."

Gersen protested politely. "But you must be tired."

Still looking away and with a trace of a flush coming over her face, Alice said, "No. Not really. In fact, I'm—well, lonely."

Gersen bowed formally once again, in acquiescence. "In that case I'll be happy to come up with you." He took her arm; they went to the lift and rode up to the fourth floor.

Alice opened the door and walked into the room, rigid as a prisoner.

Gersen followed warily. He halted in the doorway and surveyed the room. Alice watched incuriously, not even troubling to inqure the reasons for his vigilance.

Reassured, Gersen came slowly forward. He closed the

door. "Henry," said Alice breathlessly. "May I call you Henry?"

"I've told you so already."

"I forgot. Isn't that idiotic? Let me take your hat and coat.

Gersen tossed the hat into a chair and relinquished his coat. "That's a relief. The Pontefract tailors have no concept of the human form."

"Sit down, Henry—there."

Gersen obediently eased himself down upon the couch. Alice brought a silver tray from the sideboard. "What is all this?" asked Gersen.

"Candied flower petals. Hydromel crystals. This is Liquor of Life, from Sirsse." She poured clear green tincture into a pair of small bowls. "At home, lovers drink Sirsse together," said Alice. "Of course we've not lovers, you and I, but . . ."

"But what?"

"Oh—nothing particular."

Gersen tasted the liquor, which seemed heady and subtle. Alice asked, "Do you like it?"

"It's unusual, certainly. And very fragrant."

Alice settled beside him and sipped from her own bowl. "It makes me feel shuddery." Gersen was surprised to find his arm around her shoulders; he had intended to maintain his decorum. She relaxed against him and he kissed her—rather more than sheer decorum might have dictated.

Alice looked at him with pupils dark and dilated. Gersen asked, "What's wrong? Have I offended you?"

"Oh no." She laughed nervously. "You frighten me, just a little. You're so different from Mr. Lucas at the office. I don't know how to describe it."

"There's definitely only one of me."

She poured out more of the liquor. "Drink."

"The lovers' potion?"

"If you want to call it that."

"Do you have another lover?"

"No . . . What of you?"

"I'm quite alone."

Alice put up her face and he kissed her again. Her dress fell apart at the front, revealing her torso and a small round breast. She seemed not at all perturbed.

Gersen heaved a deep sigh. "This can't go any further."

"No?" Alice touched his cheek.

"I can't dispel a cruel suspicion."

Alice stared at him in consternation. "What do you mean?"

"I'd be very hurt to learn that you were cultivating me only to gain information about the contest. Absurd, of course."

Alice sat tense and pale. "Absurd, indeed."

"Well, then, could we be lovers if I told you nothing whatever about the contest?" .

"This becomes so intellectual . . . I couldn't love someone who places no trust in me."

"In other words—no."

"But I don't want it to be that way," said Alice earnestly.

Gersen reflected a moment. "It seems that, to demonstrate my trust, I must tell you everything I know."

"If you wish."

"Very well; why not?" Gersen stretched his legs out and put his hands behind his head. "There's really not much to tell. The persons in the picture have been identified, all except one, whose identity is known to us under a different name." From his pocket Gersen brought a list, from which he read names: "Yest, de Trembuscule, Utz, Bilfred, Vidol, Sparkhammer, Gray, Gadouth, Gieselman, Martiletto; all correct except 'Sparkhammer,' who is know by dozens of other names. No one has submitted his real name. Does that surprise you?"

"No. Why should it?"

Gersen tossed the list upon the table and leaned back once. "Because he would seem to be a notorious criminal named Howard Alan Treesong."

"Howard Alan Treesong? That can't be true!"

"Why not?"

Alice had no answer.

"The people in the photograph are all dead—except number six, who is Treesong. What does that suggest to you?"

Alice, with her thoughts far away, responded with a gloomy shrug. "I don't understand any of this."

"There's another aspect to the matter," said Gersen. "If number six is Howard Treesong—and he surely is—I'd like to interview him. *Extant* could very profitably use such a piece, or a short autobiography. I wish I knew some way to get this message to him. I want him to communicate with me."

Alice stared across the room and away into nothingness. Gersen rose to his feet. He picked up his coat and hat. Alice looked up and spoke in a husky half-whisper. "Are you going?"

Gersen nodded. "I've told you everything I know."

"But you haven't!" Alice blurted despairingly. "How did you get the photograph?"

"I walked into the *Cosmopolis* library: I looked into the trash basket and found this photograph. No one could tell me anything about it, and so the *Extant* contest was born."

"Who put the picture into the trash basket?"

"A young and foolish clerk."

"Still—why did you choose this particular photograph? There must have been many others equally suitable."

"Someone unknown had written 'Treesong is here' on the picture. I became interested because there are no known likenesses of Treesong available. I felt that the picture would have considerable news value. As it happens, that is the case."

Alice sat silently. Gersen went to the door. "Good night."

Alice looked at him with a tired gaze. "I wonder how much you know of me."

"Not a great deal. Is there anything you want to tell me? Trust works both ways."

Alice gave her head a sad shake. "I haven't anything to tell."

"Good night then."

"Good night."

Alice sat where Gersen had left her, leaning back on the couch, legs stretched out, a wintry expression on her face. She ran her fingers through her orange hair, pushing the curls back from her forehead into a tangle. For ten minutes she sat deep in reverie. Then, rousing herself, she went to the telephone and made a complicated connection.

A voice spoke. "Alice, so early? You're a pair of fast workers."

Alice responded in a level voice. "I have your information. The persons in the photograph are as follows—" She read names from the list Gersen had left behind.

"What is the source of these names?"

"All the different entries. There's also at least one entry listing the names all correctly, except one."

"And which name is that?"

"Mr. Lucas said that 'Sparkhammer' seems to use many

different names: Fred Framp, Bentley Strange, Howard Alan Treesong . . . I've forgotten the rest."

A silence. Then in a different voice, calm and meditative, "What did Mr. Lucas make of this?"

"I think he's anxious that Mr. Sparkhammer, or Mr. Treesong, should get in touch with him for an interview. He wants to publish Mr. Treesong's autobiography."

The response was prompt and definite. "He is doomed to disappointment. Mr. Sparkhammer, or Mr. Treesong, whatever his name, has no taste for such a vulgar antic. How did *Extant* come into possession of the photograph?"

"Mr. Lucas found it in a trash basket in the *Cosmopolis* library. A clerk had thrown it away."

"Odd, most odd . . . Are these facts?"

"I think so."

"How did the photograph arrive at *Cosmopolis*?"

"I didn't think to ask; I suppose it came in whatever way is usual."

"And what led him to select this particular photograph?"

"Someone had written on it: 'Treesong is here.' That attracted Mr. Lucas's attention."

"So he proposed a contest to identify Mr. Treesong and his colleagues."

"That is what he told me."

"Did he say why?"

"He said he very much wanted to publish Mr. Treesong's autobiography. As I told you, he wants Mr. Treesong to get in touch with him."

"Small chance of that. Mr. Treesong is very busy with urgent affairs." Mr. Strand became silent, for so long an interval that Alice began to fidget. Then: "What else did he tell you?"

"Not very much. He knows that the photograph was taken at Wild Isle, and that everyone died of charnay except Mr. Sparkhammer."

Another long silence. Then: "Very good, Alice. In the main you have done well."

"I can go back home? And you will do as you promised?"

"Not yet! Oh dear no, not yet! You must remain at your post! Keep your eyes and ears open. This Henry Lucas person, what do you make of him?"

Alice spoke in a bleak voice: "I don't know what to make of him. He's a contradiction."

"Hmmf. That tells me nothing. But no matter, continue as before. Tomorrow I am going away; and for a day or so you will not be able to reach me. Continue your intimacy with Mr. Lucas. I have a feeling that there is something more here, beyond what he has told you."

"For how long?"

"In due course I will let you know."

"Mr. Strand, I've done all I can! Please—"

"Alice, I have no time for your complaints. Continue as before and all will be well. Is this understood?"

"I suppose so."

"Good night then."

"Good night."

Chapter 7

Excerpt from an address by Nicholas Reid, Fellow of the Institute, Phase 88, at the Madera Technical College:

The Institute is dedicated to human excellence. We try to augment beneficial processes and discourage those which are morbid and septic.

Our credo derives from the history of the human race, which evolved across millions of years in the natural environment.

What happens when a salt-water fish is transferred into fresh water? It goes into spasms and dies. Consider, then, a creature whose every sense, capability and instinct have been shaped by the natural environment, by interaction with sun, wind, clouds, rain; the look of mountains and far horizons; the taste of natural food; contact with the soil. What happens when this creature is transferred to a synthetic environment? He becomes neurotic, a victim of hysterical fads, willful hallucination, sexual perversion. He deals with abstractions rather than facts, and so becomes intellectualized and incompetent. Confronted with a real challenge, he screams, curls into a ball, closes his eyes, befouls himself and waits. He is a pacifist who fears to defend himself.

From *Better Understanding of the Institute*, by Charles Bronstein (82):

Urbanized men and women experience not life but the abstraction of life, on ever higher levels of refinement and dislocation from reality. They become processors of ideas, and have evolved such esoteric occupations as the critic, the critic who criticizes criticism, and even the critic who criticizes criticism of criticism. It is a very sad misuse of human talent and energy.

From *The Institute*: *A Primer*, by Mary Murray:

Our tutelary genius is the titan Antaeus.

Urbanity is an unnatural habitude.

Are we elitist, as it is often asserted? Well, we surely do not consider ourselves the dregs of society.

We approve of contrast, social disequilibrium, extremes of wealth. Often we are accused of sponsoring chaos; however, this has never been admitted.

The Urbanites Strike Back!

"Elitist prigs!"

"If they like the Pleistocene so much, why don't they wear skins and live in caves?"

"Residents of very lofty and very remote ivory towers which they confuse with 'natural habitat.' "

"I'd rather push a pencil in an air-conditioned office than push a wheelbarrow in the mud."

In almost the same terms:

"I'd rather pick flaws in someone's manuscript than pick tomatoes in the hot sun."

Again:

"I'd rather drive my Fissel Flasher than a balky mule."

Gersen stood at a window of his sitting room at Penwipers, brooding down across old Tara Square. The time was midnight; Tara Square was dark and still. Starlight illuminated the roofs of Pontefract, casting black shadows down tall gables, under crooked eaves and thousands of crotchety chimney pots.

Gersen's mood was reflected in his posture; he felt morose and drained of energy. The great scheme had failed. The program had gone with precision: Howard Treesong had reacted as positively as Gersen could have hoped; in Alice Wroke he had found a conduit leading to Treesong. Then, almost casually, defeat. For whatever motives—pride, press of affairs, the workings of his uncanny wariness—Howard Treesong had refused to consider the publication of his autobiography, or so much as an interview.

There was no further leverage to be found in the contest. In the morning he would put Mrs. Ench in charge of the entire project.

What next? Alice Wroke remained his single avenue of access to Howard Treesong, but the linkage had become fragile and uncertain.

Two questions remained unanswered. How did Howard Treesong control Alice Wroke? Why had Howard Treesong poisoned nine people with charnay?

The answers were probably to be found at Wild Isle, but, so Gersen reflected glumly, the information would most likely be stale and useless.

Of far more interest: what was Howard Treesong's present 'urgent business'?

Of this Alice Wroke evidently knew nothing. No other source of information suggested itself.

Gersen looked over the starlit roofs. In the pubs of Partee Old Town lights would still be burning. He looked toward St. Diarmid's Inn and wondered if Alice Wroke was still awake.

Gersen turned away from the window and stood motionless. Then he threw off the Penwipers shirt, donned a dark gray spaceman's blouse, pulled a soft cap down over his forehead and started for the door . . . A chime at the communicator turned him back. He stood frowning at the instrument. Who would be calling him at this hour?

The screen came alive and presented the long pale face of Maxel Rackrose. "Mr. Lucas?"

"Speaking."

Rackrose spoke in a carefully languid voice. "The information you wanted—authentications and so forth—has come together, except for a few bits and pieces."

Maxel Rackrose spoke with such hushed restraint that Gersen instantly became alert. Rackrose said without any great conviction, "I do hope I haven't jerked you from your bed?"

"No. I was on my way out the door."

"Then why don't you step over to the office for a few minutes? I think you'll be interested in what's turned up."

"I'll be right there."

The *Cosmopolis* offices were never closed; work proceeded every hour of the day, every day of the year. A tall glass door whisked aside at Gersen's approach; he entered the foyer, where luminous slabs of colored glass blacked out a Mercator map of Earth.

Gersen rode a lift high into the North Tower and so to the offices of Maxel Rackrose, who now used the title Superintendent of Miscellaneous Operations. The outer chamber, which reflected Rackrose's pose of fastidious sophistication, was an exercise in the most exquisite excesses of the High Clapshott style. The inner room, where Rackrose spent most of his time, was a jungle of disorder. A long table supported stacks of books and periodicals, papers, photographs, oddments, curios and perplexing trifles of junk. There were several stools, a communicator, a complicated device for the brewing of tea, another for the projection of kaleidoscopic patterns on the wall, an attenuated statue of a nude woman nine feet tall, whose belly opened on the hour to permit a bird to step forth and cry "cuckoo."

Rackrose, a tall angular young man in expensive if unconventional garments, with a long somewhat equine face, lank blond hair and heavy-lidded blue eyes, greeted Gersen in a carefully offhand manner. "Sit down, if you will." He waved a limp white hand toward one of his precious antique chairs. "Perhaps you'd take a cup of tea? And a biscuit?"

"That would be nice."

With tea poured and anise cakes set forth, Rackrose settled into a chair beside a kidney-shaped table. "And how goes your contest?"

"Quite well. One entry names nine of ten, and if no one does better I think we'll nominate him the winner. What of your authentications?"

Rackrose leaned back, pressed the tips of his fingers together, looked toward the ceiling with pursed lips.

"In accordance with your instructions, I processed all available information. I started with the Index[1] and information from our own files. I may say that there was no trouble with authentication. The subjects are persons of substance and reputation. Except for number six. None of his purported names correlates with anything other than disreputable activities. In short, he seems to be a criminal."

"What of the others?"

"Aha! That's where we make an interesting discovery. I found recurring references to the Institute, and such remarks as 'said to rank high in the hierarchy,' and 'an apparently high-ranking Fellow.' In fact, Beatrice Utz is identified as '103.' Artemus Gadouth was the Triune.[2]" Maxel Rackrose

---

[1] A directory of identities, originally compiled by the IPCC and continually augmented by other agencies. The Index includes the records of history: social welfare registrations, military rosters, passenger lists of interplanetary vessels; birth, marriage and death records; telephone directories; school and university graduation lists; criminal identifications; the memberships of clubs, associations and fellowships; names culled from the daily news by automatic scanners.

[2] The Institute grades its Fellows with Ranks 1 through 111. Number 111 is the Triune. Ranks 110 and 100 are always empty.

Ranks 101 through 109 are limited to a single Fellow. With the Triune, these ranks make up the Dexad, though as often the nine Fellows from 101 through 109 are known as the Dexad.

Fellows advance from 101 to Triune in order of precedence.

Three Fellows only occupy Rank 99. When a vacancy occurs in the

paused to allow Gersen to reflect upon the implications of his information.

Gersen studied the photograph, which he already knew in minute detail. A startling suspicion formed in Gersen's mind, an idea strange and terrible. "Ten faces; could it be the Dexad?"

"The same idea occurred to me," said Rackrose.

Gersen reflected a moment. Rackrose knew nothing of the charnay poisonings, nor did he realize that number six was Howard Alan Treesong. He asked, "Who ranks highest locally?"

Rackrose frowned toward the ceiling. "There's a hermit out on Boniface, who is supposed to rank high. I've heard he's in the Dexad. If so, this picture would not seem to be the Dexad, because there's no one here from Boniface."

"Who ranks high in Pontefract?"

"I'm not sure. Let me ask Condo; he knows such things." Rackrose spoke into the communicator using a soft voice only a trifle louder than a whisper. He made notes on a pad of pale pink paper. "Good enough." He turned back to Gersen with a page torn from his pad. "Her name is Leta Goynes. She lives at 17 Flaherty Crescent, out in Bray, and she might be as high as a 60 or 65."

Gersen took the address to his own small office, which was far less splendid than that of Maxel Rackrose. At his communicator he placed a call. A moment passed, then an unemphatic female voice spoke. "Leta Goynes here."

"I'm sorry to disturb you at this late hour, Mrs. Goynes. My name is Kirth Gersen, and I want to consult you on a matter of great importance."

"Now?"

"Unfortunately yes. It's Institute business of extreme ur-

Dexad, usually by reason of death, surviving Fellows elect one of the three 99's to fill the vacancy.

From the three Fellows in Rank 98, one is elected to Rank 99. Similarly, Fellows advance up the ranks from 90. Below 90, there is no limit upon the Fellows allowed into each rank.

To achieve Rank 89 is difficult. To attain Rank 99 is much more difficult. A Fellow elected to Rank 101 has a good chance of becoming Triune. This is not necessarily true in Rank 99, where a Fellow who has made enemies among the Dexad may never be advanced.

gency. If you'll allow me, I'll come directly out to your house."

"Where are you now?"

"At the *Cosmopolis* offices."

"Take Transit to Bray Junction; a cab will bring you out to Flaherty Crescent."

As Gersen approached the cottage at 17 Flaherty Crescent, the door slid back; backlighted in the opening stood a dark-haired woman, sturdy, solid and obviously in good physical condition. She gave Gersen a cursory inspection and stood back. Gersen entered; the door closed behind him. "This way," said Leta Goynes. and led him to a neat parlor. "Tea?"

"Yes, please."

She poured and handed Gersen a cup. "Sit anywhere you like."

"Thank you." Gersen seated himself; Leta Goynes remained standing, a rather handsome woman in her early maturity, her black hair cut close to her head, her eyes dark and direct under strong black eyebrows. "There is no Kirth Gersen known to *Cosmopolis*."

"For a good reason. I call myself Henry Lucas, Special Writer."

"You are a Fellow?"

"No longer. At Phase 11 I discovered that the Institute and I often worked at odds with each other."

Leta Goynes, smiling faintly, inclined her head in a terse nod. "So then?"

Gersen handed her the contest photograph. "Have you seen this? It appeared in *Extant*."

"I haven't seen it before."

"What do you make of it?"

"Nothing particular."

"You recognize no one?"

"No one."

"It might well be the Dexad. Artemus Gadouth is this gentleman. He is Triune, as I suppose you are aware."

Leta Goynes nodded. "I've never met him."

"This is Sharrod Yest . . . Dianthe de Trembuscule . . . Beatrice Utz, rank 103 . . . Ian Bilfred . . . This gentleman calls himself Sparkhammer . . . Sabor Vidol, rank 99 . . . John Gray . . . Gadouth . . . Gieselman, rank 106 . . . Robun Martiletto." Gersen paused.

Leta Goynes said, "This is not the entire Dexad. There are three persons—those numbers five, six and seven—who are probably 99. Last month we lost Elmo Shookey. This banquet procedes, so I presume, the elevation of a 99."

"The elevation may not have occurred," said Gersen. "All except number six were poisoned by charnay."

Leta Goynes's face became cool and faintly scornful. "The Institute is not only strong; it is flexible. Normal adjustments are being made."

"In this case the adjustment will not be so easy. The survivor, number six, poisoned the others. His name is Howard Alan Treesong."

Leta Goynes stared at the photograph. "That is terrible information—if it is true. And I see that it must be true . . . How did he gain rank 99?"

"Through fraud, extortion, fear, mind-bending—so I suppose. Certainly he never rose through the ranks. But a more important question: What members of the Dexad are missing from the picture? And where are these members?"

Leta Goynes managed a harsh cold laugh. "Under the circumstances that becomes highly important information."

"True. And I might be one of Treesong's colleagues."

"Or Treesong himself."

Gersen handed her Jehan Addels's business card. "Telephone this man. He is a local resident of good reputation. Ask him whatever you like about me."

Leta Goynes went to the communicator. "First I will ask someone about Jehan Addels."

She made a set of guarded inquiries, watching Gersen meanwhile from the corner of her eye. Then she telephoned Jehan Addels. After some delay he responded, displeased that his rest had been disturbed. Gersen spoke to him: "This lady is Leta Goynes. Answer any questions she cares to ask."

Leta Goynes questioned Addels for fifteen minutes, then slowly turned away from the communicator. She had gradually resumed that manner typical of the Institute's upper ranks: a serene and exasperating indifference to events, including personal convenience.

"Addels gives you a remarkable reputation." She thoughtfully sipped her tea, then spoke in a pensive voice: "The Institute tends to ignore ordinary social problems, even criminals as egregious as Howard Treesong. Still . . ." Leta Goynes set her chin. "I will give you your information. Three of the Dexad are not present in the photograph. They are 101, 102 and 107. The death of 107 was the occasion for the conclave. 101 lives in isolation on Boniface, at a place called Athmore Violet, in the wildest part of World's Moil. His name is Dwyddion and he is our Triune, although he may not know it, since he sees no one and refuses to communicate."

"And what of 102?"

Leta Goynes smiled a strange crooked smile. "His name is Benjamin Wroke. He drowned in the Shanaro Sea. Last week his body was washed up on the beach at Cele, which is near Wild Isle."

Chapter 8

From *Everyman's Guide to the Stars*:
Vega; Alpha Lyrae:

. . . The three inner planets, Padraic, Mona, Noaille, are cinders of scorched stone, baking in the austere glare of the Great White Star. Noaille holds one face steady to Vega, and is noteworthy for the rains of liquid mercury which fall on the dark side, flow to the hot side where they vaporize and return to the dark side.

Next are the inhabited worlds: Aloysius, Boniface and Cuthbert. Cuthbert is humid and unpleasantly marshy, with few areas comfortably habitable; in part due to the numerous insects which give Cuthbert its sobriquet: "Bug-Hunter's Paradise."

Aloysius is next in orbit, temperate, if damp, and most densely populated of the Vegan worlds.

The early history of Aloysius is dominated by rivalry between religious sects; the effects of the hatred and warfare so engendered persist to the present, most especially in the countryside, in the form of provincial suspiciousness. The cities Pontefract, New Wexford, Yeo are relatively cosmopolitan.

Boniface, outermost and largest of the habitable worlds, is gloomy, dank, and like a caricature of the other two, exaggerating all the harshness and oddities of its sister planets. The oceans are bedeviled by awful storms, the land masses are notable for an extravagant topography: vast plains supine to the force of winds and rain; mountains, caves, crags, chasms; broad rivers flowing from sea to sea. Here and there the land allows habitation, though never ease or comfort.

From earliest times the shrewd and provident folk of Aloysius, wresting value from dross, used the inhospitable wastes of Boniface as a penal settlement, and here were discharged the atheists, incorrigibles and irredeemables of the Vegan worlds.

Arriving at Port Swaven, the convicts were processed at a staging compound operated by the Order of St. Jedasias. A certain Abbot Nahut, through divine revelation, received instruction in a new regimen to which arriving convicts must be subjected, the better to prepare them for life on Boniface. The methods were drastic and unique. Many of the survivors suffered genetic damage which stabilized, and a new human species was thereby more or less accidentally created. These were the "Fojos," one of the curiosities of the human universe. The typical Fojo was tall, with thin arms and legs, big hands and feet, gnarled heavy features and a shock of white quills in place of hair. The Fojos became functionally the indigenous race of Boniface and migrated to all the most sheltered nooks, crannies and lonely valleys of their harsh world.

In a few little towns: Slayman, Cashel Creary, Nahutty, Kaw Doon, Fiddletown, a few ordinary men and women operate shops and agencies and perform technical services, dealing with the Fojos in a state of mutual distaste.

The Order of St. Jedasias is long extinct, but by
one of the more acrid cosmic ironies, the Fojos still
espouse a variant of the Jedasian creed; and in every little Fojo village exists a square Jedasian
church.

Time suddenly had become a critical factor, inasmuch as
Dwyddion, hermit and new Triune, must surely represent one
of Howard Treesong's "urgent affairs." Gersen made all possible haste, from Leta Goynes's cottage to the spaceport,
aboard his *Fantamic Flitterwing* and away into space.

The automatic pilot swung the boat high over Vega and
down on the opposite side, to where Boniface coasted in orbit. A primitive world, with nothing of value to be plundered,
looted or kidnapped, Boniface lacked all entry controls; Gersen dropped unchallenged down to the harsh blue-black and
white disk.

Gersen searched the *Vegan Gazetteer*, but found only a
single vague reference to Athmore Violet. The Skak Range
ran diagonally across a section known as World's Moil, in the
middle of St. Crodecker's continent. Along the southern
flanks of the Skak, the river Meaughe meandered down
Meaughe Vale, where Gersen noted the town Poldoolie,
which might well be a source of local information.

The surface of Boniface, obscured by clouds and camou-
flaged by cloud shadows, revealed no obvious landmarks.
Gersen oriented himself with the help of radio beacons, calculated the coordinates of the town Poldoolie and slanted
down into the heavy atmosphere.

Over Meaughe Vale the sky was clear. Gersen located
Poldoolie, a huddle of stone structures beside a growth of
purple voitch.[1] Gersen descended in a spiral and landed the
Flitterwing in a soggy meadow a quarter-mile east of the
town.

The time was local noon. Gersen stepped from the *Flitterwing* into a dank cold wind smelling of mud and rancid vegetation.

Out from the town bounded a dozen gangling ragamuffins,

---

[1] A single organism, comparable to a gigantic lichen, voitch supports
a black mat ten feet thick on tawny or pale gray stalks fifty feet tall.
Certain growths of voitch are poisonous, others predatory and carniv-
orous. The benign specimens furnish food, drink, fiber, shelter and
pharmaceuticals.

the larger thrusting the smaller aside, the smaller cursing and tripping the larger. All wore dirty white smocks which they hiked up as they ran, revealing white legs and knobby knees. Their heads were narrow, their facial structures crude and gnarled. From each narrow scalp rose a bush of stiff white spines. The first to arrive halted two feet from Gersen and screamed: "I'm the guardian; I'm here first; the others are smashers, pay them naught! I'm Keak; for me the gautch."

"Gautch? What is gautch?" asked Gersen.

"That is my payment. I want either five SVU or five picture books."

The other boys cried out in eager voices: "Give him books for gautch! Good books, with bosers! Yetch bosers!"

"Bosers? What are bosers?"

The question evoked strangled guffaws. Keak wiped his mouth and explained. "Bosers—with the wide areas and no clothes on. Yetch: they're the good bosers!"

"I see," said Gersen. "And suppose I pay neither coin nor pictures of naked bosers—then what?"

"Then the smashers—those ugly chuts yonder! They'll muck up your ferberator crystals and pour stale dog-piss into your air intakes. So pay up and I'll fend them off."

Gersen considered. "How can you control so many smashers?"

"They know better than to flout me. Cukkins! Tell what I'll do to you."

"Faith, and I smash so much as a twittle, he'll shove me head up my own bum. He's a scarfer, is Keak, and he knows how to do it."

Gersen nodded. "Well, Keak, I see that you mean business. Still, I think I had better make sure of everyone. This way, then, around the boat; I've got fine things in the cargo hatch for lads like you."

"Eh?" asked a small youth. "What sort of fine things?"

"What of boser books?" asked Gersen. "Dozens of them, all rotten scurrilous!"

"That's the talk!" cried Keak. "Let's have a look!"

"This way." Gersen went around the ship, followed by the youths, loping and hopping. Gersen slid open the cargo port and drew down the ladder. He pointed to Keak. "First choice goes to you; quick now, I can't waste time."

Keak hopped up the ladder, followed by the others, with Gersen at the rear.

"There's naught for light in here," croaked Keak. "Make light! Show us bosers."

"Wide arse, big udders."

Gersen touched a button; light came to the chamber, which was starkly empty.

"Hey!" called Keak. "There's naught here!"

Gersen grinned. "Only a clutch of young blackguards. I'm going now about my business and I'm locking you in. If you make any mess I'll fly you into the mountains and turn you out, and you won't be home for supper tonight. So mind your conduct!"

Gersen backed down the ladder, closed and locked the hatch. He set off across the dank meadow and presently found a lane which flanked a stagnant drainage ditch choked with magenta slime.

At the outskirts of town he passed a small cottage, raised from the bog on posts. Under the porch crouched an old man, sorting rocks from a sack into three piles.

Gersen called out, "Hoy! Can you direct me to Athmore Violet? I can't find it on my map."

The old man merely crouched in the shadow. Thinking that he had not been heard, Gersen approached. The old man threw a cloth over his rocks and, spraddling on long legs like an ungainly spider, scrambled back into the muck under his house.

Gersen turned away and continued along the lane, passing another cottage, somewhat more substantial, with a black energy unit on the roof, surmounted by a religious fetish. In the gateway of the low wall stood a man wearing a tall conical hat.

Gersen halted and tendered an affable greeting. "Good day, sir."

"Yes, yes," replied the Fojo in a patronizing drawl.

Gersen jerked a thumb toward the first cottage: "Why does the old man hide under his house?"

The Fojo chuckled at Gersen's naïveté. "He is a miner; isn't that clear? Those are his new ores. Look under the house; notice how his eyes gleam! He carries a bylo-by. Had you touched his ores he would have blown away your head and ears."

"I only want information. Where is Athmore Violet? My map doesn't show it."

"Naturally not. At Athmore Violet Bugardoig mines alexandrites!"

"I am not interested in alexandrites. I want to find a man who lives nearby. Can you direct me to Athmore Violet?"

The Fojo jerked his thumb toward the town. "Bugardoig is the man to ask."

"I'm in a hurry. I don't want to waste time looking for Bugardoig."

"Rest easy; he will find you as soon as he notices your vessel on his water meadow, and he won't waste time."

"What of yourself? Do you care to earn a hundred SVU? Help me find my friend."

"Near Athmore Violet, you say. That must be the hermit of Voymont."

"He is a solitary man, true."

"Athmore Violet and Voymont: perilous parts, if only because of Bugardoig's mines."

From inside the cottage came a hoarse voice: "Take the money, Lippold. Do as required! It is a small thing."

Lippold made no acknowledgment of the advice. Apparently he had lost interest in Gersen and stood staring serenely off across Meaughe Vale. Overhead the sky broke apart and Vega darted light of resplendent clarity across the landscape. Objects came alive with color: swamp gorse in maroon and ocher, the mountains behind Poldoolie blue-black and white; the voitch, purple, with an inexplicable blue-green umbra below. The clouds closed like a trap; Vega-light was gone. Lippold stood unmoved by the sudden splendor and its equally abrupt disappearance. Gersen turned away and continued toward the town: an irregular huddle of stone huts, styes, stables and sheds, a dozen shops and agencies, a tavern, a squat Jedasian church.

Above, clouds from east and west collided. They swirled and churned; rain began to fall. Gersen looked over his shoulder; Lippold, in a blur of rain, stood as before.

Gersen ran into town and took shelter under the eaves of a shuttered mechanic's shop. Only the tavern seemed open for business.

Gersen waited a moment. The rain continued to fall in gray sheets, momentarily illuminated with flashes of lightning. Gersen saw tall figures loping through the drench toward the tavern, pausing at the door to shake and kick off the wet, then enter. For a moment the rain paused. During the lull Gersen ran up the street to the tavern.

He entered a long room, with a counter to one side, benches and tables to the other. A line of high windows with panes of yellow mica allowed a dreary light into the room. At the tables sat groups of Fojos, hunched over cups of mulled liquor. The pungence of hot brew mingling with the sour steam of wet clothes and damp flesh brought a twitch to Gersen's nostrils.

As he advanced into the room, all conversation halted and all heads turned and rows of milk-blue eyes scrutinized Gersen. Each man wore a stocking cap pulled down over his spike of hair; similar caps hung on poles beside each table. Gersen nodded politely to the company and went to the counter. The barman, wiping great hands on the dirty towel tied around his stomach, approached. "What is your want?"

"I'd like a few words with someone named Bugardoig," said Gersen. "Is the gentleman here at the moment?"

"There's no Alois Bugardoig here; and what are you needing from him that you wouldn't be better without? And will you not wear a hat? Where's your manners?"

"Sorry, I don't own a hat."

"No matter, you'd look a silly jape with the prut hanging past your cheek like a spent coigel. Aha, who is this?"

Into the tavern lumbered a man, thick and heavy, with slit pale blue eyes almost closed by bulging apple-red cheeks. He went to a pole, took off a "prut" and with a deft twist brought it down over his spike of hair. Gersen turned to the barman: "Is that Bugardoig?"

"Ha ha! That's cause for laughter, or—should you be Bugardoig—a great twinge of rage. That is Looke Hollop, and he empties the town swill. Notice his arms. He's a strong man, is Hollop, but never like Bugardoig. Are you drinking? Do you like our boiled twirps?"

"What else do you serve?"

"Little else. It's good enough for us; are you for fluting and luting with your nose over our good twirps?"

"Never," said Gersen. "Be good enough to serve me a portion."

"Well said. Jocko! A battern of twirps for this outlander. And here, since I'm taking pity on you, let me wrangle up a semblance of decency for your head." The barman stuffed paper into a soiled and oily prut and pulled it down over

Gersen's brow, so that the stuffed part wobbled first to one side, then the other. "Not good," sad the barman, "but better, especially since your business is with Alois Bugardoig, who is a rare stickler for the niceties of life; in fact, he's sworn never to harm another man on the Holy Day, can you believe it? Some declare he's only that much worse other days. Oh, worry, who is this?"

Into the tavern came a Fojo with a great barrel chest and a face splayed and gnarled like a jungle fungus. Gersen asked: "Is that Bugardoig?"

"Him? Never. That's Shirmis Poddle. Shirmus, what's it to be? The usual?"

"The usual, since there's naught better. I wonder where is my brat? He should have been out back tiddling the deckers and not a flap of his shirttail. Well, no matter. It's his bones I'll bruise and not my own."

The barman slid across a jar of heavily spiced twirps. "Drink in joy, Shirmis. Today so far has been quiet."

"Is that surly thing on his way? Or will I have a moment's peace?"

"Only the High Eye sees so far. Hush! Do you hear him now?"

Shirmis again looked toward the door. "That's only thunder. Still—" he raised his jar and drank "—you've roused my nerves. I'm away for places more serene."

The barman watched him depart and gave a sad shake of the head. "Fear is a strange sense and can't be explained. Ah then, is that yet thunder, or is it Bugardoig shaking his leg?"

A Fojo entered the tavern, his shoulders filling the doorway. Twin buttresses of ropy muscle arched up to support his jaw, so that the head seemed more narrow than the neck. His mouth was a gash, his nose a jut of cartilage.

Gersen looked to the barman. "And there . . . ?"

"There you see Bugardoig, and today he has flame in his eye. Someone has treated him poorly, and it may be hard for all of us. Is your prut on straight?"

"I hope so. What does he drink?"

"The usual and several more like it."

"Serve up a double order." Gersen turned toward Bugardoig, who stood looking among the patrons of the tavern with an air of glowering purpose. Turning toward the bar he took notice of Gersen, and gave an exaggerated jerk of displeasure. "And what is this here, with hat askew and face like a gargoyle?"

"A friend in Pontefract asked me to seek you out. He suggested that I put down my ship in your water meadow, as you are notoriously generous. Incidentally, I have ordered a double portion of liquor on your behalf."

Bugardoig lifted one mug in his right hand, drained it; he took the second mug in his left hand, poured it down his throat with equal facility, and set the empty containers back on the counter.

"And so to business. Since I make no exceptions, pay me now and at once a hundred SVU for landing fees, demurrage, and berthing for the month."

"First, let us discuss a larger matter," said Gersen. "Have you a few hours to spare at this moment?"

"On what kind of business?"

"Profitable business."

"Explain yourself."

"Near Athmore Violet lives an important man whom we must visit at once."

"Eh? Who is this? The crazy hermit on Voymont?"

"He is not altogether crazy," said Gersen. "In fact, he has recommended you as most qualified to take me to Voymont, since your properties are nearby."

Bugardoig uttered a great boom of laughter. "Not so nearby that I care to risk my life on Voymont. So pay me my fee and go to Voymont alone. If you approach Arthmore Violet, expect my intense displeasure."

Gersen nodded slowly. "Well then, come along to my boat; I carry no money on my person."

Bugardoig contorted his face into an astonished scowl. "Must I plod the wet marsh because you have been fool enough to forget your money?"

"Whatever you like," said Gersen. "Wait here. I will go for the money and bring it to you."

"Ha!" roared Bugardoig. "I am not to be tricked so readily. Come; if I must, I must. To your ship, and I will collect a surcharge of ten SVU."

"Hold a moment!" bawled the barman. "I want a three-piece[1] for the liquor!"

---

[1] A coin worth three-quarters of an SVU.

Gersen put a coin on the counter and signaled to
Bugardoig. "Let us hurry before the rain returns."

Bugardoig grumbled under his breath, then followed Gersen from the tavern. They walked back along the lane under
a plum-colored sky, past the cottage where Lippold stood as
before, past the hut of the miner, who was nowhere to be
seen, and out upon Bugardoig's water meadow.

They approached the *Flitterwing*. Gersen said to
Bugardoig: "Wait here. I will jump aboard and fetch the
money."

"Don't waste my time with foolishness!" said Bugardoig.
"Open up. You won't stray beyond the clutch of my finger-
nails until I heft what is due me."

"The Fojos are a suspicious race," said Gersen. He climbed
the ladder and opened the port, with Bugardoig close at his
heels. "This way," said Gersen. At the after bulkhead of the
saloon he slid open a door, gestured to Bugardoig. "Through
here."

Bugardoig shoved impatiently past and into the cargo hold;
Gersen slid the door shut and engaged the clamps, even as
Bugardoig realized his error and hurled himself against the
door. Gersen pressed his ear to the panel and heard strident
voices. Grinning, he went to the controls, took the boat into
the air and flew away up Meaughe Vale. Below, the river
moved south like a sullen gray snake through terraces
splotched with various sorts of vegetation: gray goiter bush,
purple voitch, pale green wax plant, black smut-trees. Min-
arets of pink and yellow land-coral thrust a hundred feet
into the air; poisonous orange smears delineated colonies of
wandering musk.

Ten miles slid behind. Gersen dropped the boat upon a
meadow of broad-leaved silver-grass. He alighted from the
boat and walked to the cargo hatch and slid it open, lowered
the ladder. He called; "Keak! Keak! Speak up!"

A surly voice replied: "What do you want?"

"How much mess have you created?"

A short pause; then in airy tones, cracking up into falsetto:
"I personally? Nothing of consequence."

"Keak! Listen carefully—very carefully indeed! I am now
about to let the brats go free. All but you. We will look over
the cargo hatch. If conditions offend me, I will carry you two
hundred miles into the mountains. There you, and you alone,
will scour that cargo hatch until it glistens and smells sweet

as the roses of Kew. Then you will go your way and I will go mine."

Keak's voice came somewhat tremulously: "Conditions are tolerably good. I notice a bit of mess here and there—"

"You had better clean it now, while you still command help, and while you are still close to home."

"We have no cleaning stuffs."

"There is water in the meadow. Use your shirts."

Keak uttered a furious spate of barking orders. The boys came blinking and winking down the ladder. Then appeared a pair of massive legs, next a great torso and finally the head of Alois Bugardoig. At the base of the ladder he halted to stare at Gersen, his cheeks pulsing in and out, his mouth a giant scarlet polyp. Slowly he hunched his shoulders and started for Gersen, who burnt a line of crackling dazzle almost across Bugardoig's toes. "Don't provoke me," said Gersen. "I'm in a hurry."

Bugardoig drew back a pace, his face flushed and dismal. Gersen waved the gun toward Keak. "Faster! Remember how fast you ran out from town?"

Half an hour later Gersen took the boat aloft, leaving a disconsolate group of shirtless boys staring up after him. As he watched they turned; and tucking elbows against skinned white chests, loped off down the valley.

Bugardoig now sat in the saloon, a cord limiting his scope of action. Knots of muscle played up and down his cheeks, his eyes showed as cracks of blue glitter. Bugardoig clearly was not one to show a tolerant or even fatalistic face to adversity.

Gersen took the ship high under the first fleeting layers of cloud. He turned to Bugardoig. "Are you acquainted with Dwyddion?"

"The hermit? Certainly I know him. He lives over Voymont from Athmore Violet. Have I not said he was crazy?"

"Crazy or not, we've got to get him away from Voymont or he'll be killed."

"And this is important?"

"Quite important. So, where is Voymont from here?"

"Yonder. Across the Skak."

"And what are the landmarks?"

Bugardoig uttered a rasping groan. "Ah, the inconveniences I owe this evil yetch and his gun . . . What if I am struck down by lightning?"

"That then will be your fate."

Bugardoig heaved himself erect and looked out the ports. "Go west and a slarsh-tit[1] north. Voymont is beyond those three sharp peaks. Notice that black shadow? That's the Pritz, across from Voymont, with Airy Gulch between. Notice the devil's-light! Ah, there's weird tricks along the Pritz!"

Gersen took the *Flitterwing* high, across ascending ramparts of dreary black rock, and over an awesome badlands of crag and crevasse. To the west loomed the Pritz. Lightning flashes up and down its face became ever more noticeable.

A jumble of confused ridges passed below, which Bugardoig named in a despondent voice: "The Shaggeth . . . Morney's Tooth, and yonder, Athmore Violet . . . Hunckertown Trabble, with a bore of palladium . . . Mount Lucasta; there's the head of Poorleg's River . . . Now the Voymont . . ."

The *Flitterwing* cruised out over an enormous gulch, with a silver trickle of water far below.

"Below is Airy Gulch," said Bugardoig.

The *Flitterwing* hovered and settled slowly. From churning clouds spasms of lightning clawed the Pritz. Gersen asked in a voice unconsciously taut: "Where is Dwyddion?"

"Lower your vessel into Old Airy . . . There, yonder, the ledge, where only a madman would live."

Gersen slid the *Flittering* close to the Voymont, settled through gusts of wind.

Bugardoig pointed a red-knuckled finger. "There, Dwyddion's house. I now have done my undertaking; take me back to Poldoolie."

"We'll stop only long enough to make sure of Dwyddion."

"Bah," grumbled Bugardoig. "I am tempted to pound your head with my fist, gun or no gun."

"Be patient," said Gersen. "We will not be long. In fact, the faster the better."

The *Flitterwing* drifted close to the mountainside. Dwyddion's house was a simple structure: a block of welded stone and glass, perched precariously on a ledge. To the north the ledge had been widened by an artful piling and wedging of large boulders, creating first a viaduct a hundred feet long, then a small shallow landing area: a place open

[1] Slarsh: Fojo term for a preadolescent girl. Slarsh-tit is a vulgar colloquialism for "trifling amount," or "to an almost negligible degree."

and exposed to view. South of the house the ledge became a path leading to a cramped level place in the angle of a crevice. Here sat a small black flyer, and beyond, half excavated into the stone, a structure which Gersen assumed to be a workshop. This area was concealed and unobtrusive. He lowered the *Flitterwing* to a landing behind Dwyddion's black flyer.

Bugardoig made a sneering criticism of Gersen's choice of landing place. "Are you yetch so foolish? Why do you not use the convenient area? Is it too easy and obvious an operation?"

Gersen replied in a measured voice: "A criminal is coming to kill Dwyddion. I don't want him to know that I'm here."

Bugardoig gave a rattling snort of derision.

Gersen opened the port and jumped to the ground. "I can't leave you alone in front of those controls," he told Bugardoig. "Something strange might happen. You'd better come along with me."

Bugardoig folded his massive arms. "I stay here."

"Right now!" said Gersen. "There's no time to waste."

"For crazy yetch business any time is a waste," growled Bugardoig. "Get along with you."

"Then it's the cargo hatch for you."

"No."

Gersen held out his hands. "Watch me." He jerked his right bicep; into his hand as if by magic appeared a projac. "You know what I can do with this." He jerked his left bicep and displayed that complicated weapon known as a dedactor. "Is this familiar to you? No? It discharges three sorts of glass needles. The mildest causes a maddening itch of three weeks' duration. I will use ten needles on you unless you make a very quick move to the cargo hatch."

"At last you persuade me," said Bugardoig. He groaned, belched and with maddening deliberation lowered his bulk to the ground. "I'll go with you and watch your tricks."

Gersen looked around the sky. "Let's make haste."

He set off along the ledge with Bugardoig ambling behind.

A door at the back of Dwyddion's house slid ajar; in the shadow stood a tall thin man. He took a step forward and his features became clear: a dome of a forehead with a high receding mat of dust-colored hair, black eyes brooding in shadowed eye sockets, gaunt cheeks, a delicate pointed chin:

a face implying great intellectual force and a cheerless disposition. He inspected his visitors without amiability.

Gersen halted. "You are Dwyddion?"

"I am he." Dwyddion's voice was deep. "Do not the terms of this place suggest my earnest desire for solitude?"

"Death is also solitary. You must listen carefully as we have very little time. I am Kirth Gersen; this is Alois Bugardoig, a gentleman of Poldoolie, who consented to guide me here."

"To what purpose?"

Gersen again searched the sky, and again saw only dark overcast and low clouds whirling down the wind.

A gust howled across the mountainside, pelting their faces with drops of half-frozen rain. Dwyddion made an impatient sound, hunched his head between his shoulders and retreated into his house. Gersen and Bugardoig followed; with the poorest possible grace Dwyddion allowed them to pass.

They had come directly into the main room of the house. Gersen received an impression of austere proportions, neutral colors, humorless and marginally comfortable furnishings. The message of the room was ambiguous. Here might be the expression of Dwyddion's personality, his overview of existence, or he might simply have subordinated the room to the view from its wide windows; the vast gulch blowing with winds and mists, the Pritz and the incessant play of purple-white lightning.

Dwyddion spoke coldly: "Again may I inquire the reason for your intrusion?"

"Certainly. You were notified in regard to a recent conclave of the Dexad at Wild Isle?"

"Yes. I chose not to attend. In discussions I find myself consistently a minority of one, and my presence seems unnecessary."

Gersen held out his photograph. "You know all these men?"

"Of course."

"And this person here?"

"He is Silas Sparkhammer, a 99. I consider him intelligent, spontaneous, extremely inventive, and totally unsuitable for the Dexad."

"I agree entirely," said Gersen. "His name, incidentally, is Howard Alan Treesong. He poisoned the Triune and the entire Dexad with charnay. There were two exceptions: Benjamin Wroke, whom he drowned, and you, who must now be considered the new Triune. Upon your death, Treesong becomes Triune, and he is now on his way here to murder you."

Dwyddion stared, blinking from the photograph to Gersen. "All are dead?"

"All."

"Ha hum. I find this simply incredible."

"No doubt. It is shocking news. But we have no time to waste. You must come with us—" Gersen gestured toward the door.

Dwyddion drew back. "I know nothing, I have no facts. I cannot act so abruptly . . . Who, then, are you?"

"I'll tell you everything as soon as we're away from here. Come now."

Dwyddion gave his head a fretful shake. "No, of course not. This is sheer hysteria. I can't—"

Gersen gestured to Bugardoig. "Seize this fellow, carry him out." With Dwyddion safe and out of the way on the *Flitterwing*, an ambush of Howard Treesong would become feasible. With luck, the affair could be brought to its finish on this very day.

Bugardoig blinked, then advanced upon Dwyddion, who cried out in a choked voice of outrage: "Stand back!" He flailed out with his fists as Bugardoig stepped forward. Bugardoig uttered a grunt of annoyance for the foolish position in which he found himself. He seized Dwyddion, slung him aloft and over his shoulder. Bugardoig growled at Gersen: "And what now? I am bored with this nonsense."

Gersen opened the door. "Carry him to the ship, and quickly. It's a thankless task, agreed." Bugardoig stalked out upon the ledge with Gersen close behind.

Three men who had been advancing upon the house stopped short. The person on the left was sleek as a seal in a suit of black velvet. His face was round and white and distinguished by an ornate artificial nose wrought from gold filigree. At the center stood Howard Alan Treesong, wearing green trousers, plum-red coat, flapping black cape and black cheese-slice hat. To the right a chisel-faced man with a black skin and black beard stared at Bugardoig in wonder.

Treesong called out in a quick gay voice: "Hola! What goes on here?"

Gersen brought forth the projac. He aimed at Treesong only to find Bugardoig in front of him. Leaning aside, he pulled the trigger; the bolt struck into Treesong's long taut thigh. Treesong whirled to the ground in a flutter of his black cape. Gersen dropped to his knee and fired again, but Treesong had slid over the edge of the viaduct, and lay among the boulders where he gave vent to a set of peculiar many-voiced outcries.

Gersen fired at the black-skinned man and killed him just as he aimed his own weapon. Gold-nose, dropping to the ground, fired a bolt which tore open Bugardoig's great corded neck. Bugardoig toppled like a tree and fell upon Dwyddion, who fretfully pulled himself free and crawled away, while Bugardoig lay pumping vivid red blood across the stones.

Gersen fired again. Gold-nose jerked, cursed, rolled over the edge of the viaduct. Gersen rose to stand in a wary crouch, watching for motion. Treesong had halted his remarkable multivocal yammer; Gersen ran a few steps forward and searched over the declivity, hoping to surprise Treesong. He saw nothing. Treesong had evidently taken shelter behind a squat boulder of gneiss.

Gersen ran crouching across the viaduct. He saw motion and dropped flat. A bolt sizzled through the air a foot above his head. Gersen fired his projac; rock splinters sprayed the head and neck of Gold-nose, who screamed in pain. He lost his footing and slipped down the slope. Gersen watched in fascination as Gold-nose rolled, slid and tumbled, slowly gathering momentum to become a toppling limp object, bounding, rolling, falling free to strike the rock walls, glance away and disappear into the murk.

Gersen clambered back upon the viaduct, in time to see a small airboat raise from the landing-plat and slant into the sky. Howard Alan Treesong had not taken shelter behind the boulder; he had crawled back through the rocks and so had made his escape.

For ten seconds Gersen stared after the airboat. So near, and now so far. His intrigues and strategems gone for naught, and poor Bugardoig a corpse, now drained of blood. He turned to Dwyddion, who stood to the side, watching Gersen with an unreadable expression.

"Get into the ship," said Gersen gruffly. "We've got to leave here in a hurry."

"I see no reason—"

Gersen put his anger and frustration under icy control. "That was Howard Alan Treesong. He came to kill you. He used a ship's boat. Somewhere not too high hangs his ship; in fact it's already dropping to pick him up. As soon as he's aboard, the ship will destroy your house and us as well, if we are fools enough to wait."

Dwyddion gave a fatalistic shrug, but made no further protest. The *Flitterwing* rose into the sky and flew off to the west. Down from the clouds eased a dark hull, toward Voymont. "There's his ship. We're not away too soon."

"I understand none of this," gloomed Dywddion. "It is an outrage that I, who seek only seclusion, should be harassed, coerced and inconvenienced.

"Sad," said Gersen. "Still, if it's any satisfaction to you—and to Bugardoig—we have blown Treesong's master plan sky-high, and we have also shot him in the leg."

"What plan is this?"

"With you dead, he would have become Triune. He's already tried for the IPCC and failed—although the way is still open to him. He rules the criminals of all the major worlds. There is his power base. In ten years he would be emperor of the Oikumene."

"Humm . . . At Pontefract, before the day is out, I'll appoint a new Dexad. The man is a megalomaniac!"

"He is all of that." Gersen reflected upon Howard Treesong's outcries in what seemed a multitude of voices. "He is something very strange indeed."

Chapter 9

Three recollections, vivid beyond all others, in connection with Dwyddion's house on the Voymont persisted with Gersen to haunt him all the days of his life.

First, the Pritz itself, hunched to the attack of a thousand furious lightning bolts, and Airy Gulch, reverberating to wind and thunder.

Second, the corpse of Bugardoig, face astounded by the unthinkable tragedy which had overtaken him, his topknot daubed red with his own blood.

The third recollection, strange and marvelous, would be the many-voiced babble of lamentations and threats produced by Howard Treesong as he lay among the rocks. "—by the sibyls of Hades, such pain!" "—no matter, no matter—" "—that mad dog; who knows him?" "Not I." "Nor I." "Enough! *Elhur padache!*" "Staunch Green!"

The *Flitterwing* once again swung high around Vega. Dwyddion sat stiff and resentful, mouth drooping, face glum. Presently he began to turn sidelong glances toward Gersen. But Gersen sat in silence, occupied with his own problems.

At last Dwyddion broke the silence. In a dignified voice he

said: "I would be interested in learning the reason for your involvement in this business."

"There's no great mystery," said Gersen. "I hold something of a grudge against Treesong. It's as simple as that."

Dwyddion managed a sour chuckle. "Something of a grudge, eh? What occurs when you're seriously offended? . . . Well, no matter, I suppose I should feel grateful to you."

"Probably so."

"Ah, you concur? Then allow me formally to tender my gratitude . . . I may have been solitary for too long a time. For a fact, with the Dexad destroyed, I have no further cause for isolation. The secret now is known only to me."

Dwyddion sat musing and twitching his long white fingers. Now that he had started talking he found it hard to contain his loquacity. "You probably wonder why I chose isolation. From bitterness and disillusionment—there is the answer. Or, if you prefer, I learned 'the Secret.' Perhaps I was callow, perhaps naïve—but no one had ever faulted my zeal. There was never such a swotsman[1]. I was very early selected as an 'Exemplar' and cited for my 'nobility and ease'; I spent all my time at monstrances and on walking tours. I've trudged a thousand landscapes; I've exhorted countless granges. The places I've seen! Berenskaya, Kotop, the Long Hills, Old Home and Prairie Lands, the Green Star Swantees, the Polders of Pedder-Dulah: I've walked them all! I was jailed at Chlodie on Marskens; the Factors of Pollardich on Copus shaved my head; I became resident Thwarterman at Vasconcelles. Perhaps you recall the crusade against electric sports in Myra, on the south continent of Alphanor? What is its name?"

"Trans-Iskana."

"Do you remember the crusade?"

"No."

"I led the march and we did great things, but not without suffering. Oh! when I recall the toil, the heat, the derision and abuse, not to mention insects, crawlers, and bane-bugs! But we thrust on through to Cattlesbury and won the day . . . How long ago it seems! And suddenly I was rank 50, and 60! I directed the campaign against pesticides on Wirfil; I worked

[1] Institute argot: a person who energetically strives to climb the ranks rapidly.

as liaison officer with the Peas and Beaners at New Gorcherum; I served with the Natural Jungle League of Armongol. All considered me the definition of an Institute activist; I was compelling, trenchant, sublimely assured that my ideals were the best of all possible ideals. My rank soared aloft: through the 80's and 90's and now no more campaigns, no more programs—now I was concerned with policy. I had time to rest, to think. I went before the Dexad; I watched their deliberations and I joined their banquets, and at last I was appointed 99. Suddenly I was in line for the Dexad. I met the other 99's, my rivals and my peers. One was Benjamin Wroke, a person not unlike myself, who had arrived at his status much as I had. We had much in common, yet we never achieved full amicability: which, after all, could not be expected when three men vie for the Dexad. The other 99 called himself Sparkhammer. He was a man I could not fathom; he was impenetrable to the usual processes of analysis. I found him by turns charming, repellent, soothing, infuriating. He demonstrated both competence and confidence; his decisions were effortless. He might have been considered a certainty for the Dexad, except for a certain flamboyance which hurt his chances. Both Benjamin Wroke and Silas Sparkhammer yearned for the Dexad—Sparkhammer almost shamefully so. Cloyd Free, rank 104, died in the Kankashee jungles. The Dexad voted in Benjamin Wroke and brought Sabor Vidol up to 99. Sparkhammer could barely conceal his fury. Only two weeks later, Hassamide was murdered by a Thracian footpad. I was elevated into the Dexad and Ian Bilfred was raised to 99. Sparkhammer congratulated me with grace and composure; in truth, he was far too anxious and everyone knew it. As for me, the Dexad meant nothing. I perceived suddenly—in the space of ten seconds—that this supreme achievement—I refer to membership in the Dexad—was factitious. I had overshot my goals. I saw my old self as a child playing games. It was a point of view, so I now suspected, in which the Dexad quite concurred. I had invested thirty-two years of toil and sacrifice in a cause which the leadership regarded at best with indulgent approval. Mind you, these were the best intellects of the Oikumene; they were neither corrupt nor dishonest! I gradually understood that in the processes of maturity and wide purview, they discerned that the strength and virtue of the Institute lay not in its goals, nor in the hopeful achievement of these goals, but in its operative function as a system into which persons like myself could spend their energies, and in so doing leaven an otherwise ponderous society."

Dwyddion paused and stared off along an avenue of memories, his mouth trembling in a bitter smile. Gersen asked: "You changed, so you say, in a space of ten seconds. Was that not abrupt?"

"Yes . . . Well, why should you not know? I was approached by Rob Martiletto, the 108. He said: 'Dwiddion, you are now Dexad. Needless to say you have earned the rank. May I ask if, in your appraisal of the Dexad, you have noticed what I shall call a transcendental serenity?'

" 'Yes, I have noticed something of the sort. I ascribed it to age and a waning of energy.'

" 'That is not altogether the explanation. The jump from 99 to 101 is farther than from say, 70 to 99. This is because the Dexad shares a secret, which now I will impart to you. In the Dexad you advance a long step past the rationale which brought you up to 99. The new ideology is contained in the Secret.' He then told me the Secret. The ten seconds to which I referred passed by. I said, 'Sir, not only can I not endorse your views; I will not seat myself with the Dexad. In short, I now and forever resign from the Institute.'

" 'Not possible! You have sworn to serve for the duration of your days, and so you must.'

" 'Good-bye,' I said. 'You will see me never again.'

" 'Where are you going?'

" 'Where no one will ever come to seek me out.'

"Martiletto showed neither surprise nor resentment; in fact he seemed amused. 'Well then, do as you must. Solitude may bring you a new perspective.'

"I went away. I sought and found solitude; and I must say it has been until today the most peaceful time of my life."

"And the Secret?"

"It is implicit in what I have said. The Dexad perceived society as separated into three elements. In order of consequence, they were humanity at large, the Institute and the Dexad. Humanity and the Institute were seen as opposing forces in a state of dynamic equilibrium. The Dexad functioned to maintain the tension, and to prevent either side from overwhelming the other. The Dexad therefore has often acted in opposition to the Institute, creating situations constantly to outrage and stimulate the membership. That is the Secret."

"Now you are Triune, and you will appoint a new Dexad. How do you regard this point of view?"

Dwyddion uttered a short bleak laugh. "I have discovered something about myself. The 'Secret' embarrassed me. I saw myself across thirty-two years: the earnest swotsman, the sweating dupe controlled by Institute cant, reverent toward Triune and Dexad, contemptuous of the general population. Then I learned the Secret, to my distress. Now that I am Triune, I must either impart the Secret to the next Dexad or suppress it."

Gersen said, "You are not yet free of Treesong. Today he was thwarted and hurt. He will be crazy for revenge."

"Revenge?" cried Dwyddion, with as much ordinary human emotion as Gersen had yet seen him display. "When he came to kill me? Absurd. It is I who demand revenge, for the murder of my fellows, for the great indecency perpetrated upon the Institute."

"Let me offer advice," said Gersen. "At Pontefract you must make a public disclosure of events. The role of Silas Sparkhammer, 99th of the Institute, will no longer be possible for Treesong."

"I intended to make a statement."

"The sooner the better. In fact, when we reach the Pontefract spaceport, we can call into *Cosmopolis*."

Chapter 10

Feature article in *Pontefract Clarion*:

INSTITUTE TRIUNE DESCRIBES
FANTASTIC MURDER BANQUET

Accused: Howard Alan Treesong

Entire Leadership Poisoned; Plot to Control
Institute Ascribed to Notorious 'King of Criminals,' 'Demon Prince' Howard Alan Treesong.

"I personally escaped death by a combination of
luck, quick thinking and the assistance of my aide,"
declared Dwyddion, formerly of Institutional rank
101 and now Triune, a title indicating rank 111.
"I did not attend the banquet," said Dwyddion. "I
learned of the event through Institute intelligence.
I was informed that the notorious criminal Treesong,
by some means, had preempted to himself rank 99,
naturally not in his own identity. He called himself

Sparkhammer, and in due course I will discover the deception by which he gained rank 99.

"Needless to say, his spurious ranking is canceled.

"I have appointed a new Dexad from a roster of authentic rankings. The work of the Institute proceeds.

"I did not attend the murder banquet, for a number of reasons. The Dexad and the Triune met at Wild Isle, on the planet Cytherea Tempestre, to elevate one of three 99's to the Dexad; and to enjoy a banquet including charnay, which is a delicacy known only on Cytherea. I have tasted charnay and find it delectable, but if not prepared properly it is a deadly poison.

"Howard Alan Treesong obtained charnay, extracted the poison, injected it into the already prepared, certified wholesome fruit, which was then served to Triune, Dexad and the candidate 99's. Treesong himself abstained from eating, or perhaps ate wholesome fruit. Benjamin Wroke, rank 102, who like myself chose not to attend the banquet, was subsequently drowned by Treesong.

"Why did he perform such an atrocious act, when he still might have been elevated into the Dexad? Because twice already he had been passed over, and probably had received information that he was to be rejected again, in favor of either Vidol or Bilfred. When a 99 is gainsaid for the third time he must face the bitter fact that he will never attain the Dexad, and so might as well retire from candidacy.

"Treesong chose, rather, to murder all ranks above him, whence, by Institute law, he ascended to the highest rank left open: in this case only 109, until I could be disposed of. I, naturally, being of higher rank, would precede him to Triune."

Gersen rubbed his face with sallow skin tone, arranged a hairpiece of effusive black curls over his own short black pelt and donned his exquisite garments, to achieve once more the semblance of an indolent wastrel.

He set off across Tara Square. The day was gray, and a gray mist hung on the air. The folk of Pontefract marched stolidly past. Their black and brown costumes made a muted richness against the wet stone and old black iron.

Gersen turned into Corrib Place, halted to inspect the *Extant* offices. Nothing seemed amiss. The aged structure, black with grime, seemed as placid as ever. The duration of his absence could be measured in hours; the psychological time seemed far longer . . . He crossed the street, entered the building and went directly to the contest workroom. Today, so he recalled, saw the end of the contest; the work load had decreased significantly and only a half-dozen sacks of mail lay in the bin.

Mrs. Ench bustled forward to greet him. "Good morning, Mr. Lucas!"

"Good morning, Mrs. Ench. Any startling developments?"

"Not yet, Mr. Lucas. The Cytherea entry is still the closest. But have you seen the newspapers this morning? It's absolutely remarkable!"

"Yes, most amazing."

"How will it affect our contest?"

"In no way whatever, or so I hope. We are lucky that our deadline is today. Otherwise we might have multitudes of opportunistic winners."

"We still might have some."

"We'll simply have to judge each entry on its own merits."

"Quite right, Mr. Lucas."

Gersen turned away but Mrs. Ench called him back. "Oh, Mr. Lucas, one interesting letter—at least I consider it interesting. I set it aside for you, since it concerns our number six." She handed Gersen an envelope.

"Thank you, Mrs. Ench." Gersen read the letter. "Interesting!" He read the letter a second time. "I suppose it has no particular bearing on our contest, as the newspapers have established Sparkhammer's true identity."

"My feeling exactly. Our contest seems remarkably timely. Is it all a coincidence?"

Gersen laughed politely. "In case anyone asks, we are all dumbfounded by the new developments."

"No one has asked, but many may be wondering."

"That's as may be. The publicity can't do *Extant* any harm."

Gersen went on into the front office. Alice sat quietly at her desk. She wore a simple black shirt and jacket, upon which the tips of her orange hair rested and then curved upward. At the sight of Gersen she made an abrupt motion toward the newspaper on her desk, then restrained herself.

"Good morning, Mr. Lucas."

"Good morning, Alice. You've seen the news, evidently."

Alice feigned no misunderstanding. "Yes." She looked down at the journal. "It is—interesting."

"No more than that?"

Alice only gave a noncommittal shrug.

Gersen said, "Treesong is a terrible man. He is one of the 'Demon Princes.' "

"I have heard the name, certainly," said Alice stiffly.

Gersen said, "There's mention of a 'Benjamin Wroke' who drowned in the Shanaro Sea. I hope that he is no connection of yours."

Alice looked up with somber eyes, then turned away. "Yes. He is a close connection."

"That's a great pity. You have my sincere sympathy."

Alice made no reply. Gersen went to his desk. He sat down and studied Alice's profile. "I still wish very much to meet Howard Alan Treesong."

Alice's chin rose an eighth-inch. She spoke a bitter monosyllable. "Why?"

"He is now more than ever a superb subject for an interview."

Alice lowered her chin to its original position. "Do you think it wise to publicize the exploits of such a man?"

"Certainly. Sooner or later he will come to a bad end. How do such men function? What are their motivations? How does he regard himself?"

"He would never allow you to write undignified things about him."

"He could write the copy himself, for all I care. What with the contest and the murders, we'd sell a hundred million copies."

Alice abruptly rose to her feet. "I don't feel well. If there's nothing for me to do, I think I'll rest for an hour or two."

"Just as you like," said Gersen. He rose politely to his feet. "I hope you're better soon."

"Thank you." With a final swift glance toward Gersen, skeptical and dubious, Alice left the office.

Gersen sat back. He brought out the letter tendered him by Mrs. Ench and read it for the third time.

Director of *Extant* Contest:

Please consider this letter as my entry in your contest.

I can definitely identify one person in the photograph.

This entitles me to one-tenth of a share in the contest prize, which I claim.

That person marked "Number 6" was born at Home Farm, near Gladbetook, in the Land of Maunish. He was named by his mother: Howard Alan, after the television wizard H. A. Topfinn and Arblezanger, in remembrance of her grandfather. With his patronymic he was and is Howard Alan Arblezanger Hardoah and so do I identify him. He has not been a close son, and indeed left us some years ago. I have heard that he is successful and doing well and I hope to see him shortly at the school reunion to which he has been invited.

In any case, I render this identification and I will expect my share of the contest money at once.

I am Adrian Hardoah,

at Home Farm
Gladbetook, Land of Maunish
Moudervelt
Van Kaathe's Star

Gersen reflected a moment, then called Information Service. Moudervelt he found to be the only populated planet of Van Kaathe's Star. It was a world somewhat larger than Earth, with a single continent sprawling two-thirds of the way around the equator. The world was old and its soil was mellow. The mountain ranges of its youth had eroded low, leaving wide prairies and meandering rivers. Moundervelt had first been settled by a variety of small groups: religious sects, clans, sporting associations, philosophical societies and the like. They had quickly exterminated the race of semi-intelligent beings in residence, parceled out tracts of land, established frontiers for their 1,562 realms, and for century after century occupied themselves with their own affairs. The Land of Maunish occupied a section of the Goshen Prairie, in the eastern midlands of the great continent. The capital, Cloutie, maintained a population of three thousand. Eighty miles north in Fluter Township on the banks of the Wiggal River was Gladbetook, with a population of three thousand. Maunish had been settled by the Partitioners of the Pure Truth; the Teachings discouraged space travel, and the nearest spaceport lay three hundred miles south, at Theobald Station, in the Land of Lelander.

Gersen turned away from the communicator. Howard Treesong had been born a country boy, in one of the most placid backwaters of the human universe. Gersen decided, upon reflection, that the fact had no general significance. There were many country boys who never became criminals . . . He turned back to the communicator and made connection with room 442 at St. Diarmid's Inn. Alice would be arriving at her own room just about now.

His timing was exact. He heard the door open and Alice's steps as she crossed the room. For a few moments she moved here and there, rather listlessly, then came to rest.

She sat five minutes arranging her thoughts. Then he heard her speaking, in a voice resolute and steady. "Alice Wroke here."

A minute passed. Then Howard Treesong's voice replied, in tones strident and harsh: "Yes, Alice, I hear you. What have you accomplished?"

"As much as possible."

"I am satisfied only with achievement."

"Where is my father? According to the newspapers he is dead."

"Do not presume to question me. Make your report."

"I can report only what you already know. Mr. Lucas told me again that he is anxious to interview you."

The voice became even more harsh. "He knows you are in contact with me?"

"Certainly not. He is as callous as you are. He wants to

publish your biography, or your autobiography, so that he can sell a hundred million copies of his journal."

"And he considers me an altruist?"

"I doubt that, but then I am only reporting his remarks. Do as you see fit."

"Just so."

Alice hesitated, then asked, "The contest is over. I have kept to the terms of my bargain. Is my father truly dead?"

Treesong's voice, changing once more, became flat yet throaty, acrid yet thick. "You now know my name."

"Yes."

"And you know who I am."

"I have heard of you."

"Perhaps you divined my great scheme."

"You planned to be Triune of the Institute."

The stridency returned to Treesong's voice. "That plan has hatefully and viciously been thwarted. Benjamin Wroke— who was he? What did he matter? Naturally he is dead, and why did I trouble myself? The plan is broken, by the journalists and their contest!"

"So he has gone?"

"Who? Wroke? How could you think otherwise?"

"You assured me otherwise."

A rasping laugh. "People believe whatever they want to believe."

"I am now done with you."

"Go your way. You are destructively beautiful; you have brought dissent among the colors of my soul. Red lusts; Blue feels a melancholy longing, while Green would cause you pain. But nothing will be done; I have taken injury and I suffer. There is no time; also you have soiled yourself; you bedded with the journalist. Granted, at my behest, but you should have pleaded and made outcry."

"I showed poor judgment," said Alice tartly.

When Treesong responded his voice was stern and sullen. "I am about to depart. Vega has not been kind; nor was it ever. I am wounded and sore, but in due course I will set things straight—and then! My pain will be remedied a thousand times over."

"What happened to you?" Alice spoke with ingenuous interest.

"We met ambush. A demon in the shape of a man sprang out of Dwyddion's house and fired his projac into my leg."

"I should think you'd be expecting such things."

Treesong seemed not to hear the remark. Another brief silence, then a new voice, clever and electric: "The *Extant* contest ends tomorrow?"

"No. Today."

"And there is yet no winner?"

"That's correct."

"Then these are your instructions: 'Do not call me again.' "

"I am free of you! Save your instructions!"

Treesong ignored the interruption. "Continue as before." But the conversation had ended.

At noon Vega burnt away the overcast, leaving the sky suffused with bright milky haze. Alice returned to the office looking pale and drawn.

"You're feeling better, I hope?" asked Gersen.

"Yes, thank you." She went to her desk and seated herself. She had changed into a gray-green frock with a prim white collar which her orange curls barely brushed: the colors of some exotic desert flower, thought Gersen. She became aware of his attention and gave him a quick glance. "Is there anything I should do?"

"Not really. The contest is essentially over. There have been interesting developments, don't you think?"

"Definitely so."

"Still, it's not much better than a standoff. Treesong failed to take over the Institute. On the other hand, he's still alive and his career goes on. Your father is dead, which is your private tragedy. If you had known that Sparkhammer was Howard Alan Treesong, you could never have hoped otherwise."

Alice turned in her chair to stare at Gersen. "How did you know that Benjamin Wroke was my fahter?"

"It's on your application," said Gersen. He smiled a rather lame smile. "Also, not to put too fine a point on it, I tapped into your conversations with Treesong."

Alice sat like a statue. "Then you knew—"

"From the moment you walked into the office. Even before. I knew when I saw you across the street."

Alice flushed suddenly pink. "And you must have known . . ."

"So I did."

"But still . . ."

"What would you think of me if I had taken advantage of you?"

Alice showed a strained, meaningless smile. "What difference does it make what I think?"

"I don't want your self-esteem to be damaged—especially for the wrong reasons."

"This is an idiotic conversation," said Alice. She rose to her feet. "And it is idiotic for me to stay here any longer."

"Where are you going?"

"Away. Am I not discharged?"

"Of course not! I admire your courage! When I look across the room, I like to see you sitting there. Furthermore—"

The desk communicator chimed. Gersen touched a button; a voice spoke: "Howard Alan Treesong calling Henry Lucas."

"Henry Lucas here. Do you have a face?"

"I do indeed." Upon the screen appeared an image: a face with a high square forehead, clear hazel eyes, a fine straight nose, long chin, wide easy mouth, an expression of prideful verve and vivacity. Gersen pulled the black curls of his hairpiece forward and down across his white cheeks, half-closed his eyes and dropped his jaw, in order to project an impression of aristocratic languor. Alice watched in sardonic amusement as Gersen transmitted the image to Howard Treesong.

The two men studied each other. Treesong spoke in a rich flowing voice. "Mr. Lucas, I have been following your contest with interest, since, as you know, I am included in the photograph."

"So I understand. Naturally it augments popular interest in the event."

Treesong said airily: "I am not sure whether or not you intend to flatter me."

"For the purposes of this occasion I am a journalist, which is to say, an automaton, without personal feelings."

"If so, then you are unusual. But no matter. Since you make no specific bans or debarments, I wish to submit my personal solution to your contest. Be kind enough to note my identifications, or better, ask your remarkably beautiful secretary to do so."

Gersen said thoughtfully, "I doubt if this could be considered regular procedure. All our other entries have arrived in written form."

"You make no stipulation to this effect, so why should not a verbal identification be valid? I can use the prize money as well as the next person."

"Quite so. Our award ceremony takes place shortly. If you were adjudged the winner, could you be on hand to accept the prize?"

"A bit awkward, I'm afraid. Unless the occasion were celebrated in the far Beyond."

"That might be troublesome, from our point of view."

"Then you must send the money to an address which I will supply. Now for the identifications."

"Quite so, quite so . . . Alice, take notes."

"I will identify as you have numbers. One is Sharrod Yest. Two is that acidulous harridan Dianthe de Trembuscule. Three, the corpulent Beatrice Utz. Four is the once-voluble Ian Bilfred, whose agile tongue, alas, is now forever stilled. Five is the overeager Sabor Vidol. Six is that person known on this occasion as Sparkhammer, but more generally known as Howard Alan Treesong. Seven is John Gray. Eight is that otiose lummox the Triune, Gadouth. Nine is Gieselman; ten, Martiletto. I hope that I am the first correctly to identify these folk."

"I'm afraid not. As soon as Dwyddion's revelations were made public, dozens of opportunists swarmed into our office with correct identifications."

"Pah! Greed is rampant everywhere! Another score to be settled with Dwyddion!"

"Something may still be salvaged. I want to publish your biography, at terms to be arranged. You are a unique individual and your memoirs should interest our readers."

"It is something to think about. I have often felt the need to express my views. The public regards me as a criminal. By ordinary definition, I am a very paragon of the trade; I recognize no peer. By the very nature of my accomplishments, I have created a new category by which I and I alone may be judged. I will not now enlarge upon the idea."

"In any case, public interest will not be diminished."

"I must consider the matter carefully. I don't like to station myself in a designated place at a specific time. If you will reflect upon the conditions of my existence, you will perceive that the need for vigilance is one of its very few disadvantages."

"Yes, so it would seem."

"Certain folk do not yield gracefully to my instructions; they thereby incur penalties. This is sheer simple fact. I am meticulous in regard to rewards and penalties, I assure you. I usually take the rewards and others must make do with the penalties, but no matter. Is not the cosmos a more vital and adventurous place for my presence? Of course! I am indispensable."

"All this will fascinate my readers. I hope you agree to the interview."

"We shall see. At the moment I am pressed for time. I have a rendezvous to keep upon a distant planet and I must make my arrangements. That is all for now."

The screen went dim. Gersen leaned back in his chair. "Treesong seems to have an elastic disposition."

"He changes from minute to minute," said Alice. "He terrifies me. Still, I hope to see him at least once again."

Gersen was intrigued by her lackluster voice. "Why so?"

"I'll try to kill him."

Gersen stretched his arms into the air. The narrow-shouldered coat constricted him. He pulled it off and threw it aside. Then he took off his hairpiece and threw it after the coat. Alice watched him sidelong, but made no comment.

"He is cautious," said Gersen. "I was lucky to get a single shot at him out on the Voymont."

In a soft wondering voice Alice asked, "Who are you?"

"In Pontefract I'm known as Henry Lucas, a writer for *Cosmopolis*. Sometimes I use a different name and do different things."

"Why?"

Gersen rose, sauntered across the room to her desk. He reached under her arms, pulled her up so that her face was close. He kissed her forehead, her nose, her mouth, to which she remained passive.

He eased the pressure of his arms. "If Treesong calls to ask about me, you can't tell him if you don't know."

"I will tell him nothing in any case. He has no more power over me."

Gersen kissed her again, to which she yielded but again made no response. She drew back. "Then you want me to remain here?"

"Very much so."

She turned and drew away from him. "I have nothing better to do."

"Then you'll be here when I get back?"

"Where are you going?"

"I'm going out to a strange old world, to take part in a social occasion."

"Where Howard Treesong is going?"

"Yes. I'll tell you all about it when I return."

Alice asked wistfully. "When will that be?"

"I don't know." Gersen kissed her again, and now she responded, and for a moment relaxed against him. Gersen kissed the top of her head. "Good-bye."

Chapter 11

Life, Introduction to Volume II,
by Baron Bodissey Unspiek;

As we traverse the river of human time in our wonder boats, we notice recurring patterns in the flow of peoples and civilizations . . . The disparate races coalesce only when territory is limited, cramped and crowded, with compressive social pressures. Strong, exact governments are typical of these circumstances; they are both necessary and welcome. Conversely, when land is vast and easily available, as in the broaching of a new continent or a new world, nothing can keep different sorts of people in close contact. They migrate to new places and particularize, whereupon languages mutate, costumes and conventions elaborate, aesthetic symbols take on fresh meanings. Now the public mood turns inward; government imposed from another place cannot be tolerated. The processes, as the race wanders from its native star, are of infinite richness and a source of endless fascination . . .

Moudervelt: *Then and Now*, from *Studies in Comparative Anthropology*, by Russell Cooke:

Had the astute Baron chosen to adorn his famous *Introduction to Volume II* with examples, he might well have selected the remote world Moudervelt, orbiting Van Kaathe's Star, as a felicitous paradigm for the illumination of his general principle.

Moudervelt is a world benign and fertile, with an expansive land area. The flora is generally compatible with Earth stock; the fauna offers no menace except for a few predatory sea creatures.

Moudervelt is an old world. The ancient mountain ranges are now forested hills; rolling plains extend horizon to horizon, under blue skies and flotillas of tall white cumulus. Great slow rivers wander the prairies, where the soil is deep and the climate fair. Except for rivers, the land lacks natural boundaries, but boundaries and borders aplenty have been created, to delineate 1,562 separate dominions, each jealous of its identity, each cherishing its own rotes and rites, each celebrating its distinctive cuisine and scorning all others as filth and scum, each considering itself the single home of civilization among 1,562 barbaric, incomprehensible and unpleasant neighbors.

Moudervelt knows no true cities. Most of the lands maintain a spaceport. Commerce is carried on the rivers, which are all interconnected by canals. Only a few land routes connect the states.

Moudervelt is by no means isolated from the universe. It exports a considerable quantity of special foodstuffs for the use of former inhabitants,[1] and imports technical goods, special tools, a few books and periodicals: in total bulk, no great amount. Moudervelt by and large is self-sufficient.

From *Popular Handbook to the Planets*, 330th Edition, 1525: Moudervelt, Van Kaathe's Star:

[1] Ships trading in offworld foods roam everywhere across the settled worlds. Old Earth supplies perhaps a third of all such comestibles. The wines of Earth are especially prized.

(After the usual exposition of physical data and an historical summary, the text devotes a paragraph or two to each of the 1,562 dominions.)

Maunish, at the center of Goshen Prairie, occupies an area of about 40,000 square miles and supports a population of about a million, descended from a mission of the Pure Truth Partition. The areas bounded by the Dalglish River on the south and east, by the Land of Puck to the west, Amable and the River Bohuloe on the north, the lands of Ganaster and Erquhar to the east. The principal town is Cloutie.

Notice to Offworld Arrivals: There are no spaceports within the confines of Maunish. Indeed, space vessels, aircraft, hoppers or sky-riders flying at an elevation over forty-nine feet are prohibited. Entry must be made by surface transportation at an authorized checkpoint. Border controls are strict, as are import regulations. Bring in no weapons, intoxicants, erotic materials, medicines, except those personally required. Border searches are thorough; penalties are severe.

Gersen lowered the *Flitterwing* down upon Theobald Station. Farmlands punctuated by white houses spread away from the town in all directions. The Dalglish River crawled in great loops across the landscape, finally to swerve to the north and disappear.

The spaceport projected no detectable beacon or signal. Gersen isolated it from adjacent fields only by virtue of three spacecraft already on hand; a pair of small cargo carriers and a bedraggled old *Sissle Wanderway*.

Gersen landed the *Flitterwing*, made his usual arrangements and jumped to the ground. He found himself at the center of a sunny open field sodded with blue-green turf. Cool country air blew in his face; there was no sound except for a slight hiss from the *Flitterwing's* recharging respirators. A hundred yards across the field, shaded under a pair of sprawling trees, he saw a small shed, upon which rested a sign:

Central Space Terminal
Theobald Station, Land of Lelander
All Incoming Traffic Report Here.

Inside the shed Gersen discovered a small fat man dozing at a table, the remains of his lunch spread before him. He wore what once had been a smart uniform of black, tan and red twill; but for breeches and boots he had substituted a white knee-length skirt and sandals.

Gersen rapped on the table; the official woke abruptly. Almost before opening his eyes he groped for his cap and pulled it over his balding pate. He looked Gersen over with a bland expression. "Sir?"

"I am an item of 'Incoming Traffic.' The sign directed me here."

"Yes. Yes indeed. Well, there are a few formalities incident to entry . . ." He secured a form, put questions to Gersen, noted the responses.

He completed the form and filed it in a box. "That is all, sir, except for the landing fee."

Gersen said, "First, a bit of information. I am actually en route to Maunish; are there any hindrances to travel?"

"None whatever. The borders are open."

"I can rent a vehicle?"

"Certainly. I will rent you my own car, and my son will drive you."

Gersen's ears were attuned to almost imperceptible hints and implications. He looked sharply at the official. "At what rent?"

"Oh—nothing unreasonable. Ten SVU per diem."

"No extra charges or supplements?"

"None. Do you take me for a scarper?"

"He will drive me to Cloutie and elsewhere in Maunish at my convenience?"

The official showed an expression of indignant wonder. "Into Maunish? You must be joking! To the Maunish border, no farther! How could I risk my car in that nation of stoneheads; where girls strut around with bare elbows and men show their teeth while eating? They drive like catatonics; the air stinks with their pickled ramp. To the border, no farther. Perhaps you can secure onward transportation at that point."

"Well then, what are the public conveyances between the two countries?"

"Nothing to suit a wealthy offworlder. You would be forced to ride the Trans-World bus with bumpkins returning to Maunish."

"That will suit me well enough. I have ridden in worse company."

"If that is your taste, you are in luck. The afternoon car passes by in a matter of minutes. Now as to the landing fee, a vessel such as yours is rated at 200 SVU per week, payable a month in advance."

Gersen laughed. "I have important friends in the neighborhood. They warned me that public officers tend either to larceny or daydreaming." He produced five SVU. "This will have to do."

The official took the money with poor grace. "It is not regular but I suppose that exceptions are possible for the sake of good public relations . . . Yonder comes the Trans-World."

Along the road came a rickety triple-jointed omnibus, riding on eight great air-wheels. Gersen flagged it down, paid another five SVU to the driver and found a seat.

For hours he rode across a gently rolling land of fields, rivers, ponds and orchards. White farmhouses sprawled under luminescent foliage of pink, rose-red, orange and yellow. The farmers seemed prosperous; life could not be totally bad in the Land of Lelander, even if the girls might not show their elbows.

A line of dark blue and black foliage wandered across the horizon, where the Dalglish River swung east to delineate the Maunish frontier. A hundred yards short of the boundary the bus halted. From a station house marched a sergeant and six soldiers in fine uniforms.

The sergeant boarded the bus, put several questions to the operator, who jerked his thumb toward Gersen.

The sergeant signaled to Gersen. "This way, sir, for just a moment. Bring your luggage."

Gersen took his small traveling bag and followed the sergeant from the bus and into a shed. The sergeant took the bag, hefted it, looked at Gersen with a smile. "I see that you are attempting to smuggle a Model 6A projec into Maunish." He untaped a pair of grips from the handle to the traveling bag. "This is not a new trick; we are alert for it. Here I merely confiscate the weapon. Across on Maunish you would be placed in a cage, submerged in the river for three hours, or until you were thoroughly drowned. They are barbarically strict in this regard. Give me the other parts, please."

Gersen opened the bag and produced the other components, which he had disguised by various methods. "There you are, sergeant. I thank you for your warning." He jerked his right forearm and a throwing blade appeared in his hand. "You had also better take custody of this." He shook his left arm, producing an air-tube for shooting glass needles. "And this."

"Very wise, sir."

"Please don't sell them at once. If I return this way—and I plan to do so—I will buy them from you myself."

"That is often the situation, sir."

Gersen returned to the bus, which at once proceeded across the wide Dalglish on an iron bridge and so entered the Land of Maunish.

The road slanted off across a marsh of brown mud and purple reeds, passed through a grove of giant pawpaws which emitted a fetid sweetness into the air, burst out into the sunlight, and now the countryside had altered. Yonder, across the river was Lelander; here was Maunish; nothing was quite the same. The bus halted at the Maunish border station, in the shade of an enormous ling-lang tree, with blue foliage and a gnarled contorted trunk six feet in diameter. As before guards marched out to meet the bus. Here they wore uniforms of gray and green instead of red, black and tan. They were a people notably different from the short soft-featured Lelanders; here they were tall, spare, with lank brown hair and bony faces.

At a signal from the sergeant the passengers alighted and one by one they entered a long shed, where each was examined and searched at three separate stations. In Gersen's case they were brisk, impersonal and extremely thorough. They ignored his offworld origin. His professed trade, journalism, aroused only slightly more interest. "What do you expect to learn in Maunish?"

"Nothing of consequence. I am coming here as a tourist."

"Then why not call yourself a tourist?"

"It is no great matter, one way or the other."

"Perhaps not to a tourist, nor to a journalist, but we are security officers responsible for the decency of Maunish. To us the roles are very different. In the first place the tourist may stay at the Hotel Bon Ton in Maunish, while journalists must spend each night at the police station."

"In that case I am definitely a profound tourist. I agree that the differences are significant."

"Apparently you carry no contraband."

"Apparently not."

The official showed him a wintry smile. "You will discover that many of our good Maunish customs become persuasively practical, upon acquaintance. Still—and I can assure you of this, since I have traveled widely; I have visited thirty-nine distinct and separate domains—Maunish is a haven of tolerance compared to such as Malchione or Dinkland. Our statutes are simple and reasonable. We forbid the advancement of polytheism and the display of white flags. We prohibit offensive belching and other breaches of the public peace. Our schedule of crimes is ordinary enough; you need only conduct yourself with discretion to avoid trouble." He signed Gersen's certificate of admission with a flourish. "There you are, sir. The freedom of Maunish is yours!"

Gersen boarded the bus, which suddenly lurched into motion; the border station under the sprawling blue linglang was left behind. The landscape was now that of Maunish, different from that of Lelander; whether by reason of psychic shift or immanent character or altered references Gersen, who had experienced such shifts many times before, had no way of knowing. The country seemed bigger, the sky more open. In a new clarity of atmosphere the horizons seemed both far and near, in a curious visual paradox. Along the plain trees grew in private clusters and copses, each to its own kind: ginsaps, orpoons, linglangs, flamboys; the shadows below were a dense darkling black which seemed to glimmer with a strange rich color without a name. The farmhouses were both less frequent and older; high and narrow for no obvious reason, and set far back from the road in jealous seclusion . . . The country became softer. The bus rolled through orchards with black trunks and effulgent pink or yellow foliage, across brimming rivers, through hamlets and at last into Cloutie, to halt in the central square. The sides swung up; those passengers with business in Cloutie alighted, among them Gersen. He looked around him with interest. To the young Howard Treesong Cloutie would have seemed a most important place, the center of the civilized universe, where he might be brought once a year on some special occasion. Across the square Gersen saw the Hotel Bon Ton, an ungainly four-story structure, high and narrow, with a heavy overhanging roof and a pair of two-story wings.

If Howard Treesong were traveling to Gladbetook to take part in his school reunion, quite possibly, like Gersen, he might choose to lodge at the Bon Ton. The time for caution had arrived, and indeed might already have passed him by ... At a haberdasher's shop Gersen changed into local garments: a shirt of heavy green cloth, bag-breeches gathered at the knee, gray wool stockings and black broad-toed shoes, a wide-brimmed, low-crowned black hat, tilted somewhat to the back of the head. The local mannerisms—a slow stiff-legged gait with arms at the sides and face turned squarely forward—were less readily simulated. He would still be noticed as an outlander, but less readily.

He crossed the square to the Bon Ton Hotel and entered a dim lobby smelling of years upon years of waxed wood, moldering leather, heavy cushions and unnameable local exudations. The lobby was deserted; the reception desk was dark. Gersen knocked at a wicket until a small old lady appeared from a back room. In a shrill voice she demanded his business.

Gersen replied with dignity. "I wish to take lodging for a few days."

"So indeed; where will you feed?"

"Wherever I find the best meals."

"Those are far away, over at the lake, where folk forget Stricture and pamper their guts. You must ingest what we choose to serve here, in our dining room."

"Whatever is proper."

"It is very proper." The old woman peered at him slantwise. "What are you doing here? Are you for selling *things?*" She contrived to invest the word with an emphasis at once lubricious and minatory.

"No, I am selling nothing."

"Oh." And after a pause, "Nothing whatever?"

"Nothing whatever."

"That's a pity," she declared in a voice suddenly bright and garrulous. "I always say that a body should buy and sell as they choose, despite the Health Agency. Where are you from? I can't place you. You're not a Mandyke? Nor a Booder?"

"None of those."

"Do you burn fires or pour waters?"

"No, never."

"Very well; you may have the Smiling Sunrise Room." The woman's face became so beatifically innocent that Gersen instantly was prompted to ask: "What are the rates?"

"It is our best room, reserved for important dignitaries. It rents at a corresponding level."

"How much?"

"Eighty-three SVU per diem."

"That is far too much. Let me see your schedule of rates."

"Well then, five SVU . . ."

Gersen was pleased with his room, which included the lowest of the central verandahs, a bathroom paneled in white wood, an adjacent sleeping cubicle, a small gymnasium.

The time was now late afternoon. Gersen descended to the street, looked right and left, then set off to inspect the town. The south end of the square was dominated by a stone statue and, behind, a tall austere structure, evidently a church or temple. A plaque at the base of the statue identified the lordly form as Bandervoum the Didram, who held aloft a carpenter's try square that he might gauge the souls of the dead. Behind the church grew a line of heavy black deodars; gaps in the foliage revealed a field on which stood a throng of white statues.

Near the church Gersen discovered a small stationer's shop selling a miscellaneity of small objects. On a rack he noticed several copies of *Cosmopolis*, of assorted dates, and an *Extant*. The *Extant* cover displayed a picture of ten men and the caption:

WHO ARE THESE MEN?
NAME THEM CORRECTLY AND WIN 100,000 SVU!

Gersen entered the shop. Behind a pair of parallel counters, to right and left, stood a pair of small girls, dressed in long-sleeved black frocks. Their black hair was tied into topknots, so tightly drawn that their eyes seemed to bulge. Into the hair a pair of coral-russet fronds had been fixed. On the counter Gersen found for sale a pamphlet entitled:

THE LAND OF MAUNISH
OFFICIAL MAP AND SURVEY
This authoritative rendering includes all roads, towns, rivers, bridges, frontier posts, together with physiographic details.

Price: 25 centums.

Gersen took a copy of the map and paid over a coin. The girls protested instantly! "Sir! The price is two SVU!"

Gersen indicated the printed notation. "The price is set at 25 centums."

"That is for local residents," said one girl.

"Outlanders must pay a surcharge," said the other.

"Why is this?" asked Gersen, wondering how the girls knew him for an outlander in his new Cloutie clothes.

"Because the map includes valuable secret information," said the girl to the right in an earnest voice.

"Extremely valuable to an enemy army," said the girl to the left, even more grave.

"But surely your enemies already possess maps of Maunish?"

"Perhaps not all of our enemies."

"Perhaps not with so much secret detail."

"In that case," said Gersen, "your map is far more valuable than a mere two SVU."

"True, but no one would pay such a price," said one girl.

"They would prefer to use any old thing," said the other girl.

"Well, it so happens that I am a local resident and not an enemy," said Gersen. "I live at the Bon Ton Hotel; therefore I am eligible for the lower rate."

The girls stood silent, considering the theoretical basis of Gersen's position; before they could formulate an argument, Gersen was gone.

Gersen sat on a bench and studied the map. He found Gladbetook forty miles to the north, on the banks of the Sweet Trelawney River.

Gersen continued around the square. Along the way he noticed a sign:

PANTILOTE GARAGES
Vehicle of Quality! Sale or Hire:
By Hour—By Day—By Week

Apply at our correctly managed workshops. You will observe and approve the dutiful exactitude of our processes.

29 Didram Rummel Street

Gersen located Didram Rummel Street and the Pantilote Garages, where, after considerable formality, he succeeded in renting a three-wheeled runabout, which had been constructed on the premises from miscellaneous bits and pieces.

Evening was already darkening the skies. The way to Gladbetook seemed too long a journey. Gersen arranged to call for the vehicle on the following morning, whereupon he would drive across Goshen Prairie to the early home of Howard Alan Treesong.

Chapter 12

From the Teaching of Didram Bodo Sime, 6:6

(Obloquies against the Toper and his Drink)

Motto:
It is not good to inebriate nor to souse, using swillage, near or far beers, or distillations.

Expansion:
The toper is a fuming bore, a loon, a mongrel, a social mockery. Often he soils his clothes and commits malditties. He smells and belches; his familiarities trouble all decent folk. His songs and tirrilays offend the ears. He often gives breath to scurrilous conjecture.

The toper suborns good fruit and gives it to decay, and the good person who wishes to enjoy the sanivacity and good savor of the wholesome fruit is bereft and must raise this out-

cry: "Why have you despoiled me, O toper,
of my fruit and given it to filthy decay?"

The toper performs foolish dances. He postures
like a clown and cleans his ears with broom-
straws. He is prone to perform pugnacities upon good and earnest folk who chance to halt
upon their way to chide him for his folly.

North of Cloutie the countryside became wild and desolate, first because of the Junifer River boglands, then by reason of long ledges of black rock which made the land fit only
for grazing. For the first time Gersen saw indigenous fauna
of Moudervelt: two-legged toadlike creatures bounding high
after flying insects; a band of lizard-foxes, with gray-green
pangolin scales and a single optic orb. They reared high to
watch Gersen pass by; when he slowed the car they advanced
with dancing sidelong steps, for purposes Gersen could not
guess. He drove on, leaving the troop staring after him.

With the Rock-Wallows behind, the solitude persisted.
Empty steppes spread away to the horizon: a land gently rolling, without trees, lonesome and forlorn in the sunlight.

Finally, across the north, appeared a dark line: the trees
along the banks of the Great Swomey River. Once across the
river the land again became settled. Gersen drove through
half a dozen hamlets, as like to each other as eggs: a main
street, a few cross streets, an inn, several shops, a school to
the side, a hall, a temple, a varying number of houses and
cottages.

Close on midmorning Gersen arrived at Gladbetook: a village much like those others along the road, if perhaps a trifle
larger, a condition signaled by the Dankwall Tavern on the
outskirts of town as well as the more pretentious Swecher's
Inn on the central avenue.

Gersen halted the runabout to the side of Swecher's Inn,
an ancient agglomeration of twenty guest rooms of various
sizes on different levels. The public chambers were no less irregular, with sloping ceilings, black woodwork and windows
stained violet by a hundred years' exposure to Van Kaathe's
Starlight. The stone exterior could hardly be seen for vines.
Along the front, citizens of the town sat at their ease under
an arbor.

At a desk in the entry hall stood a man seven feet tall and thin as a cane, with waxen cheeks and cavernous eye sockets. "Your needs, sir?"

"Lodging, if you please. I prefer a suite of several rooms."

The innkeeper inspected Gersen with raised eyebrows and sagging mouth. "You are alone?"

"Quite alone."

"And you want several rooms?"

"If such a suite is available."

"It seems an immoderate taste, if I may say so. How many rooms can you occupy at once? In how many beds do you plan to sleep? How many sanitary requirements are essential for your health?"

"No great matter," said Gersen. "Give me a single room with a bath . . . Has my friend Jacob Bane arrived?"

"To Swecher's? No."

"Not yet? Any outlanders at all besides myself?"

"No one here by the name of Bane, nor any other name. You are the first to check in today. Please settle in advance for your accommodation. A person who arrives like a way-wisp from some far corner of the universe can depart as easily without paying his bill."

Gersen was taken to a dim room with blue walls and a black ceiling which seemed higher than it was wide. A stand supported a basin of water with a scrub brush. A pad of gray felt covered the bed, with a similar pad on the floor. Glancing into the bathroom, Gersen discovered a state of disorder. The innkeeper anticipated his complaints. "At the moment this is the best we can offer. The inn is heavily booked for an occasion two nights hence. To bathe, use the pan and the brush. For your other needs, go to the latrine down the hall." The innkeeper departed.

Luck is with me, Gersen told himself. *The Dankwall Tavern is probably worse.*

Gersen wasted no time in the room. He descended to the street, looked right, in the direction he had come, then turned left and strolled into Gladbetook's modest business district.

At Golcher Way he turned left, crossed the Sweet Trelawney River by a mossy stone bridge. On the side stood a statue in the likeness of Didram Runel Fluter, who held aloft in one hand a short curved knife, in the other a severed set of male genitalia. Behind stood the church. A sign read:

PARTITIONERS POSITIVE OF CREATIVE TRUTH
"There is no retreat!"
"There is no looking aside!"
"There is only the Truth and its Teaching!"

A cemetery occupied the field opposite, which was bordered by heavy deodars. Everywhere stood statues honoring the dead: simulacra carved with uncanny skill from glossy white marble or synthetic stuff. The statues stood in groups and companies, arranged as if in a colloquy of consolation for the grievous event which had been their common lot.

A quarter-mile along the road another bridge crossed the broad, slow Swanibel River, on its way to meet the Sweet Trelawney; beyond Gersen saw the Gladbetook High School . . . He halted and reflected a moment. The time was something short of noon. He turned and went back along Golcher Way into town.

At a meat market Gersen asked directions to the farm owned by Adrian Hardoah.

"Turn left at the corner by Swecher's," he was told. "Make out of town; you'll be on Virle Way. Go four miles to the crossroads, turn right on Bausger Lane. The second farm on the left, that's the Hardoah place, with the big green barn. What do you want from Hardoah? Don't think for money; he's tight as a constipated duddle on a cheese diet."

Gersen made a noncommittal reply and went his way.

In the runabout he set out along Virle Way to the north. Four miles across the prairie he came upon the crossroads, and turned right into Bausger Lane. A mile along the road and a hundred yards back from the road, he saw a farmstead surrounded by garoms and pepper-nuts, the foliage fluorescing in the light of Van Kaathe's Star. Another mile along the road he noticed a small cottage to the left of the road—the Hardoah farm? It seemed somewhat modest and even ramshackle, nor did he notice a green barn. On a bench in the sunlight sat an old woman, small and thin, with a peaked wrinkled face. Beside her hung a coil of coarse string, from which she tatted a patterned cloth, working her stiff fingers with painful intensity.

Gersen halted the vehicle and alighted. "Good day, madame."

"Good day, sir."

"Would this be the Hardoah place?"

"No, sir. By no means. You'll find the Hardoahs yonder, a mile along the road."

Fifty yards to the side of the bungalow Gersen noticed a dilapidated old structure, obviously derelict, surrounded by a copse of blue-black ginsap. "That looks to be an old school-house," said Gersen.

"It is indeed and where I taught thirty years, and sat here another twenty years watching the place fall apart. Nowadays they take children over the hill to the new school at Leck."

"You've lived here all this time?"

"Aye, indeed. I've never had a man. I drink water and whey and pot-liquor. I follow Teaching close as close can be, and I was judged a good teacher of the young."

"You taught Howard Hardoah, then."

"I did that. Do you know him?"

"Not well."

The old woman looked off through the air, seeing scenes across the years. "I've often wondered what chanced with Howard. He was an odd little boy, and moody. I've his picture somewhere, but I'd never find it. He was like an elf-child; in fact, I remember him now at the school pageant, where he represented the elf, all dressed in green and brown, and an elfish little elf he was: wry and fidgety and with an eerie face. Ah yes, and wasn't he naughty with little Tammy Fluter, the fairy! She cried out and Howard was brought up short, and no doubt roundly punished by his father. They were Fundamentals, that's the strictest of the Partitioning, and mostly died out now. You're not a Fundamentalist?"

"I'm totally ignorant of the sect."

"They espoused a strong creed, and quite sensible if all were said that need be said. They asserted man's sins could be bred out by careful choice, and brother married sister and cousin married cousin, so to achieve the best. Did you notice the statue to Runel Fluter the Didram in town? Well, he was master of the creed, and did the work that needed to be done, but little thanks he got, especially from those he considered unworthy. Oh, those were rare days, with Teaching ever so strong! Now there's none left in these parts but the Hardoahs, and they don't practice the old ideas."

"Howard must have been quite a handful."

"Sometimes, yes. Or he might be sweet as sweet could be. He had overmuch imagination. How he loved flowers and how his little mind worked! One day he sorted the flowers out by color, for the Battle of the Flowers; and such wild antics never did you see, with petals flying and the cries of the corpses. From hither to yon went Howard, charging his Red troops against the Blues, with roses dying in great gallantry and bluebells triumphant over the vervains. Ah me, what a day! Then he went up to high school and did poorly, or so I'm told. He was small and young and no doubt the big boys bullied him a bit. Then he went at odds with the Sadalflourys, and naturally that was a scandal."

"How so?"

"Mmf—hm. I shouldn't be talking so much, but it's long ago and times have changed, though the Sadalflourys are still important folk. Howard took a fancy to one of the girls, I think it was Suby. She naturally jilted him and Howard did something very reprehensible, and the Sadalflourys were in a passion of rage, only Howard hastily departed and traveled offworld."

Gersen bent over the woman's tatting. "That's beautiful work."

"It's my best, I say no more, and it earns my victual."

Gersen gave over ten SVU. "You can start such a cloth for me. If I don't come back, well and good, sell elsewhere, without a thought."

"But thank you, sir!"

"Not at all. I've enjoyed your talk, and now I must be on my way."

A mile along the road Gersen came to a farmstead with a conspicuous green barn to the side. He halted the runabout and surveyed the house, a queer tingle of imminence coursing along his skin. The house was like many another; three stories high, built of pink clapboard with blue trim at the windows, a high roof broken by gables and dormers. In the kitchen garden a tall man in blue trousers and a black shirt worked a cutthroat hoe. Noticing Gersen and the runabout, he paused in his work to stare.

Gersen drove into the yard and was approached by the tall men, evidently Adrian Hardoah. His hair was yellow-brown streaked with gray, cut with no attention to style; his face was long, bony and weatherbeaten. He examined Gersen with neither cordiality nor interest. "Sir?"

"This is Home Farm?"

"So it is."

"And you are Adrian Hardoah?"

"That is right." Adrian Hardoah spoke in a soft deep voice, with careful pace and precise enunciation.

"I am Henry Lucas; I represent *Extant* Magazine and I have come here from Pontefract on Aloysius."

"Ah! That was the contest magazine." Hardoah's voice took on a more lively note.

"True. Among millions of entries, you were the first correctly to identify subject number six, who is, of course, your son."

Adrian Hardoah instantly became defensive. "That should make no difference. Identification is identification."

"No argument whatever. In fact, I have come to award the prize."

"That's grand news! How much?"

"By our rules, the first accurate single identification gains three hundred SVU. I carry that sum with me."

"Blessings on us, with the help of the Didrams! And would you know that you just missed Howard himself by no more than an hour? He's come for his school reunion."

Gersen smiled and shrugged. "An odd coincidence, certainly. But it's nothing to me, one way or the other. He just happens to be a man in a photograph."

"He's doing well, is Howard, though he left us no coin, and it's been many long years since he went out from home. But come inside; the woman must hear the good news. Truth to tell, I clear forgot the matter and never even thought to ask Howard of his great publicity. Folk must be looking at him everywhere, with his picture out like that."

"Few folk are so observant, sir." He followed Adrian Hardoah up the stairs and into a tidy kitchen. A woman almost as tall as Adrian looked around. Her face, with a hundred elusive hints of Howard Treesong, fascinated Gersen. Under a wide square forehead her eyes were set a trifle too closely; a long straight nose hung over a pale mouth and a near-invisible chin: characteristics which for better or worse gave her an unrelenting and secretive look, with no indication of ease or humor.

Still, to Adrian's report of his winnings, she responded with a totally ordinary gurgle of pleasure. "Well, isn't that fine! So Howard has warded us willy nor nilly!"

"So it seems. Well, then, what of a taste of tea? And a good scone? What do you say to that, Mr. Lucas?"

"I'd say thank you very much."

At Adrian's gesture, Gersen seated himself at the table. He brought forth a packet of notes and began to count them out. Adrian spoke reverently. "To think that by the flick of chance, no more, did I look toward that photograph, and only for its being in that outworld jinket *Extant*. And who won the grand prize?"

"Persons of the group are essentially strangers who chanced to meet at a pleasure resort. An attendant at the resort was first to supply the names. Your son Howard also submitted an accurate identification, but too late."

Reba Hardoah smiled a caustic smile. "Isn't that just like Howard? He always fell short, by just so much! A pity . . . Hist! I do hear Ledesmus. He'll be Howard's older brother, a different sort altogether. He'll have the farm when we ford the Flowing River."

Ledesmus halted in the doorway, surprised to see the offworld visitor. He was bulkier than his father, with apple cheeks and heavy-lidded eyes which gave his face a look of sly humor. Adrian spoke out: "Ledesmus, step forward to meet Mr. Henry Lucas from a far planet. He has brought us an account of money."

Ledesmus pursed his lips to whistle. "Phee-oo! What a day! First Howard, down from nowhere, and now Mr. Lucas."

"Coincidence," said Gersen. "Still, it's a pity I missed him, as I am ordered to write an article on the folk in the photograph."

Adrian spoke in a voice of dispassionate judgment: "There's not much to say about Howard. He never worked a good stint around the farm. He dreamed away his schooltime and I daresay he's nothing very much today, for all his travels."

"Now then," said Reba, "don't be too near with the boy. You've always known him to be eerie-like."

Gersen asked, "Do you expect him back?"

Adrian responded curtly, "No."

"Strange that he should come so far to stop by for just an hour or two."

Reba tried to explain. "Well, we expect conduct just a bit

indecorous[1] from Howard. Still we grieve to see him stray from Teaching. If only he would shake the star dust off his heels and come back home to work the fields with Ledesmus. That would give us joy."

Ledesmus, showing his sly grin to Gersen, said, "He won't be back. He is more indecorous now than ever."

Adrian agreed. "He won't be back. He came out and looked the old place over. All he'd say was: 'It's the same. But it's not the same.' He spent as much time out in his old office as he did with his mother."

"His office?"

"The old pump-shack yonder, where he'd take himself with his books and papers and colored pens."

Ledesmus said soberly, "Howard read too much for his mentality, a lot of crazy offworld stuff. He had a chair and a table, and halfway through the night he'd be out there burning lights, until we called him to bed. Regular werd[2] was Howard."

"Where is he staying now?"

Adrian said dubiously: "He mentioned friends he wanted to visit."

Ledesmus gave a jeering laugh. "Friends? Howard? There was nobody but poor Nimpy Cleadhoe, and he's no more."

"Now then," said Reba in mild reproach, "you don't know everything, Ledesmus."

Adrian said, "He came mainly for his school reunion. Still, a person would think he'd want to bide at home. After all, it's here he was born and here he was bred, and this is the dirt that made up his bones."

Gersen pushed the sheaf of SVU certificates over to Adrian Hardoah. "There you are, sir, and our gratitude for participating in the contest. I suppose you'll want to subscribe to *Extant*?"

Adrian pulled at his chin. "We'll give thought to the matter. It's an offworld jinket and beyond our concerns. If I can't fathom the acts of the False-head Ulms in next land to north of us, how can I hope to understand the doings at Alpheratz,

---

[1] The word *vardespant* lacks contemporary equivalence. It includes the notions of obstinacy, perverse wrong-headedness, a jeering attitude toward somber rectitude.

[2] A man-shaped supernatural being who prowls by night and sleeps underground by day. According to Maunish folklore, it hides in the shadows, waiting to pounce on children and carry them away.

or Caph? No, we'll study our own knowledge. Which, after all, is Pure Truth. So the Didrams tell us."

"Blessed be the Teaching," murmured Reba.

Gersen rose to his feet. "I'd like to look about your farm, if I may. It will serve as background for the article I must write on Howard."

"Certainly. Ledesmus, show the gentleman about."

Gersen and Ledesmus went out into the yard. Ledesmus peered sidelong at Gersen. "So now you must write of Howard? Who wants to read of him?"

"There's great interest in the contest. I'll mention your father and mother and, naturally, you."

"Indeed now. There'll be my picture and all?"

"Unfortunately not. I don't have a camera with me . . . You're older than Howard?"

"Aye, three years."

"Did you get along well?"

"Well enough. Father allowed no bickers. I did the work and Howard dreamed away in his office."

Gersen stood irresolute. The spoor of Howard Alan Treesong was strong but seemed to lead nowhere. "I'd like to look into Howard's office."

"Right yonder. It's changed not at all in thirty years. We pump irrigation water from the pond for orchard and truck. House water we draw up from the well; that's another pump."

Ledesmus led the way to a shed ten feet long by eight feet wide. He pulled at the door, forcing it open against the screech of corroded hinges. Two windows admitted light and showed a dusty clutter.

"Place hasn't changed much," said Ledesmus. "Yonder is his table, and that's the very chair where he planted his bewalkus. These shelves held his books and papers; he was neat, was Howard, with everything just so."

"And where are the books and papers?"

"Hard to say. Some are back to the house, some destroyed. Howard was fidgety with his things; when he took to far ports little enough was left behind. Howard liked his secrets."

"Had he friends? What of girls?"

Ledesmus made a guttural sound of scornful amusement. "Howard never had the knack for girls. He talked too much and acted too little, if you get my meaning. He liked little young girls, and he played dirty on one or two, but don't print that." Ledesmus looked over his shoulder toward the house. "Father never heard these tales. He'd have skinned Howard for wallpaper. It didn't mean much; Howard just wanted to try out the equipment; after all, that's why it's there, aren't I right? Teaching is a bit vague on this score, but if Sarter Martus didn't want girls for to play on, he'd have wrought them with snap-teeth, like fish traps, if you get my meaning. His great love was a girl called—what was it now? She drowned in Persimmon Lake . . . Zada Memar, a pretty thing . . . Friends? There was Nimpy Cleadhoe from down the road. He and Howard roamed the woods together and went out for nuts; and he was somewhat a friend. Father didn't like it because old man Cleadhoe was then town marmelizer."

"What's a marmelizer?"

"You've seen the cemetery, where dead folk stand? They're all marmels. It's low work, with dead stuff and all. Still, they're gone now, and that was Howard's friend, if friends they were." Ledesmus turned Gersen a sheepish smile. "I ruined that friendship, me and my foolishness."

"How so?"

"Well, Howard treasured a red writing book and he was most private of it. One time Nimpy called him out of his office and sent him to see Mother, over something or another. I reached through the window and took the red book and tossed it over the pump. Well, as luck would have it, the book slid behind the siding. I went back of the barn and waited. Howard came out and went to lock up his book and couldn't find it, and then I never saw such crazy doings. He began talking in funny voices and hopping around. Then he saw poor innocent Nimpy, and jumped him. I ran out and pulled him away before he killed the boy. That was Howard's friend and he wasn't a friend after that; in fact he never come back. Howard went off to summer Teaching, and I forgot about the book. Let's see if it's still there." Ledesmus stepped over the pump, pulled aside the wallboard and thrust down his arm. "Hope I don't grab the hot end of a cang[1] . . . I got it." He held up a red notebook and tossed it to Gersen, who took it out into the sunlight and glanced through the contents.

---

[1]Indigenous stinging insect, reaching a length of four inches.

Ledesmus came from the pump room. "What's in the book?"

Gersen handed it over and Ledesmus flipped through the pages. "Nothing important . . . What kind of writing is that? I never saw anything like it before."

"It's hard to make out."

"Whatever, it's tomfoolery. What's the use of writing what nobody can read? . . . Here's pictures: dukes and kings in fancy dress. Silly rigobands at a carnival. Father thought Howard was copying out the Organon. I thought he was making up girl-stuff. Howard fooled us all."

"It would seem so," said Gersen. "I'll take it off your hands for a souvenir of Gladbetook. Would you take ten SVU for your trouble?"

"Well, I don't know—" Ledesmus hesitated, then took the money. "I guess it's nothing Father would want. Just don't speak of the matter."

"I'll say nothing, and you don't mention the book to Howard should you see him before I do. I wonder where he's staying."

Ledesmus shrugged. "I think he planned to stay here, until he had words with Father, and he left as soon as he arrived. He might be at Swecher's Inn since that's the best in town."

Once more in Gladbetook, Gersen went to the arbor in front of Swecher's Inn and found a seat at one of the tables, his back to the lowering afternoon sun, his black shadow across the scrubbed pinkwood table. A tall, gangling boy, all arms, legs and neck, came to inquire his needs. "How, sir?"

"What are you serving for lunch?"

"Lunch is out, sir. Just a bit too late. I could get you a dish of maunce, with a crust of our good bread."

"What is maunce?"

"Well, it's a kind of put-together, from herbs and river-fish."

"That will do me very well."

"And will you drink?"

"What's to be had?"

"Whatever you choose, sir."

"I'd like a pint of cold beer."

"That we don't serve, sir, cold or warm."

"In that case, show me the card, or the list."

"Nothing of the sort here, sir. People know what they like without reading about it."

"I see . . . What are those folk yonder taking?"

"They have our chilled gruel seepings."

"And those folk to the side?"

"They take tanglefoot soak."

"What else can be had?"

"Kidney tonic. Nibbet. Soursap toddy. Belchberry sprig."

"What is nibbet?"

"Vitalizing tea."

"I'll try nibbet."

"At once, sir."

The boy departed and Gersen was left to ponder his situation. Near at hand, perhaps within earshot, was Howard Alan Treesong; Gerson could feel the weight of his presence. If Gersen could lure him a few steps out of town, perhaps through mention of the old red notebook, and drown him in the Sweet Trelawney, there would be a satisfactory end to the affair. Unlikely that all would go so well . . . The serving boy brought a platter of fish stew, bread and a pot of tea.

Gersen poured the tea, tasted, to discover flavors to which he could put no names. One of the ingredients seared first the tongue, then the entire oral cavity. The servant boy, hiding a grin, asked politely: "Sir, is nibbet to your taste?"

"Excellent." Gersen had devoured white curry in the Lascar Quarter of Zamboanga; he had drunk pepper rum in Mama Potts's Swillery at Sairle City on Copus. "Incidentally, I'm expecting a friend from offworld. He doesn't seem to be here at the inn. Are you reserving rooms for Mr. Slade or any other foreigners?"

"That I don't know, sir."

Gersen produced a coin. "Find out, but discreetly, as I want to surprise my friend. He's coming for the school reunion."

The boy scooped up the coin and departed. Gersen stolidly ate the maunce as he had eaten dozens of other such dishes across the inhabited planets.

The boy returned. "Nobody like that here, sir, and we're holding no rooms."

"Where else could he be?"

"Well, there's Dankwall Tavern down the road, but their rooms are poor; and there's Ott's Resort out on Skooney's Lake, where rich owls go to roost. Else, there's nothing closer than the inn at Blurry Corners."

"I see. Where is the telephone?"

"In the office, but first pay for maunce and nibbet—I've had such tricks played on me before."

"Just as you like." Gersen laid down coins. "On second thought—" Gersen gave the boy another SVU "—be so good as to call first Skooney's Lake, then the Dankwall Tavern, and inquire as to offworld visitors here for the school reunion. Mind you, discreetly now! Don't so much as mention me."

"As you say, sir."

Minutes passed. Gersen essayed another taste of nibbet. The boy returned. "No one known, sir. The reunion is mostly locals, though there'll be a few in from foreign places. Ditty Jingol's uncle is in from Bantry and some others from Wimping. Your friend will likely be along tonight. Anything else, sir?"

"Not just now."

The boy departed. Gersen brought out the red book. On the front was a title, carefully printed in block letters:

THE BOOK OF DREAMS

Gersen opened the book and concentrated his attention upon young Howard Hardoah's handwriting . . . An hour passed, two hours.

Gersen looked up, turned, gauged the height of Van Kaathe's Star. Late afternoon. He slowly closed the book and tucked it into his pocket. He beckoned to the serving boy. "What is your name?"

"My name is Vitching, sir."

"Vitching, this is an SVU. It is for you. Presently there will be another. In return I want you to perform a service for me."

Vitching blinked. "All very well, sir, but how? I can't counterwink Teaching. I'd blight all my good deeds of the past."

"You'll find no conflict with Teaching. I want you to watch for that offworld person I mentioned to you."

"Well—one thing with another, I see no reason why I can't do this work."

"Remember, the work must be done in secrecy! If one word leaks out, I'll be seriously angry."

"No need to fear, sir."

Gersen transferred the SVU to the skinny-fingered hand. "I am now going out to walk about the town."

"Precious little to see, sir, for folk like you who have been to Cloutie."

"Well, I'll still look about. Mind you, not a word to anyone of our business."

"Right, sir."

Gersen set out along the street, and now he felt conspicuous in his citified Cloutie clothes. He paused at a clothing shop and looked over the merchandise. A tray beside the door displayed sharp-toed black boots. On a rack hung scarves, hats and high gaiters in moleskin gray, embroidered with green and red. He entered the shop and fitted himself out in Gladbetook style: a high-shouldered coat of black furze, loose-bottomed trousers, gathered at the knees with black straps, a wide green hat fitting low over his forehead instead of tilted back, Cloutie-style. Looking in the mirror Gersen saw a bumpkin sufficiently bland and moony to deceive any offworld eye.

Leaving the shop, he turned down Golcher Way. He crossed the Sweet Trelawney, passed Didram Runel Fluter, the Orthometric Church and, opposite, the cemetery where marmels of the dead stood with their kindred. With uneasy side glances Gersen marched past, in the uncanny conviction that blank white eyes shifted to watch as he went by. A quarter-mile beyond, he crossed the Swanibel River, and once again stood before the school, a structure conforming to the most elaborate tenets of Maunish architecture. Each side extended a wing capped by a baroque tower; a heavy, steep-faced roof culminated in a belfry of fluted brass, surmounted by a tall brass finial. In the silver-gold light from the setting Van Kaathe's Star each detail, each crotchet, bracket and ornament was picked out in strong contrast. Over the gate a sign read:

25th Anniversary Reunion
Welcome the return
of the famous Galloping Flatfish Class

Galloping flatfish? An old pleasantry, a special joke to be apprehended only by members of the class . . . An effort to think of Treesong in this environment, walking this road, climbing the school steps, peering from the tall windows . . .

Between the north wing and the Swanibel extended a paved pavilion, a place for students to idle, gossip, survey the river. A dozen men and women worked on the pavilion now: hanging festoons, arranging tables and chairs, decorating the speaker's platform with banderoles, tall gilt fans and tassels.

Gersen sauntered into the driveway, climbed broad steps of polished red porphyry, crossed a piazza, approached a line of bronze and glass doors, one of which stood ajar.

Gersen entered, found himself in a long central hall that ran east and west. At the far end, Van Kaathe's Star poured level light through other glass doors. On the walls to either side hung a succession of group photographs: graduating classes reaching far into the past.

Gersen stood listening. Silence except for a wisp of music, rising, falling, halting abruptly. A nearby door stood open. Looking through, Gersen saw a tall thin-faced man with a bush of white hair and a pair of girls, each of whom played the flageolet in time to majestic sweeps of the man's long arms.

Gersen moved away and looked up at the photographs. He saw a date fifty-two years past. As he proceeded along the corridor the dates approached the present. Gersen halted at the photograph displaying the class of twenty-five years before and studied the young faces gazing forth, some proudly posing, others grinning sheepishly, still others sullen and bored with the entire procedure . . . Voices and footsteps. From the music room came the instructor and his pupils. The instructor stared suspiciously at Gersen. The girls, after an incurious glance, departed. The instructor spoke in a voice stiff and pedantic: "Sir, the school is not open to visitors. I am now leaving and must lock the door. May I ask you to leave?"

"I have been waiting for you, sir. Might we speak together a moment?"

"Concerning what?"

Gersen began to develop an idea which had just entered his head. "You are professor of music here at the school?"

"Here I am Professor Kutte. I give lessons; from little musical barbarians I create the majesty of an orchestra. Away from here, I am Valdemar Kutte, Master Musician, and Director of the Grand Salon Orchestra." Valdemar Kutte raked Gersen up and down with eyes sharpened by decades of instructing children in the correct fingering of piano, lute, harp, flageolet and liltaphone. "And who are you, Mr. Offworlder, so I see?"

"How do you see that?" asked Gersen. "I thought to look an ordinary Gladbetooker."

"Not with those clumsy boots. And you wear your trousers low. Here we cultivate style, not slackness. Without intent to offend, you seem like someone dressed for a charade."

Gersen laughed ruefully. "I will try to profit by your instruction."

"Good day, sir. We must depart."

"One moment. Is the Grand Salon Orchestra playing at tomorrow's festival?"

Valdemar Kutte responded curtly. "They have engaged no orchestra whatever, owing to financial stringencies."

"Circumstances would seem to warrant the presence of your orchestra."

"Perhaps so. As always there is someone to hold a tight hand on the purse strings—usually the most affluent of the persons in authority."

"This is how they become affluent."

"Yes, perhaps."

"How long have you been musical director here?"

"Far too long. I celebrated my twenty-fifth anniversary three years ago. I may add that no one took notice of the 'celebration' save myself."

"So then you instructed these folk?" Gersen indicated the photograph on the wall.

"Many of them . . . Some had will but no talent. Some had talent but no will. Many more lacked both. A very few displayed both qualities, and these I remember."

"What of this group? Who were the musicians?"

"Aha. Darben Sadalfloury had a nice touch on the tantalein. I believe that he still plays. Poor Mirtisha van Boufer—she labored four years on the varience but always played flat. Howard Hardoah, he was most adept but undisciplined. Alas, I believe that he might have gone far."

"Howard Hardoah? Which would he be?"

"Third row down on the end, the lad with the brown hair."

Gersen scrutinized the young Howard Alan Treesong, who showed a not ill-favored face with a square forehead, wide and high, neat light-brown hair, an intense blue-gray gaze. The candid and wholesome effect was flawed by a foxy chin, a drooping girlish mouth and a nose somewhat too long and too thin.

"—Fadra Hessel of course plays loitre to this day at the catechisms. I confess my memory brings forward little else. Sir, we must depart and lock the school."

The two made their exit; the door was locked. Valdemar Kutte bowed. "A pleasure talking to you, sir."

"One moment," said Gersen. "A pleasant concept has come to mind. I have strong sentiments toward this particular class, and I, as an anonymous benefactor, will engage an orchestra, to augment the joy of the occasion. Can you suggest such an orchestra?"

The instructor stood erect, eyes snapping. "Fortuitously, I can do so. I refer you to the Valdemar Kutte Grand Salon Orchestra, which I personally supervise. It is the only conceivable choice. True, there are other local groups: scattleboggers, bang-and-bump groups and the like, but I control the single musical organization worthy of the name this side of Cloutie."

"And are you available for the evening in question?"

"By chance, I am quite free."

"Then consider yourself engaged, as of now. What will be your fee?"

"Well, let me think . . . How many pieces will you require? Generally, I present two tarables, on the right and left; zumbolt, soprano pipe, gamba, cornet, vibre, fiddles, a guitar and flageolet, in the classical manner. For an engagement of this sort I ordinarily ask two hundred SVU but—" Professor Kutte looked dubiously at Gersen's attire.

"I won't quibble," said Gersen. "You are hired, at two hundred and fifty SVU. My only stipulation is this: I want to become a member of your orchestra for this engagement only."

"Eh? You are a musician?"

"I can't play a note. I'll tap quietly on a drum and not disturb anyone."

"You would disturb us all! The drum is a baby's noisemaker!"

"What would you suggest?"

"This is preposterous. Why cannot you merely listen from beyond the fence?"

"I want to participate close at hand. Still, if you can't—"

"No! We will find a way. Can you play so much as a tin whistle?"

Gersen could not help but feel humiliation at his incompetence. "I have never so much as tried."

"Bah! This is bathos. Come with me. We will see what we can do."

Chapter 13

The only good drummer is a dead drummer.

—Valdemar Kutte
Director, Grand Salon Orchestra
of Gladbetook

In Valdemar Kutte's studio, Gersen was handed a long wooden flute. "A child's instrument," said Kutte disdainfully. "Still, to sit with the Grand Salon one must play, if only a wooden pipe. Now, fingers here, here, here. So. Now blow."

Gersen achieved a sour tone.

"Once more."

Three hours later Gersen had learned one of the five basic scales and Kutte was fatigued. "For now, that is enough. I will number these stops: one, four, five and eight. We shall play simple tunes: promenades, gallops, an occasional ramble. You will play one-five one-five one-five-eight one-five-eight, in time to the music, occasionally four-five-eight, or one-four-five. When we use a different mode I will furnish you a different instrument. I can do no more. Please pay me my fee in advance, plus twenty-four SVU for three hours' intensive instruction."

Gersen paid over the money.

"Now then! Take this flute. When opportunity offers, practice. Play the scale. Play simple progressions. Above all: learn one-five-eight one-five one-five."

"I'll do my best."

"You must do better than your best! Remember, it is the Grand Salon Orchestra with whom you play! Even though 'play' is a pretentious word for your level of achievement, and you will of course be making only soft sounds. I hope that all will go well. It is an eccentric situation, but for a musician, life is a succession of remarkable events. We will meet here tomorrow, at middle afternoon. Then you will go to Van Zeel's store to be fitted in proper musician's uniform, as worn by the Grand Salon Orchestra; I will instruct him before you arrive. Then, after securing your uniform, come here and I will supply further instructions, as best I can. Who knows? This occasion may make a musician of you!"

Gersen looked doubtfully at the flute. "Perhaps so."

Once more at Swecher's Inn, Gersen dined on lentil paste, a stew of pale meat and herbs, a salad of river reeds and a half-loaf of crusty bread. Vitching, the serving boy, reported no success in his investigations but Gersen rewarded him suitably.

Darkness fell on Gladbetook. Leaving the inn, Gersen wandered up the main avenue to the center of town. At each corner of the square a tall post supported a white-green globe around which careened dozens of foot-long pink insects, with eight soft wings to either side like the oars of a galley.

The shops were dark and empty. The haberdasher had neglected to move his tray of boots inside, and his scarves hung as before, where anyone so inclined could purloin the entire selection. Other merchants seemed equally casual; the folk of Gladbetook were evidently not addicted to larceny.

In the center of town night life was nonexistent. Gersen returned along the main street, past Swecher's, to the Dankwall Tavern, where in the common room, to the light of a few dim lamps, a half-dozen farm workers drank sour-smelling beer . . . Gersen returned to Swecher's Inn, went up to his room, where he softly practiced the flute for an hour, until his lips failed. Then he brought out *The Book of Dreams* and puzzled over its crabbed script. Apparently young Howard had evolved a set of heroic tales, involving a company of heroes, whose persons Howard had depicted with loving care and in the most intricate detail.

Gersen put the book aside and tried to make himself comfortable upon the unyielding bed.

In the morning he followed Kutte's instructions. He practiced the flute, and presented himself to Kutte's studio on the extension of Golcher Way a hundred yards south of the square. Kutte heard him play the scales without enthusiasm.

"Now try one-four-five."

"I haven't reached that stage yet."

Kutte raised his eyes to the ceiling. He heaved a sigh. "Well, what must be, must be: that is the lesson all musicians learn. I have spoken to Mrs. Lavenger. She is chairman of the reunion. I told her that an anonymous benefactor had hired the Grand Salon Orchestra and she was very pleased. We must arrive tomorrow afternoon at the fourth hour and arrange ourselves. We will play before the supper when the guests drink liquor outland fashion, and during supper. After supper there will be encomiums and congratulations, then several dance promenades, and no doubt the stylish folk will take punch, which is not my habit, needless to say. As an outworlder, you have probably seen inebriation in your time?"

"I have so, indeed."

"Glory to the Teaching Didrams! Think of that! Still, you seem a relatively sound man!"

"I seldom, if ever, drink overmuch."

"But is not the stuff pernicious?"

"I've heard opinions in both directions."

Kutte seemed not to hear. He knit his eyebrows thoughtfully. "Where, to your knowledge, is the most intolerably drunken den of the Oikumene?"

Gersen considered. "Not an easy choice to make. A hundred thousand saloons from Earth out to Last Call clamor for that distinction. Twast's Place on Krokinole can hold its head high, Dirty Red's on the pier at Daisy's Landing, on Canopus III, is another well-known resort."

"How fortunate are we in Gladbetook! Our decency is the envy of the cosmos! However, and I say this with regret, tomorrow night our reputation may become tarnished. The Sadalflourys, the van Bessems, the Lavengers—all surely will taste essences and stings. But none will trouble us, so I feel assured or at least hopeful. Once more—let us hear those scales . . . Now: one-five-eight. One-four-five. One-five one-five . . . One-four-five . . . Harp on the Sacred Ram! Stop! It will have to do; today I can hear no more. Practice diligently tonight. Concentrate on sound-production, on tone, justness, pitch, timbre, clarity, precise attack and sonority. When you alter tones, raise one finger, depress the other simultaneously, not after a lapse of a second or so. Practice finger placement. When you seek to put a finger on four, let it be four, neither two nor six. Cultivate verve; avoid that dreary flatness which now pervades your articulation. Is this all clear?"

"Perfectly."

"Good!" cried Valdemar Kutte heartily. "Tomorrow will show us hope and improvement."

On the following afternoon the orchestra assembled at Kutte's studio. Kutte distributed scores, took Gersen aside and listened as he played his parts. Kutte had arrived at a state of fatalistic calm and made no expostulations. "It will have to do," he said. "Play very softly and all will be well, especially if essences flow freely."

Kutte led Gersen before the other musicians. "All, pay heed! I wish to introduce my friend Mr. Gersen, who has become an amateur of the flute. He plays experimentally on this single occasion only. We must all try to be polite to him."

The musicians turned to look at Gersen and muttered among themselves. Gersen submitted to the attention with as much aplomb as he could muster.

The orchestra set off down Golcher Way, each man carrying his instrument, except Gersen, who carried five flutes, turned in various modes. All were dressed alike, in black suits—high-shouldered coats and bag-bottom breeches—gray gaiters, pointed black shoes, flat-crowned black hats with down-drooping brims.

The group approached the school and Gersen grew ever more uneasy. The scheme which originally had seemed so ingenious now, as the critical moment approached, he saw to be inconvenient, cranky and uncertain. If Howard Treesong gave the musicians more than a cursory look, he might recognize Henry Lucas of *Extant*, which would create an awkward situation. Howard Treesong would undoubtedly arrive well-armed and with an entourage. In contrast, Gersen carried five flutes and a kitchen knife bought the same morning from an ironmonger.

The orchestra filed into the pavilion, placed their instruments upon the platform and waited while Valdemar Kutte conferred with Ossim Sadalfloury, of the locally important Sadalfloury family: a portly and jovial man in a fine suit of dark green gabardine.

Valdemar Kutte rejoined the orchestra. "A collation will be set behind the pavilion for our convenience. It will include braised navets and conserve; there will also be tea and raisin water."

At the back of the group someone muttered and laughed; Kutte glared and spoke with meaningful emphasis. "Mr. Sadalfloury realizes that we are all valetudenarians and respects our convictions. No essences or fermented products will be served to the orchestra, as that in any event would detract from its performance. So now, up on the platform: hup, hup, hah! Lively and smart, everyone!"

The musicians seated themselves on the platform, arranged music, tuned instruments. Kutte placed Gersen in the back row, between the zumbolt and the gamba, both instruments played by large blond men of phlegmatic disposition.

Gersen arranged his flutes in the order Kutte had dictated. He played a few tentative scales, contriving to seem musicianly; then he sat back and watched the old classmates as they entered the pavilion. Many were local residents; others had arrived from outlying townships. A few resided in far lands, and a few had made the journey to Gladbetook from offworld. They greeted each other with cries of marveling surprise and brassy laughter, each astonished to discover how the others had aged. Hearty salutations were exchanged between folk of equal social standing; greetings more carefully measured took place between persons of disparate status.

Howard Hardoah, as these folk knew him, was not yet in evidence. When he arrived, what then? Gersen had not even the vestige of a plan.

At the fourth hour of the afternoon the reunion officially began. The tables were already filled with groups. To the right of the bandstand the gentry had tended to collect; to the left sat farm-folk and shopkeepers. A few tables to the far left were occupied by river-folk, who lived on barges, the men wearing brown corduroy, the women coarse-woven pantaloons and long-sleeved blouses. The gentry, so Gersen noted, sipped liqueurs from exquisite little flagons of blue and green glass. When a flagon was empty, it was dropped with a mannered gesture into a basket.

Valdemar Kutte, carrying a fiddle, stepped up on the platform. He bowed to right and left, then turned to his orchestra. " 'Sharmella's Dance,' the full version. Easy but lightsome, not too much vigor in the duets; are we ready?" Kutte glanced at Gersen, waved a finger. "The fourth mode ... No, not that one ... Yes, correct."

He jerked his elbows; the orchestra broke into a merry bounce-about, with Gersen blowing the flute as he had been taught, though quietly.

The piece ended. Gersen gratefully put down the flute. It might have gone worse, he thought. The basic rule seemed to be to stop playing when everyone else stopped.

Valdemar Kutte bespoke another tune, and as before signaled Gersen in regard to the proper instrument.

The tune "Bad Bengfer," was familiar to everyone present. All vigorously sang the choruses and stamped their heels on the floor. The song, so far as Gersen could determine, celebrated the escapades of Bengfer, a drunken roustabout, who fell into the cesspool at the back of Buntertown. Convinced that he had fallen into a vat of "Nip-doodle Beer," he drank to satiety, and when Van Kaathe's Star rose to illuminate the scene, astonished passersby discovered Bengfer's rotund belly protruding above the banks of the cesspool. An unsavory song, thought Gersen, but Valdemar Kutte conducted his orchestra with gusto. Gersen took advantage of the general confusion to blow more daringly into his flute, receiving only a warning glance or two from Kutte.

A gentleman from a table to the right came up to the bandstand and spoke to Valdemar Kutte, who responded with a peevish if obsequious bow.

Kutte addressed the company. "By request, Miss Taduca Milgher will sing for us."

"Oh no!" cried Taduca Milgher from her table. "Utter terror!"

She was urged to the platform while Valdemar Kutte stood smiling sourly.

Taduca Milgher sang several ballads: "A Lonesome Bird

Am I," "My Little Red Barge on the River" and "Pinkrose, the Space Pirate's Daughter."

The tables were full; the latecomers apparently had all arrived. Gersen began to wonder if Howard Treesong would after all be on hand for the occasion.

Taduca Milgher retired to her table. Supper was announced, and the orchestra went to enjoy their collation behind the service screen.

Evening had come to Gladbetook. A hundred fairy lamps hanging from a bamboo trellis illuminated the pavilion. At their tables the patricians dined at leisure and took their liqueurs. Folk who interpreted Teaching more earnestly sat over pots of tea, but missed very little of what went on at the stylish tables.

Unreality, thought Gersen. Where was Howard Treesong? *Near at hand!* came a sudden message from his subconscious, harsh and strong. Gersen looked across the edge of the pavilion, out over the river meadow . . . Time seemed to freeze. Unreality dissipated. Now was the true, the real Now. Near the river three men stood motionless, looking toward the pavilion. Gersen turned, looked off toward the road. By the fence, faces and garments blurred by twilight, stood three other men. Gersen knew by their postures that these were not men of Gladbetook.

All was changed. To this moment the reunion had been an occasion of froth and fancy: exaggerated, quaint, absurd. Beyong the glimmer of the fairy lamps were fancies of another sort, brooding and sinister. Gersen went to the edge of the pavilion and looked to the south. He discerned other shapes, inconspicuous under a copse of elms . . .

Kutte called his orchestra back to the platform. "Now then! We will play "Rhapsody of Dreaming Maidens." Mind now! Grace and delicacy."

Revelry among the reunited schoolmates had reached a mellow state of joviality and good fellowship. Friends called to old friends across the pavilion, recalling escapades, feats and jokes. Social rigors were loosening; badinage included folk along the length of the pavilion: "—never, never! It was Crambert all the while! I was censured and blamed—" "Hoy there, Sadkin! Remember the stink-flower in Miss Boab's bouquet? What a lark, eh?" "—most fearful scandal ever! That was a year before your time! He was known as 'Pussy-britches' ever after." "What happened to 'Pussy-britches'?"

"Drowned in the Quade Canal, poor chap. Fell from his barge." "Worse scandal yet was Fimfle's periscope; remember that?" "Aye, so I do. Over the transom into the girl's dressing room, for knees, elbows and all between." "What a thought was that!" "Fimfle! What a sorry chap! Where is he tonight?" "Not a clue." "Hey there, whatever happened to Fimfle?" "Don't mention the horrid little fellow." —This from Adelie Lagnal at the Sadalfloury table.

A sound like the lowest tone of an enormous gong—was it real? or subliminal? Gersen felt it, but no one else seemed to notice.

In the entrance stood a tall, square-shouldered figure. Tight trousers of green velour encased his long strong legs; over a loose long-sleeved white shirt he wore a black vest with purple and gold fobs. His ankle-boots were pale brown leather; a soft black cap was pulled askew across his wide high forehead. He stood in the entrance, smiling a twisted smile. Then with exaggerated self-effacement, he went to a vacant table nearby and seated himself, still smiling his twisted smile. From the Sadalfloury table came a hoarse choked whisper, which penetrated a sudden silence: "It's Fimfle himself!"

Howard Alan Treesong, or Howard Hardoah, slowly turned his head and looked toward the Sadalflourys. Then he glanced toward the bandstand. His gaze passed over Gersen and fixed upon Valdemar Kutte, and his smile became a trifle wider.

The school chums resumed their conversations. Back and forth went the badinage, but not so easy and not so free, as eyes turned curiously toward Howard Hardoah.

At last Morna van Hulgen, one of the chairwomen, took herself in hand and, approaching, gave him a hearty and only faintly false welcome, which Howard Hardoah accepted graciously. Morna van Hulgen gestured toward the buffet table, proffering supper. Howard Hardoah smiled, shook his head. Morna looked uncertainly around the room, from group to group, then turned back to the suave man at the table before her. "It's so nice seeing you after all these years! I'd never have known you—except you haven't really changed! The years have been kind to you!"

"Very kind indeed. I am happy with them."

"I don't remember your particular friends . . . But you mustn't sit here alone. There's Saul Cheebe; you remember him? He's sitting with Elvinta Gierle and her husband from Puch."

"Of course I remember Saul Cheebe. I remember everyone and everythting."

"Why not join him? Or Shimus Woot? There's so much to talk about." She indicated the tables which were well to the left end of the room.

Howard Hardoah glanced briefly toward the tables in question. "Saul or Shimus, is it? Both, as I recall, were lummoxes, dull and dirty. I, on the other hand, was a philosopher."

"Well, perhaps so. Still, people do change."

"Not so! Consider me, for instance. I am still a philosopher, even more profound than before!"

Morna made uneasy movements preparatory to edging away. "Well, that's very nice, Howard."

"So then, with these considerations in mind, what groups would you recommend that I join? The Sadalflourys yonder? Or the van Bouyers? Or for that matter, your own?"

Morna pursed her lips and blinked. "Really, Howard! I'm sure that you'd be welcome anywhere, it's just that, well, at school, you know, and I thought—"

"You thought of me as a poor vagabond of space, returning, tired and forlorn but full of sentiment, to rejoin Shimus and Saul at our class reunion. In some respects, Morna, time is like a magnifying lens. As a boy I never so much as tasted liqueurs or essences. I brooded upon these illicit delights, and the pretty little flasks became objects of fascination and wonder. Be so good as to signal for the steward, Morna, and sit with me. Together we will taste Nectar of Phlox and Blue Tears and Now-You-See-Me."

Morna drew back a step. "There is no general steward here, Howard. The drink you see has been privately supplied. And now—"

"In that case I will accept your invitation." Howard Hardoah jumped to his feet. "We will join your table, and no doubt Wimberly can spare a flask or two from his basket." With a debonair gesture he urged Morna across the pavilion to the table she shared with her spouse, Wimberly, Bloy and Jenore Sadalfloury, Peder and Ellicent Vorvelt.

The group gave Howard Hardoah a cool and minimal welcome. His response was an easy salute. "Thank you all. Morna has commended me to this noble old Blue Tears, and

I will gladly take a dram or two. Gentlemen and ladies, my best regards! Let the festivities proceed!"

"There is no formal program," said Jenore. "Are none of your old friends here?"

"Just yourselves," said Howard Hardoah. "No program, you say? We must see about that. After all, a reunion should be memorable! Thank you, Wimberly, I'll try another gill. Hey there, Director Kutte, strike up a tune!"

Valdemar Kutte performed a rigid inclination of the head and shoulders. Howard Hardoah chuckled and leaned back in his chair. "He has altered not a whit; same dry old frump. Some of us develop in one direction, some in another. Right, Bloy? You've developed outward; indeed, you're quite corpulent."

Bloy Sadalfloury became red in the face. "It is not a matter I care to discuss."

Howard Hardoah had already passed on to a different subject. "So many Sadalflourys in Fluter Township I can't keep the various branches separate. As I recall, you are of the senior line."

"That is correct."

"And who now is head of the family?"

"That would be my father, Mr. Nomo Sadalfloury."

"He is not present tonight?"

"He is not a member of this class."

"And what of Suby Sadalfloury who was once so beautiful?"

"You are evidently referring to my sister, Mrs. Suby ver Ahe. She is present."

"Where is she sitting?"

"At the table yonder, with her husband, and others."

Howard Hardoah swung about and inspected the dark-haired matron at a table twenty feet away. He rose to his feet and went to lean over the group. "Suby! Do you recognize me?"

"You are Howard Hardoah, I believe." Suby ver Ahe's voice was cool.

"I am he. And who are these others?"

"My husband, Paul. My daughters, Mirl and Maud, Mr. and Mrs. Janust of River Vista, Mr. and Mrs. Gildy of Lake Skooney and their daughter Halda."

Howard Hardoah acknowledged the introductions and returned to Suby. "What an event, meeting you again! I am happy now that I came. Your daughters are as lovely as you were at their age."

Suby's voice was colder than ever. "I am surprised that you should wish to bring old events to mind."

Paul ver Ahe said, "Astonishing that you should choose to appear at all!"

Howard Hardoah showed a plaintive smile. "Was I not invited? Is this not my class and my school?"

Paul ver Ahe said gruffly, "Certain things are best left unsaid."

"Quite true." Howard drew up a chair and seated himself. "If I may, I'll try a flask of your Ammary."

"I have not invited you to do so."

"Tush, Paul, don't be mean! Does not your mill grind out ton after ton of valuable murdock flour?"

"The mill is still in operation. I dispose of the profits as I see fit."

Howard Hardoah threw back his head and laughed. "A pleasure to meet you all." He took up Mirl's hand and kissed her fingers. "Especially you. I have an absolutely unappeasable—insatiable perhaps is not quite the word—admiration for beautiful girls, and before the evening is over we must arrange to meet again."

Paul ver Ahe started to rise to his feet, but Howard Hardoah had already turned away from Mirl. He tilted the flask of Ammary to his lips and swallowed the contents at a gulp. "Refreshing!" In proper style he dropped the empty flask into a basket.

Suby's attention had been distracted. She touched her husband's arm. "Paul, who are those people?" She pointed to the edge of the pavilion. There stood three hard-faced men wearing uniforms of gray and black with black casques. Each carried a short, heavy gun.

Mrs. Janust cried out softly: "They are everywhere! They're all around us!"

Howard Hardoah said in a negligent voice, "Pay them no heed. They are part of my entourage. Perhaps I should make an announcement, to allay curiosity."

Howard Hardoah jumped up on the bandstand. "School chums, old acquaintances, others, you will notice here and there groups of what appear to be battle troops. They are, in fact, a squad of my Companions. Tonight they wear this rather forbidding costume, which tells us that they are in a somber mood. When they wear yellow, you'll find them jaunty and gay. When they wear white, we call them 'death dolls.'

"On this occasion, attend their wise counsels, and we'll all enjoy an evening of fun. Everyone, proceed with the party! Let the reminiscences flow! Jenore Sadalfloury tells me that no entertainments have been planned. I feared as much, and saw fit to arrange a little program. Let me talk briefly of myself. Perhaps of everyone attending the dear old school I was most innocent. I laugh now to think of my illusions. Ah, that dear dreamy lad twenty-five years gone! At school he discovered a mysterious new world of illicit pleasures and tantalizing possibilities. But when he tried to explore and extend himself, he was rebuffed. Nothing went right for him. He was bullied, abused, taunted and given an odious nickname: 'Fimfle.' Bloy Sadalfloury, I believe, was first to use that expression. Am I correct in this, Bloy?"

Bloy Sadalfloury puffed out his cheeks but made no response.

Howard Hardoah gave his head a slow, marveling shake. "Poor Howard! The girls treated him little better. Even now I wince at the slights! Suby Sadalfloury played a particularly heartless game, which I will not describe. I now invite her charming daughters on a cruise aboard my ship. We will visit interesting regions of space, and I assure them that in my company they will not be bored. It is possible that Suby may be distressed and lonesome, but she should have considered the possible consequences of her acts twenty-five years ago, which resulted in my own departure from Gladbetook.

"In sheer point of fact, nothing could have been more to my advantage. I am now a very rich man. I could buy all Gladbetook and never notice. Philosophically, I am a far more definite person. I subscribe to the Doctrine of Cosmic Equilibrium: in simple terms, for every 'tit' there must be a 'tat.' Now for tonight's program. It is a little pastiche called 'A Noble Schoolboy's Daydream of Justice!' How fortunate we are to have on hand many principals to the seminal circumstances!"

Cornelius van Bouyers, chairman of arrangements, came hurrying forward. "Howard! You're talking extravagant folly! You can't be serious; in fact, you're making fun of us all. Come down at once, there's a good fellow, and we'll all enjoy the evening."

Howard raised a finger. Two Companions led Cornelius van Bouyers from the pavilion and locked him in the girls' gymnasium and he was seen no more that night.

Howard Hardoah turned to the orchestra. Gersen, twenty feet away, hoped that a wide-brimmed hat and a bland expression were adequate disguise.

Howard Hardoah barely glanced at him. "Director Kutte! It gives me great pleasure to see you tonight! Do you remember me?"

"Not well."

"That is because you flew into a rage with me and snatched away my fiddle. You said I played like a drunken squirrel."

"Yes, I remember the occasion. You used a clumsy vibrato. In the attempt for sentiment you achieved only larmoyance."

"Interesting. You do not play this style?"

"Decidedly not. Each note should be met justly and precisely, with an edge to each side."

"Let me remind you of a musician's truism," said Howard Hardoah. " 'When you stop going up, you start going down.' You have never played 'drunken squirrel' style, and it is time that you should make the essay. In order to play like a 'drunken squirrel,' while you cannot become a squirrel, at least you can become drunken. Here we have the necessary essences. Drink, Professor Kutte, then play! As you never have played before!"

Director Kutte bowed stiffly and pushed aside the proffered flasks. "Excuse me, I do not drink ferments or spirits. Teaching expressly condemns their use."

"Bah! Tonight we throw a blanket over theology, as we might cover a cantankerous parrot. Let us rejoice! Drink, Professor! Drink here or outside the pavilion with the Companions."

"I have no taste for drink, but since I am forced . . ." Kutte threw the contents of a flask down his throat. He coughed. "The flavor is bitter."

"Yes, that is Bitter Ammary. Here, try Wild Sunlight."

"That is somewhat better. Let me try the Blue Tears. . . . Yes. Tolerable. But quite enough."

Howard Hardoah laughed and clapped Kutte between his narrow shoulders, while Gersen watched sadly. So near and yet so far. The zumbold player next to him muttered, "The man is insane! If he comes within reach I'll clap the zumbold over his head; you make play with the flute and we'll have him helpless in a trice."

By the entrance stood two men: the first short and thick as a stump, near bald, with a square head and flat features; the second spare, saturnine, with short thick black hair, hollow cheeks, a long, pale jaw and chin. Neither wore a Companion uniform. "See those two men?" Gersen made a discreet indication. "They are watching and waiting for just some such foolishness."

"I am not a man to accept humiliation!" growled the zumbold player.

"Tonight you had better go carefully, or you may not awake to life tomorrow morning."

Director Kutte ran his hand through his hair. His eyes had become a trifle glassy and he lurched as he turned to his orchestra. "Play us a tune," called Howard Hardoah. "Drunken squirrel style, if you please."

Kutte mumbled to his orchestra: " 'Gypsy Firelight,' in Aeolian."

Howard Hardoah listened carefully as the orchestra played, keeping time with his finger. Presently he called out, "Enough! Now for the program! It gives me great pleasure to present tonight's entertainment. It has been germinating for twenty-five years. Since I am the impresario, and since the themes derive from my own experiences, the subjective point of view need come as no surprise.

"Let us begin! Our stage properties are at hand. I roll back the curtain of time! We are now at school with Howard Hardoah, a dear lad mistreated by bullies and fickle girls. I recall one such incident. Maddo Strubbins, I see you yonder; you seem as overbearing now as then. Come forward! I wish to recall an incident to your mind."

Maddo Strubbins glowered and sat back defiantly. The Companions approached. He lurched to his feet and sauntered toward the bandstand, a tall, burly man with coarse dark hair and heavy features. He stood looking up at Howard Hardoah with mingled contempt and uncertainty.

Howard Hardoah spoke in a harsh brassy voice: "How good to see you after all these years! Do you still play on the quadrangles?"

"No. That is a game for children, striking a ball back and forth."

"Once, we both thought differently. I went on the court with my new racquet and ball. You came with Wax Buddle and pushed me off the courts. You said, 'Cool your arse, Fimfle. You must wait on your betters.' So you played your game using my ball. Do you remember? When I protested that I had arrived first, you said: 'Sit quiet, Fimfle! I can't play my best with you caterwauling in my ear.' When you had finished, you hit my ball over the fence and it was lost in the weeds. Do you remember?"

Maddo Strubbins made no reply.

"I have long felt the deprivation of that golden day forever lost," said Howard Hardoah. "It has hung in my memory: a frustration! The price of the ball itself was fifty centums. My time spent waiting and hunting for the ball is worth another SVU, to a total of one-and-a-half SVU. At ten percent interest compounded across twenty-five years, it is exactly sixteen SVU, twenty-five centums and two farthings. Add ten SVU punitive damages for a total, let us say of twenty-six SVU. Pay me now."

"I don't carry so much money."

Howard Hardoah instructed his Companions: "Flog him well for twenty-six minutes, then cut off his ears."

Strubbins said, "Wait a minute . . . Here is the money." He paid over coins, then turned and hunched back toward his table.

"Not just yet," said Howard Hardoah. "You have only paid me for the lost ball. 'Sit quietly,' you said."

The Companions rolled forward a wooden chair-frame on which rested a block of ice. They conducted Maddo Strubbins to the chair, cut away his trousers, sat him on the ice and strapped him in place.

"Sit quietly; cool your own arse," said Howard Hardoah. "You lost my ball and I am tempted to order an excision along your own ropy scrotum, except that this is a family entertainment. One other matter . . ." A Companion stepped forward and pressed a contrivance against Maddo Strubbins's forehead; he cried out in pain. When the contrivance was removed the letter F, in heavy purple block print, remained.

"That is an indelible reminder of the odious nickname 'Fimfle,' " said Howard Hardoah. "It shall be a memento for anyone I recall using this term. It was evolved by Bloy Sadalfloury. Let us deal next with this corpulent scalawag."

Bloy Sadalfloury was stripped naked and tattooed with F's

over his entire body, except across his buttocks where FIM-FLE was spelled out in full.

"You are bedizened in style," said Howard Hardoah with critical approval. "While you are bathing at Lake Skooney and your friends ask why you are spotted like a leopard, you will respond: 'It was the fault of my malicious tongue!' Hey, Companions! A clever elaboration! Stamp his tongue as well!

"So then, who and what is next on the program? Edver Vissy? Forward, please . . . Remember Angela Dain? A pretty little girl from the lower grades? I admired Angela with all the fervor of my romantic heart. One day as I stood talking to her, you came along and pushed me aside. You said, 'Run along, Fimfle. Just pick a direction; Angela and I will go the other way.' I have puzzled over this command long and often. 'Run along.' Along what? The road? An imaginary line? A long way?" Howard Hardoah's voice became nasal and pedantic. "In this special case, we will simplify and imagine a course around the pavilion. You will run 'a long way' 'along' this course, and we will learn where emphasis lies. Four blackguard dogs will chase you and gnaw your legs should you tarry. Hurrah then, Edver! Let us watch a fleet pair of heels as you 'run along.' A pity that little Angela is not here to enjoy the evening."

The Companions took Edver Vissy to the course and set him running, with four squat hounds lurching and snarling behind him.

The zumbold player muttered to Gersen, "Have you ever seen the like? The man is mad, to play such spiteful tricks!"

"Take care," said Gersen. "He hears whispers ten minutes old and half a mile away. So far his acts are almost benign; he is in a good mood."

"I hope never to see him in a rage."

The program proceeded, as, one by one, Howard Hardoah adjusted strains and imbalances in the cosmic equilibrium.

Olympe Omsted had arranged to meet Howard at the Blinnick Pond Picnic Grounds. Howard had trudged ten miles and had waited four hours, only to see Olympe arrive in company with Gard Thornbloom. "You will now be conveyed to a far place," Howard told Olympe. "You will wait eight hours, until morning, then walk twenty miles to the Wiggal River. That you may forever remember this occasion, I have arranged a further penalty." Olympe was stripped nude to the waist; one breast was stained bright red, the other an equally intense blue, and for good measure a purple F was stamped on her belly. "Excellent!" declared Howard Hardoah. "In the future you will find it more difficult to beguile and deceive trusting young boys."

While Howard gave his attention to Leopold Friss, Olympe was led from the pavilion, and carried off through the night. Leopold had instructed young Howard to "Kiss his arse." Six pigs were brought before Leopold, and he was obliged to kiss each appropriately.

Hippolita Fawer, who had slapped Howard's face on the front steps of the school, was spanked by two Companions, while Professor Kutte played a threnody in time with her outcries.

Professor Kutte, now loose in the knees, found difficulty in applying bow to strings. Howard Hardoah seized the fiddle in disgust. "I have drunk five times as much as you!" he told Kutte. "You boast of musical competence, yet you cannot play while drunk! For shame! I shall play the tune properly." He signaled the Companions who set about spanking Hippolita, who resumed her cries while Howard played the fiddle. He began to dance as he played, lifting one of his long legs, thrusting it high and forward and giving a little kick, then prancing forward, knees bent, meanwhile playing with rapt face and half-closed eyes.

The zumbold player said dubiously to Gersen: "Truth to tell, he plays in fine style . . . A sure touch there; notice how justly he accents the woman's outcries. I am tempted to shout 'bravo.'"

"He would be pleased," said Gersen. "On the whole it is probably best not to call attention to yourself."

"I am sure that you are right."

The tune came to an end and Hippolita returned in dishevelment to her table. Howard Hardoah was in the mood for music. He faced the orchestra. "All together now, with zest, rare tones and precise execution: 'Pettyville Pleasures.' Parnassian Mode."

Gersen nudged the zumbold player. "Which flute?"

"With the brass flange."

Howard Hardoah stamped his foot; the tune began. After one rendition, Howard called a halt. "Fair, only fair! More bite with the cornet! You on wood-pipe! Why do you not play the traditional solo?"

Gersen showed a moony grin. "I'm not that sure of the part, sir."

"Then you should practice your instrument!"

"I give my all, sir."

"Once again, lively now!"

The tune was played, with Howard Hardoah performing his absurd capering dance.

Abruptly he stopped, stamped his feet, raised his hands on high, brandishing fiddle and bow in outrage. "You, on the wood-pipe! Why do you not play as you should? Why this preposterous pip-pup-pup, pip-pup-pup?"

"Well, sir, truth be told, it is how I learned the instrument."

Howard Hardoah clutched his head, deranged his hat in a frenzy of impatience. "You exasperate me to distraction, with your pip-pup-pup! Also your foolish leering face. Companions! Seize this mooncalf, take him down to the river and throw him away! Musicians of his sort the world is better without."

The Companions seized Gersen, dragged him from the platform. Howard addressed the audience. "You are witnessing an important event. The population is divided into three classes: first, fastidious persons of discrimination and taste; second, the vulgar masses, exemplified by yourselves; and third, a few wretched parvenus who mimic the style of their betters, as in the case of this wood-pipe player. His sort must be discouraged! Now—on with the music. All who wish may dance."

Two Companions frog-marched Gersen across the pavilion and down the slope toward the river. A third strolled negligently behind. Nothing could have been more to Gersen's satisfaction. Down the steps to the boat dock they marched, and out to the far end where the fairy lamps reflected in jerks and jiggles on the dark water.

The Companions seized Gersen by the arms and the seat of the pants. Gersen hung supine and limp. "It's to be one, two, three and on your way! So, here we go!"

"Here we go," said Gersen. He swiveled, broke holds, struck the man on his left a fearful blow in the neck, crushing his larynx. He struck the other across the temple with his fist and felt the crush of bone. Turning at a crouch he flung himself against the knees of the third man, who staggered, swayed, lurched backward, clawing at his sidearm. Gersen caught him in a clamp, flung him face down, planted his knees on the heavy shoulders, reached down into the man's mouth, jerked up and back and snapped the man's neck.

Panting, Gersen rose to his feet. In less than thirty seconds he had killed three men. Gersen took up one of the long-guns, a pistol, a pair of daggers, then rolled the bodies into the river.

He started back toward the pavilion. The music had halted. The Companions, coordinated by radio-communicator, by one means or another had been notified of trouble at the riverside.

Gersen glimpsed a dozen Companions running at a crouch from the pavilion. Howard Alan Treesong stood on the band-stand, scowling in his direction. Gersen raised the long-gun, aimed, fired a round just as Howard Treesong jumped from the bandstand. He whirled in midair, struck in the shoulder. Gersen fired again, and struck Howard Treesong in the groin, spinning him around again. He fell to the floor of the pavil-ion and out of Gersen's range of vision.

Gersen hesitated, leaning back and forth, almost irresistibly urged to rush forward and make sure of Howard Treesong's death . . . Danger was too close. If Howard Treesong were only wounded, as seemed likely, and Gersen were captured, it would be a grisly business. He could wait no longer. Dodging into the shade of the larch trees, he ran around the pavilion to the driveway, where he crouched among the parked ve-hicles. Three Companions ran along the front of the pavilion; Gersen aimed, fired: once, twice, three times and three bodies tumbled to the ground.

Gersen gingerly rose to his feet and craned his neck hoping for another shot at Treesong.

Danger hung heavy. Death was imminent. Gersen retreated to the road, crossed and took refuge in a copse of some dank local growth. A giant shape blotting out the stars descended upon the pavilion. Searchlights suddenly illuminated the en-tire area . . . Gersen decided to wait no longer; infrared scanners would soon be combing the landscape. He ran to the riverside, lowered himself into the water and floated away to the north, secure from infrared detection.

He swam across the river and emerged a quarter-mile downstream. He climbed the bank, sodden as a muskrat, and stood surveying the scene to the south . . . Failure once more. Bitter, galling failure. For the second time he had been

offered a shot at his quarry; for the second time he had inflicted only a wound.

Tenders drifted down from the ship and a moment later
returned. The floodlights were extinguished; the ship, now a
black mass picked out by lines of illuminated ports, rose to
an altitude of a thousand feet and hovered.

Within the ship, Treesong's brain would not be inactive.
The alarm had emanated from the dock, where the Companions had taken the inept musician. Who was this musician
whom Professor Kutte had allowed to play in his orchestra?
Obviously, the question would be put to Kutte, who would
briskly tell all he knew: the musician was an offworlder who
wished to be present at the reunion.

An offworlder? He must be captured, without fail. Inquiry
quickly would be made at inns, towns, transport agencies,
spaceports. At Theobald Spaceport, the *Flitterwing* would be
noticed, boarded. The registration, in the name of Kirth Gersen, would duly be recorded and made known to Howard
Treesong. Gersen grimaced. He climbed the bank and trotted
north to Glocher Way, then west beside the cemetery. The
death of Gladbetook, uncannily sentient in the starlight,
watched him pass.

At the main street Gersen hesitated a moment, thinking of
the runabout, but Professor Kutte represented the greater urgency and he continued along Glocher Way to Kutte's house.

Light glowed from the front windows. Keeping to the
deepest shadows Gersen approached the house. Valdemar
Kutte, in a maroon dressing gown, paced back and forth,
holding a towel to his forehead. So far, thought Gersen, so
good; the normalcy of the scene made him wonder as to the
accuracy of his projections. The spaceship might already have
departed, with the idiot musician remaining as an unsolved, if
trivial, mystery . . . Nevertheless Gersen decided to wait. Behind a hedge he found concealment and settled himself.

Minutes passed: five, ten.

The street remained quiet. Gersen stirred fretfully. He
looked around the sky, to find only stars and strange constel-
lations. He heaved a sigh, adjusted his position, his clothes
still damp.

A faint sound from above. Gersen became instantly alert.
Again! Imminence!

Down from the sky drifted a small airboat. Soft as a
shadow it dropped to a landing in the street, ten yards from

Gersen's hiding place. Three men stepped to the ground, dark shapes in the starshine. For a moment they stood in muttered conversation, evidently making sure of Kutte's house.

Gersen ran crouching behind the hedge, circled Kutte's hydrangea bushes, and waited behind the gatepost.

Inside the house Valdemar Kutte, in a posture of outrage and indignation, complained of the night's events to a small plump woman who listened aghast.

Two men came along the avenue. They turned into Professor Kutte's yard. Gersen hit one upon the forehead with an iron garden ornament, grappled the other and stabbed him to the heart.

There had been no sound. Within the house Professor Kutte continued as before, striding back and forth, flourishing his hands, pausing to emphasize some particularly heinous episode.

Gersen crept back behind the hedge to his former post. The third man stood leaning against the skycar. Gersen stepped quietly into the street behind him. Striking hard with the dagger, he cut the man's spinal cord.

Into the back of the skycar Gersen tumbled the three corpses. He took the vehicle aloft, floated across Gladbetook, now dark and shuttered for the night, and settled into the yard behind Swecher's Inn. He went quietly to his room, changed gratefully into his ordinary clothes, tucked *The Book of Dreams* into his pocket. Returning to the skycar, he rose into the night and flew south toward Theobald.

Over the Dalglish River he lowered the skycar, jettisoned the three Companions, then continued south.

The scattered lights of Theobald presently appeared below. Red and blue twinklers marked the outlines of the spaceport.

Unnoticed and unchallenged, Gersen landed the skycar beside his *Fantamic Flitterwing*. He went aboard and started up the flight systems.

He considered the skycar. If Howard Treesong found it here, near the spot vacated by a *Fantamic Flitterwing*, he would draw the natural and obvious conclusion. The depot official would supply him the *Flitterwing's* registration codes, the trail would lead directly to Kirth Gersen, care of Jehan Addels, Pontefract, Aloysius . . . Gersen overrode the safety latch, set the controls and let the skycar fly off into the night.

He returned into the *Flitterwing*, sealed the ports and left the Land of Lelander below . . . At an altitude of ten miles he hovered and searched the sky. Neither macroscope, nor radar, nor xenode detector discovered any trace of Treesong's ship, which was just as well, since the *Flitterwing* lacked armament.

Gersen flew into the far north and landed on an expanse of desolate tundra, safe from Treesong's detectors, should anyone think to deploy them.

Silence and starlight on the waste outside the observation ports. Gersen consumed a bowl of goulash and sat slumped in his chair, profoundly tired but prevented from sleep by a flux of queer moods: nervous excitement slowly waning, disappointment for his failure to kill Howard Treesong, contradicted by a grim satisfaction for the damage he had done, which would cause Treesong inconvenience, anger, fear, uncertainty and pain: not a bad evening's work. The events themselves—they could only be comprehended in terms of Howard Treesong's personality . . . Taking up *The Book of Dreams*, Gersen began to study the contents. He was too tired to persist . . . He went to his couch and soon slept.

Chapter 14

In the morning Gersen went out to drink a cup of tea in the slanting sunlight. The air carried a smoky reek of fust, mud and eons of slow-decaying vegetation. Low hills huddled across the southern horizon; elsewhere a plain, half-tundra half-bog, extended as far as the eye could see. Gray-green lichen covered the ground, punctuated by starved clumps of sedge and small black plantains with scarlet berries. The reunion at Gladbetook School seemed far distant in both space and time.

Gersen went into the saloon and drew another cup of tea. Sitting on the top step of the exit port, in the wan light of Van Kaathe's Star, he once more set himself to an examination of *The Book of Dreams*.

The tea grew cold. Gersen read, page after page, and came at last to where young Howard had stopped his writing almost in mid-sentence.

Gersen put the book down and looked off across the distance. Once, Howard Hardoah had treasured this book. For Howard Alan Treesong it would represent a memento of the sweet sad days of his youth. And far more: it defined his being; it was precious beyond calculation. Suppose he were now to learn of its existence? . . . There were dozens of permutations to the situation. Howard believed that the book had been taken from him by his friend Nimpy Cleadhoe. An all-important question: where now was Nimpy Cleadhoe?

Gersen sat thinking: of young Howard Hardoah, frail, tentative, sensitive; of Howard Alan Treesong, strong, radiant with confidence, pulsing with vitality. Picking up *The Book of Dreams*, Gersen thought to feel from the faded red cover a quiver of similar life . . . On first reading, the book had seemed a rather formless pastiche. There were personal assertions, colloquies between seven paladins, twelve cantos of narrative verse. A late chapter revealed the language Naomei, known only to the seven paladins, and included a syllabary of 350 characters, by which Naomei might properly be transcribed. Before young Howard had fully developed Naomei, the book came to its abrupt ending.

The book apparently had occupied Howard for a period of years. The initial manifesto occupied a page and a half: a statement in which a sympathetic ear might find much that was vivid and compelling, whereas a cynical spirit would hear only callow bombast. So much, thought Gersen, might be said for the entire book; final judgment could only rest upon how closely achievement matched youthful fantasy. In this light the term "callow bombast" must be discarded. "Feeble understatement," thought Gersen, was a more appropriate phrase.

The book began:

> I am Howard Alan Treesong. I profess no fealty to the Hardoah ilk; I expect none. That my birth occurred through the agency of Adrian and Reba Hardoah is an incident over which I lacked control. I prefer to claim my substance elsewhere: from brown soil like that which I now clutch in my hand, from gray rain and moaning wind, from radiance discharged by the magic star Meamone. My stuff has been impregnated with ten colors, of which five are found in the flowers of Dahane Forest and five may be struck from the Meamone scintilla.
> Such is the stuff of my being.
> For ilkness I claim the line of Demabia

Hathkens,[1] specifically from his union with Princess Gisseth of Treesong Keep, from which came Searl Treesong, Knight of the Flaming Spear.

My vistgeist[2] is known by a name of secret magic.

This name is IMMIR

May sullen rays from the dark star beside Meamone strike liver and lights of him who utters this name to scorn.

To the following page was attached a drawing worked by an unskilled hand yet infused with ardor and an earnest directness. Depicted was a naked boy standing in front of a naked young man, the boy stalwart and determined, with a bright intelligent gaze; the young man somewhat insubstantial but effulgent with a nameless quality compounded of daring, ardor, magical wonder.

This, thought Gersen, was young Howard's concept of himself and his vistgeist Immir.

The next page listed a set of aphorisms, some legible, others so erased and altered as to be unintelligible:

IN COUNTERMANDS OUT.

Problems are like the trees of Bleadstone Woods; there is always a way between.

I am a thing sublime. I believe. I surge, and it is done. I defeat heroes; I woo fair girls; I swim warm with glorious longing for the ineffable. With my ardent urge I outstrip time and think the unthinkable. I know a secret force. It comes from within,

[1] Protagonist of a heroic cycle of folktales from *The Heham Ffoliot*, a collection of sagas and fairy tales acknowledged glancingly and painfully by Teaching.

[2] A term from the jargon of Teaching: essentially, the idealized version of one's self. Teaching defines the vistgeist rather narrowly and exhorts the individual to a lifelong attempt to match the beatitude of of the vistgeist. Howard, for vistgeist, formulated an entity totally emancipated from the strictures of Teaching.

exerting irresistible thrust. It partakes of all gaiety,
of the striding gallantry of the beautiful Tatten-
barth nymphs, of the soul's conquest over infinity.
This is VLON, which may be revealed to no one.
Here is the secret symbol:

I love Glaide with the blond curls. She lives in
dreaming, as an anemone lives in cool water. She is
not aware that I am I. I wish I knew the way into
her soul. I wish I knew the magic to join our
dream-ways. If I only could talk to her by starlight,
afloat on quiet waters.

I can see the outlines; there are ways to control
the beast. But I have much to learn. Fear, panic,
terror: they are like wild giants who must be con-
quered and enslaved to my service. It shall be done.
Wherever I go they will follow at my heels, unseen
and unknown until I command.

Glaide!
I know she must be aware.
Glaide!
She is made from starlight and flower dust; she
breathes the memory of midnight music.
I wonder I wonder I wonder.

Today I showed her the Sign, casually, as if it
were of no importance. She saw it; she looked at
me. But she spoke no word.

(The next few passages bore traces of erasure with passages overwritten in a stronger hand.)

What is power? It is the means to realize wants and wishes. To me, power has become a necessity; in itself it is a virtue and balm sweet as a girl's kiss, and—similarly—it is there to be taken.

I am alone. Enemies and hurlibuts surround me, and stare with mad eyes. They flaunt their insolent haunches as they pass by on the run.

Glaide, Glaide, why did you do so? You are deprived to me, you are soiled and spoiled. O sweet soiled Glaide! You shall know regret and remorse; you shall sing songs of woe, to no avail. As for the dogskin Tupper Sadalfloury, I shall take him in the amber gondola to Slaymarket Isle and give him to the Moals.

But it is time to think beyond.

The text passed over a page, to resume in ink of heavy purple-black. The hand seemed more firm; the characters more regularly formed. The next passage was headed:

MANTRICS

The accumulation of power is a self-sustaining process. The first accretion is slow, but increases according to direction.[1] First, the requisite steps. These are an equable and careless fare, where nothing is revealed. During this phase all strictures are methodically discarded. Discipline in itself is not a corrupt concept, only discipline that is imposed rather than self-calculated. Emancipation, then, is first: from Teaching, from duty, from softer emotions, which loosen the power of decision.

(An evident lapse of time, perhaps several months. The ensuing hand was tall, spiky, angular and exuded an almost palpable energy.)

---

[1] "Direction" evidently signifies "personal control," "personal manipulation."

A new girl has come to town!
Her name is Zada Memar.
Zada Memar.
To think of her brings a blur of enthrallment
across the brain.
She moves in a cosmos of her own, colored by
her own colors and urged by her own fascinating
ardors! How can I join my cosmos to hers? How
can I share our secrets? How can we merge ourselves into a unity of body and soul and ardor?
I wonder if she knows me as I know her?

There followed several pages of extravagant speculations
upon Destiny and circumstances subsequent to a chance
meeting between himself and Zada Memar.
The next passage consisted of passionate apostrophes
addressed to the inner consciousness of Zada Memar. There
was no explicit clue as to the progress or outcome of the love
affair, except in the termination of the passage: a wild burst
of emotion directed against the environment in which
Howard Hardoah found himself.

Enemies surround me; they stare at me with mad
eyes, walking or loping past, or veering as if blown
on the wind, they flaunt their insolent challenges. I
see them through several minds, as is useful.

The time is Now. I call on Immir.
Immir! To the fore!

A blank page, and a division in *The Book of Dreams*. For
want of better terms, the foregoing could be designated *Part
One*. *Part Two* was indited in a firm round hand. The rasping
fervor of previous passages seemed under strong control.
The apparent continuity between the final line of *Part One*
and the first line of *Part Two* would seem to be misleading.

Upon that place made sacred to myself I bled my
blood, I made the sign. I spoke the word, I called
on Immir, and he came.

I said, Immir, the time is Now. Stand together with
me.

Assuredly. We are one.

Now we must set about our affairs. Let us form our company, so that each is known to each, mighty paladins all.

So it shall be. Come, stand in the ray from Meamone and by their redolent colors let them be known.

The ray struck down upon the black gem, so that a person of black splendor appeared; he and Immir embraced like boon companions of old.

Here is the first paladin; he is Jeha Rais the Wise, and far of vision. He reckons eventualities and counsels the necessary, without weakness, pity, ruth or clemency.

I give you welcome, noble paladin.

To Meamone's ray Immir showed the red gem, and a person wearing crimson amphruscules[1] joined the three.

Here stands Loris Hohenger the red paladin. He knows and works the executive arts. Without effort he does deeds wondrous to the ordinary man. He is a stranger to fear. He cries: Ah ha ha! when the falbards are raised for combat.

Loris, I accept you as my red paladin, and I promise you feats and forays to surpass any which have gone before.

That is good to hear.

Immir, who now will join us?

Immir used the green gem, and one wearing the

---

[1] Amphruscules: the enameled tablets forming the shoulder insignia and chest medallion of a Trelancthian knight.

green garments of an Idaspian grandee stepped to the fore. Tall and grave he stood with hair like midnight and eyes blazing green.

Here is Mewness, who upholds the Green: an extraordinary paladin, supple, strange and eerie in his manner of mind. He conducts the madcap exploits, he performs that which is direly unexpected. He owns to no more qualms than a lizard and makes no explanation to friend or foe. He has no peer in riddling mazes and also he is a most talented musician, proficient in the several modes.

Green Mewness, will you join us as a paladin?

With great joy, and forever.

Excellent! Immir, who now?

Immir found a fine topaz and cherished it under Meamone, and so appeared a person wearing a black halpern fetched with a yellow plume, yellow boots and gauntlets. Strung over his back he carried a lute. Immir gave him greeting and named him Spangleway the Antic.

We are fortunate indeed; here is merry Spangleway the Antic, to relieve us when the way is weary. In battle he is wily and master of terrifying artifice; only Mewness can match him for his cunning ploys and startling displays.

Immir, who else do we command?

I hold this sapphire to Meamone; I call on Rhune Fader the Blue!

A person slender and strong, as blithe and winsome as the sunny sky of memory, stepped forward.

Here is our gay Rhune, fair and strong and ignorant both of despair and defeat! Sometimes he is known as Rhune the Gentle, still he strikes hard, deep and often, but never in harsh rage, and he allows his captives easy repentance.

Rhune Fader, we welcome you; will you join us?

All the winds and thunders, all the energetics of war, all the ploys and plots of cunning cowards: none could hold me apart.

Then you are our sworn paladin.

Immir, who else? Are there more to add to this marvelous troop?

One more; a person to make out the whole.

Immir held high a white crystal. I call for Eia Panice the White!

A person appeared wearing a black cape over body armor of white sequins. His face was pallid and without humor; his cheeks were hollow and his eyes showed like glimpses of pale fire.

Immir spoke: Eia, as fearsome to enemies as death itself, speaks little. His deeds tell their own tale and terror trembles in his wake. Rejoice, paladins, that Eia is one of us; as foe he is redoubtable.

Eia Panice, I greet you and make you my brother paladin, and we shall venture through many circumstances.

That is my hope.

Immir spoke: So then, the gallant seven! Let all advance and clasp hands and may the bond be broken only by sorry death!

All averred, and so was formed the noble troop, destined to perform deeds and feats to surpass all those of yore or hence.

On the next pages the young Howard had attempted portraits of the Seven, with much evidence of painful reworking. The sketches terminated *Part Two* of the book.

There followed several pages of notes and memoranda, a few written in the Naomei syllabary. Howard apparently tired of the exertion and continued in ordinary language.

A list of descriptive titles appeared:

1. The Adventure at Tuarech
2. The Duel with the Sarsen Ebratan Champions
3. The Coming of Zada
4. The Insolent Pride of King Weper
5. Zada Forlorn
6. The Castle Haround
7. The Wooing of Zada Memar
8. The Seven Weirds of Haltenhorst
9. The Adventure at the Green Star Inn
10. The Great Games at Woon Windway
11. The Dungeons of Mourne
12. Paladins Triumphant!

Whatever text Howard Hardoah had planned for the twelve titles was not included in the book, except for excerpts and fragments which occupied the pages following. Then, abruptly, two-thirds of the way through the book, almost in mid-sentence, there was no more writing.

Gersen put the book down. He descended to the tundra and paced back and forth beside the *Flitterwing*. All could yet go well. There had been failure at Voymont, and likewise at Gladbetook, but *The Book of Dreams* might permit a third opportunity—if he used it correctly. To any obvious bait, Howard Treesong, twice-wounded, would react with hypersensitive suspicion.

The problem, then, was to deploy the bait where it would be perceived as something otherwise.

Gersen halted and stood looking gloomily south. Before plans could be formed, he must return once more to Gladbetook.

The proscriptions in regard to Maunish air space no longer troubled Gersen; clearly no one made the slightest attempt at enforcement. About the hour of noon he dropped the *Flitterwing* down from behind a low cloud and into the woodland at the back of Hardoah's Home Farm. Mindful of previous frustrations, he armed himself with care, then sealed his ship and walked to the edge of the open land. To his right spread a large pond, to his left that strip of land formerly worked by the Cleadhoes. As Gersen approached Home Farm, Ledesmus Hardoah left the barn with a bucket of feed which he tossed into the fowl-run, and then returned into the barn.

Gersen went to the door of the farmhouse and knocked.

The door slid back to reveal the gaunt figure of Reba Hardoah. She looked Gersen up and down with a blank expression.

Gersen greeted her politely. "Today I'm here on business, I'm afraid. I need just a bit more information. Naturally, I'm quite willing to pay for taking your time."

Reba Hardoah spoke in a nervous rush of words: "Mr. Hardoah isn't here at the moment. He has gone into the village."

Ledesmus, emerging from the barn, saw Gersen. He put down his bucket and ambled across the yard. "So you're back, eh? Did you hear the news about Howard?"

"News? What news?"

Ledesmus guffawed and wiped his mouth with the back of his hand. "Maybe I shouldn't laugh, but that crazy Howard come to the school meeting with a gang of thugs and made everyone jump through a hoop. Settled all his old scores, did Howard."

"Terrible, terrible," keened Reba Hardoah. "He insulted the van Bouyers and struck Bloy Sadalfloury and acted a great cruel villain. We've been properly shamed by a graceless son."

"Now there, lady," said Ledesmus, "it's nothing to pine over. Truth to tell, it gives me to laugh when I think of it. That Howard now, who'd have thought he'd turn out such a scarper?"

"It's a disgrace!" cried Reba. "Your father even now is trying to make amends."

"He's much too upright," said Ledesmus. "Howard is nothing to do with us."

"That's my point of view," said Gersen. "Still, it's a pity that he brought you such bad notoriety."

"When I go to Teaching House, I'll never know where to look," said Reba Hardoah.

"Just stare them down," Ledesmus told her. "Specify that

if they don't behave you'll complain to Howard. That should shut a mouth or two."

"What an insane idea! But give this gentleman his information; he's willing to pay for it."

"Indeed? What is it this time?"

"Nothing of consequence. You mentioned one of Howard's friends, Nimpy Cleadhoe."

"Certainly. So then?"

"What happened to Nimpy? Where is he now?"

Ledesmus frowned and looked across the field to a dismal little house under a pair of straggling ginsaps. "Those Cleadhoes were always queer folk, offworlder stock. Old Cleadhoe was queerest of all; in fact he was marmelizer for Fluter Township. I don't remember all so clearly, but they didn't take kindly to Howard fighting on Nimpy and accusing him of stealing his book; and the lady, Mrs. Cleadhoe, come over to complain to father, who had words with Howard, and Howard went away to make his career, and succeeded, as we have seen."

"Ledesmus, don't say so! It's shame on us for his awful deeds!"

Ledesmus only laughed. "I wish I'd been to see it all. Think of Maddo Strubbins with his hind parts on ice! That's rich, now!"

Gersen asked, "And what of Nimpy?"

"The Cleadhoes left, and that's all we saw of them."

"Where did they go?"

"They told me naught." He looked to his mother. "What of you?"

"They went back whence they came." Reba Hardoah jerked her thumb toward the sky. "Offworld. When the old Cleadhoes died, they called for their offworld kin to inherit the land, so the new Cleadhoes arrived. That was before you were born. We had little to do with them, and we can't be blamed, considering the man's calling."

"Town eviscerator and marmelizer." Ledesmus spoke with disgust.

Reba Hardoah hunched her bony shoulders and shuddered. "It comes to us all, Teaching or no. Still, who'd be marmelizer but someone low-caste, or offworld?"

Into the house came Adrian Hardoah. He stopped short at the sight of Gersen and stared suspiciously from face to face. "What's all this? Something to do with Howard again?"

"Not this time, sir," said Gersen. "We were discussing your old neighbors, the Cleadhoes."

Hardoah grunted and flung his hat upon the settee. "Bad stock, those folk. Never did well, never bred true. A boon that they're gone."

"I wonder where they went?"

"Who knows? Off-planet, at least."

Reba spoke. "Don't you remember? Old Otho said he was going back where he came from?"

"Yes, something of the sort."

"Where could that be?" asked Gersen.

Hardoah gave him an unfriendly glance. "The Hardoahs are the lineage of Didram Fluter. I am Instructor at the College; my mother was a Bistwider; my father's mother was a Dwint of the nineteenth generation. Otho Cleadhoe was public eviscerator, who turned a flat ear to Teaching. Am I then to be his crony?"

"Definitely not."

Adrian Hardoah gave a gloomy nod. "Go look at the marmels. The first Cleadhoe stands proudfast. His plaque tells of his birth."

"Correct and exact!" cried Ledesmus. "Trust Father for wisdom; he's never failed yet!"

Ledesmus and Gersen drove into town in the Hardoah's old power-wagon. Along the way Ledesmus discussed Howard's exploits at the school reunion. His chortles of amusement indicated neither shame nor remorse for Howard's outrageous deeds.

Ledesmus halted the wagon beside the church and led the way into the cemetery, threading the dead convocations with the ease of long acquaintance. "The Hardoahs and our other ilk are yonder. Over here stands the dross—out-worlders and persons of poor reputation."

The time was late afternoon. In the low light the two moved among the shadowed figures. Plaques bespoke their names to those who after the passage of years might have forgotten them. Kassideh . . . Hornblath . . . Dadendorf . . . Lup . . . Cleadhoe . . .

Gersen pointed. "Here's one of them."

"That's one of the old ladies. Here's Luke Cleadhoe; he'll be the first, and there's your answer: 'Born on Bethune Preserve, out in the Crow, a far world lost to the goodness of

Teaching. In his youth a notable outrider, by diligence he earned to the post of disease monitor to the wild beasts, then to First Apprentice Taxidermist. Arriving at Gladbetook, he diligently worked the farmlands and nurtured a family of several souls, all sadly impervious to the truths of Teaching.' So there you have it," said Ledesmus in triumph.

As they walked back through the cemetery toward the church, Gersen chanced to notice the marmel of a young girl. She stood straight, head turned a trifle to the side as if she were listening for a far sound, a voice or a bird call. She wore a simple gown; her head and feet were bare. Her plaque read: *Zada Memar, unfortunate child, taken from her loving family almost before her first bloom. Woe and alas for this poor maiden!*

Gersen called Ledesmus's attention to the marmel. "Do you remember her?"

"Yes indeed! At the school outing she wandered off into the woods and they found her in Persimmon Lake. A pretty thing she was!"

The sun had set low behind the line of deodars; the marmels stood in gloom.

Ledesmus said suddenly: "Time to move along! Here's no place to loiter after dark."

Chapter 15

From *The Avatar's Apprentice*, in *Scroll from the Ninth Dimension*:

Surrounding the pedestal: a low mound, agglomerated from the shards of false effigies across a hundred centuries. The latest of these, in the likeness of Bernissus, lay toppled, with one mighty leg thrust high. Marmaduke, standing to the side in a robe of brown frowst, was moved to a tear of sad recollection.

Now the effigy of Holy Mungol was brought forward and raised on high, to be exalted by the throng.

The Warkeep of Gortland climbed to the plinth. He raised his arms and called out in a brazen voice: "Victory—at last and forever! Mungol stands on high; the holy and the true guard our land! For all eternity so it will be! Let there be joy!"

The host responded with jubilation, uttering deep-throated shouts and dancing in circles. The

Wind Lords struck their shields with mailed fists;
the Bracha skirled their noblest tunes. Arrayed in
glistening mists the Prudesses rang bells and made
signs; the Little Wefkins rejoiced.

Again spoke the Warkeep. "All is complete! The
parapets are guarded by our mighty Vencedors;
Bernissus is less than nothing: the remembered
smell of a latrine in a diseased leper's nightmare!

"But of the past no more! Holy Mungol stands
on high and casts his sublime gaze across eternity.
Let each take up his loot and march in glory to his
home! Blue Men to the east; Green Men to the
west. I with my Cantaturces fare north!"

The host gave a final glad cry and dispersed,
each marching his preferred way. A single group of
seven persons set off to the south across Maudly
Waste, toward Sesset. They were: Cathres, a flat-
faced lumpkin with burly shoulders and a lewd
tongue; three Lygons Ordinary: Shalmar, Bahuq
and Amaretto; Implissimus, Knight of the Blue
Kerlanth; Rorback the glutton and Marmaduke. It
was an ill-assorted troop and a surly one, for none
had taken loot.

Faring across the waste they encountered a train
of three wagons laden with the plunder of Molan-
der Abbey. The commander was Horman the one-
eyed vagabond. He and his henchmen were given
short shrift, and the band set about dividing the
spoils.

In the front wagon Marmaduke discovered the
delightful Sufrit who had caused him such heart-
ache at the Grand Masque. To Marmaduke's dismay Cathres insisted that Sufrit be considered a
segment of his plunder, and his arguments won the
day.

With sly forethought Chathres told Marmaduke:
"Since you have expressed dissatisfaction with the
arrangements, divide the spoils as you will, into
seven lots, and each shall choose that lot which
suits him best!"

"What is the order of choosing?"

"The order is determined by lot."

Marmaduke set about dividing the booty. Sufrit

whispered into his ear: "You have been tricked. The lots will determine who chooses first, but you must choose last, as you are arranging the division, presumably, into parts of equal value."

Marmaduke uttered a cry of consternation. Sufrit said: "Listen then! Place me in one lot, alone. Divide all treasure into five lots. Into the last lot place Horman's three iron keys, his shoes, his drum and other valueless oddments. These naturally will fall to you. Make sure you keep the keys, but abandon all else."

Marmaduke did as he was bid. By trickery the salacious Chathres won first choice and with a grand flourish took Sufrit for his own. The others chose lots of gold and gems, and Marmaduke was left the oddments.

Suddenly it was discovered that the draught beasts had escaped and, worse, that all the water bags had been slashed with a knife and hung empty.

Furious talk was heard and accusations were exchanged. "How can we reach Sesset, which lies five days hence across the burning waste?" cried Chathres.

"No matter," said Sufrit. "I know of a fountain not far to the south. We will reach it by sunset."

Grumbling and already thirsty, the band took up the loot and staggered to the south. At dusk they came to a fertile garden surrounded by a high iron wall which none could scale by reason of poison spikes. A single postern afforded entrance, which one of Marmaduke's keys controlled.

"What luck!" cried Chathres. "Marmaduke's foresight has helped us all!"

"Not so fast," said Marmaduke. "I demand a fee for the use of my key. From each of you I will take your best jewel."

"I have no jewels!" cried Chathres. "Must I then remain outside to become prey to wild animals?"

"What can you offer?"

"I have only my sword, my garments and my slave girl, whom you may not have, and no warrior of honor would part with his sword."

"Then give me your garments, every last stitch and strap."

So it was done and Chathres entered the garden naked as an egg, to the amusement of all.

"Laugh now," Chathres told them. "Tonight I shall take pleasure with my slave girl. Then who will be laughing?"

For supper the band ate fruit from the trees and drank copiously of clear cold water. Then Chathres took Sufrit among the trees and set about his lascivious endeavors. But the iron walls surrounded a sacred grove and whenever Chathres attempted a lewd act a great white bat flew down to buffet him with its wings, until Chathres at last desisted and Sufrit was allowed to sleep undisturbed. Chathres, however, found no comfort in the chill air of the desert night.

The next day, still lacking water bags, the group continued to the south, Chathres annoyed by the rays of the sun as well as sharp pebbles and thornbushes.

At sunset Sufrit guided the troop to an abandoned monastery to which only Marmaduke's key gave access.

On this occasion Chathres was obliged to yield his sword before Marmaduke allowed him through the portal.

During the night Chathres again tried to use Sufrit for his pleasure, but a ghost came from the ancient stones and sat on his back, and Chathres was distracted from his intent.

In the morning the troop set off to the south, Chathres suffering greatly from sore feet, insect stings and heat blisters. Still, he never released the rope which he had tied around Sufrit's waist.

An hour before sunset the band entered a ravine which almost at once narrowed to a defile. A flight of stairs led high to a locked door, which Marmaduke's third key opened at a twist. Each of the troop passing through the portal gave up a choice gem except Chathres, who gave over to Marmaduke the rope attached to Sufrit. "She is yours, along with all my other goods. Let me pass."

Marmaduke instantly removed the rope. "Sufrit, you are free. I supplicate your love but not your submission."

"You shall have both," she told him, and they clasped hands.

The troop continued along a narrow path. From a grotto sprang a rock devil. "How dare you use my private way?"

"Be calm," said Sufrit. "We will pay toll."

For herself and Marmaduke she paid over the sword and garments once owned by Chathres. Each of the others gave up a jewel, except Chathres who cried out: "I cite my naked body in evidence! I have nothing. I cannot pay."

"In that case," said the devil, "you must step into the grotto."

The others hurried along the way, the better to escape the sound of Chathres' appalling outcries.

At last the way came out upon a pleasant land. Roads led off in several directions. The comrades took leave of each other and went their separate ways.

Marmaduke and Sufrit stood hand in hand considering the various directions. One of the roads dropped into a green vale, rose again, and slanted across the downs toward a steeple marking a dear and familiar village. Marmaduke stared in wonder. "That is the road I would travel," he told Sufrit. "Will you come with me?"

Sufrit looked along another road which led to a place she knew well, but none there did she love. "Yes, Marmaduke, I will come with you."

"Hurry then, and we'll be home before sunset!"

And so it was. They ran joyously along the road to home, while the light faded behind them. At tea, only Pinnacy asked awkward questions, but they said they'd been to a fancy dress party, and that was all there was to it.

Later, events of this particular time tended to blur in Gersen's memory: a consequence of fatigue and the necessity of constantly contriving new plans on the ruins of old. Howard

Alan Treesong had become a will o' the wisp, dancing elusively ahead, ever out of reach.

Once again in space, Gersen repressed the urge to make for Pontefract, there to ponder new schemes and perfect his acquaintance with Alice Wroke.

Instead, he brought out the *Celestial Handbook*. Bethune Preserve was the single planet of Corvus 892, a yellow dwarf, in a group of a dozen such stars. The system as a whole controlled fourteen planets, uncounted planetoids, moons and fragments of debris, of which Bethune Preserve alone supported life.

Bethune had been discovered by locater Trudi Selland. Her description of its phenomenal flora and fauna caused a public sensation, and prompted the Naturalist Society to instant negotiations, which ultimately led to purchase outright. Centuries passed, during which Bethune Preserve became in effect a planet-sized vivarium.

From the *Handbook* Gersen read:

> "At the present time Bethune Preserve is a curious mixture: ten parts nature preserve, five parts tourist attraction, three parts headquarters for the Naturalist Society, its affiliates and a dozen other organizations such as: *Friends of Nature, Leave Be, Scutinary Vitalists, Life in God Church, Sierra Club, Biological Falange, Women for Natural Procreation*. A few residential tracts had been allocated for the use of these groups, as well as scientists, students and research fellows. In practice, almost anyone who finds the conditions of Bethune Preserve congenial is allowed temporary residence, which may be extended indefinitely.
>
> "Today Bethune Preserve comprises over six hundred game and nature reserves, jealously guarded in their original state, ranging from an entire continent to that acre supporting the single and unique lillaw tree, whose provenance is a total mystery.
>
> "The Executive Trustees today are as zealous as their predecessors—sometimes heard are the words 'arbitrary,' 'pedantic,' 'vindictive,' 'capricious,' 'obstinate.' They rule the world as if it were a private natural history museum, which in fact it is."

In compliance with the local requirements, Gersen drifted close to one of the ten orbiting quarantine stations. He was boarded by four officials in uniforms of blue and green. The *Flitterwing* was searched; Gersen was questioned in regard to contraband life forms and instructed in local regulations. A pilot remained aboard to guide the *Flitterwing* down upon a plat at the Special Visitors Compound near the city Tanaquil. Here Gersen was required to post a bond and forbidden to introduce, sequester, molest, capture, modify, annoy or export living entities of any sort. He was then allowed to proceed about his business.

From the space-field Gersen rode an omnibus into Tanaquil, through a grove of enormous black-trunked trees burdened with vermilion flowers and alive with small twittering creatures, who jumped, swung and glided across high sunlit spaces. The omnibus was evidently their ancient foe; a troop followed overhead, twittering and pelting the vehicle with fruit pods.

The bus continued into Tanaquil, a town unexpectedly quaint, like a town built of children's blocks in bright primary colors. The original scheme had been conceived by the chairwoman of an ancient architectural board, who derived inspiration from the illustrations in a children's book. She had laid down the architectural parameters to which "concordance"[1] must be achieved.

Gersen took lodging at the Hotel Triceratops, a tourist inn notable for a stuffed saurian twenty feet long, with six splayed legs and two horns, popularly known as *Triceratops Shanar*.[2]

---

[1] Concordance: a concept basic to the functioning of Bethune society. The Trustees govern Bethune Preserve in "concordance" with the old regulations.

Trustees are selected from "Notable Organizations," in which membership is hereditary. These one-time naturalist groups now serve principally to denominate the aristocracy.

Caste distinctions, while mild and nonrestrictive, are real. Tourists are outcastes and lack entry into local society.

By a curious and amusing inversion of values, those persons performing physical functions in regard to the animals and other nature objects—park rangers, veterinarians, biologists, herders, plant pathologists and the like—rank low in status.

[2] Bethune taxonomy, while precise, lacks verve. Popular terms carry more impact. Shanar is one of the Bethune continents.

Gersen made inquiry of the desk clerk. "I want to locate an old acquaintance, but I don't know where he lives."

"No difficulty whatever. Apply to the Registry. There aren't all that many of us; all told, fewer than five million. But you won't find anyone there now; they'll all be at lunch."

In the dining room, which was decorated to resemble a primordial forest, Gersen was served a stolid meal, based upon standard cosmopolitan cuisine, though the individual dishes all carried picturesque local names. He drank beer from a bottle labeled SAVAGE MAULER ALE, which exhibited the picture of a hideous brute glaring at a distant tourist charabanc.

At the Registry, Gersen was efficiently provided the addresses of two Cleadhoes, both resident upon the continent Rheas, in a place known as Blue Forest Camp, within the Grand Triste Primitive Reserve.

Gersen had noticed the Halcyon Vista Tourist Service in a building adjacent to the hotel, but when he applied at the office, it had already closed for the day; it seemed that the business community of Tanaquil operated in a fashion convenient to themselves rather than their customers.

Gersen returned to the hotel and spent the rest of the afternoon on the shaded verandah, watching tourists, locals and great floating insects: wispy creatures of froth, film and trailing tendrils depending from a gas bladder. He drank a succession of gin pahits and wondered how best to approach the business at hand.

If he apprised the Cleadhoes of his plan, they might help, they might hinder or they could inflict total disaster upon him. He sorted through a hundred possibilities, then as the sun settled into the forest, he threw his hands into the air. He could make no definite plans until he knew more about the Cleadhoes.

In the morning Gersen returned to the Halcyon Vista Tourist Service, where the clerk smilingly informed him that only qualified scientists on specially approved expeditions were allowed the hire of air vehicles.

"No end of troubles otherwise, sir," explained the clerk. "Think it out for yourself! We'd have little family picnics in the middle of the Gunderson Wallows, with baby eaten by a three-armed swamp ape, and daughter raped by the game warden."

"Then how can I get where I want to go?"

"Tourists are recommended to book aboard one of the Wild Life Inspection Safaris, in a totally safe and air-conditioned vehicle. That is the easiest and best way to visit the preserves. But where do you want to go? You must understand that many areas are off-limits."

"I want to go to Blue Forest Camp in the Grand Triste Primitive Reserve."

The agent shook his head. "That is not an area developed for tourist travel, sir."

"Suppose you yourself wished to visit Blue Forest Camp, how would you go about it?"

"I'm not a tourist."

"Still, how would you do it?"

"I'd naturally take the commercial flight to Maundy River Station, and the day flight into the forest. But——"

Gersen put a fifty-SVU certificate on the counter. "I'm not a tourist, I'm a commercial traveler. I sell insect repellent. Get me the tickets. I'm in a hurry, incidentally."

The agent smiled and shrugged and put the certificate into a drawer. "It does no good to hurry here. In fact, it may even be against the law."

Blue Forest was a heavily wooded savannah, rather than an unbroken growth of trees, and occupied the basin of the Great Bulduke River, an area of half a million square miles. The forest foliage was only predominantly blue, in three hues: ultramarine, bright sky blue and pallid chalk blue. Additionally, certain trees showed foliage of beetle-wing green and a few were gray. Enormous soft-winged moths moving through the sunlight created a teasing flicker of crimson and black. Beasts were numerous. The herbivores were protected by bulk, armor, speed, agility, stench, flailing arms, bristling horns or poison glands. Carnivores displayed equipment to overcome the defenses. Various sorts of scavengers skulked through the shadows.

The junction of the Lesser Bulduke and the Haunted River occurred in a network of sloughs and swamps, inhabited by an extravagant variety of creatures: large, small, fearsome, mild, with and without yellow wattles, with and without gaping purple maws. North of the swamp rose a low tableland, the site of Blue Forest Camp.

Gersen walked from the airport to town along an unpaved road guarded by a pair of ten-foot fences, which held back

vegetation and beasts but permitted the free passage of insects. Heat and humidity oppressed the air, which smelled of
twenty unfamiliar odors: vegetation, soil, animal essences.

The fence struck off to either side at right angles to enclose
the town. Gersen went to the Corporation Circuit Hotel and
entered a lobby dim and cool. Without comment he was assigned a room by a morose young woman, who took his
money and jerked her thumb toward the hall. "Room four."
Keys were considered unnecessary.

Gersen's room was clean, cool, sparsely furnished, and
well-screened from the outdoors. An old town directory lay
on the table. Gersen turned the pages. He saw:

Cleadhoe, Otho	Residence:	20 Perimeter
	Employment:	Post-station Workshop
Cleadhoe, Tuty	Residence:	20 Perimeter
	Employment:	Commissary

Gersen went out into the little central square. The town
was quiet; few folk were abroad. Across the street a gaunt
structure showed a sign: COMMISSARY.

Gersen looked through the door. He saw an elderly man
and a portly black-haired woman with thick black eyebrows,
a heavy nose and an uncompromising manner. The affairs of
a customer occupied her attention; Gersen turned away. The
Commissary was not an appropriate place to meet Tuty
Cleadhoe.

In the center of the square a refreshment stand sold cold
drinks and ices. Gersen obtained a pint of cold fruit punch
and seated himself on a bench.

For an hour he waited while the folk of Blue Forest Camp
went about their affairs. Children trooped past on their way
home from school; persons entered the Commissary and departed. The sun dropped into the west.

From the Commissary came Tuty Cleadhoe. She walked
briskly away to the south part of town.

Gersen followed, along a lane shaded under great spread-
ing trees. Tuty Cleadhoe entered a house close by the
peripheral fence.

Gersen waited ten minutes, then rang the doorbell. The
door slid back and Tuty Cleadhoe looked out. "Sir?"

"I'd like to talk to you for a few minutes."

"Indeed." Tuty's dark eyes snapped as she looked Gersen up and down. "To what purpose?"

"You formerly were resident at Gladbetook in Maunish?"

After a short pause. "Yes. A long time ago."

"I have just come from there."

"That is of no interest to me. I have only bitter memories of Gladbetook. You must excuse me. The neighbors will wonder at my talking to a strange man." She started to close the door.

"Wait!" cried Gersen. "You lived near the Hardoah family?"

Tuty Cleadhoe looked through the narrow gap. "That is true."

Gersen found himself proceeding faster than he had intended. "Do you remember Howard Hardoah?"

Tuty Cleadhoe stared at Gersen a long ten seconds. She responded in a thick voice: "I do indeed."

"May I come in? I am here in connection with Howard Hardoah."

Tuty Cleadhoe grudgingly stepped aside and made a gesture. "Come in then."

The interior of the house was dim, stuffy and, for so warm a climate, overfurnished. Tuty pointed to a chair upholstered in rose-pink velour. "Sit, if you will . . . Now then, what is this of Howard Hardoah?"

"Recently I had occasion to visit the Hardoah farmstead, and the conversation turned to the subject of Howard."

Tuty Cleadhoe looked incredulous. "Howard lives at home?"

"No. He left long ago."

Tuty thrust her head forward. "Do you know why?"

"Trouble of some sort. That's my guess."

"If I could have put my hands on him—" she extended her hands with fingers clenching "—I would have torn him into bits."

Gersen leaned back in his chair. Tuty spoke on in a voice hissing with passion. "He came to our house; he called to our son, softly, so that we should not hear. But we heard. He called out our one chick, our boy Nymphotis, who was so meek and good. They went to the pond and there Howard drowned our little son, held him under the water.

"I had a terrible feeling; I called 'Nymphotis! Where are

you?' I went to the pond, and there I found my lovely child. I pulled out the little bedraggled corpse and carried him home. Otho went to find Howard, but he had already gone."

Gersen asked, "Howard never knew that you suspected him?"

"There was no suspicion. It was certainty!"

"But Howard never knew?"

Tuty made a fierce controlled gesture. "How could he know? He was gone. It was our tragedy."

Gersen said, "I did not know Nymphotis was dead. I'm sorry to revive bitter memories."

"You revive nothing! We live with them daily. Look!" Tuty's voice cracked with emotion. "Look!"

Gersen turned his head. In a shadowed corner of the room stood a boy formed of a glossy white substance.

"That is our Nymphotis."

Gersen turned away. "I will tell you something of Howard Hardoah and what he has become, and how justice may be done upon him."

"Wait! Otho must hear you. If you think I am bitter, he surpasses me four-fold." She went to a telephone, made a connection and poured a tumble of words into the mesh. From time to time a man's voice uttered a question. Tuty gestured to Gersen.

"Now speak! We both will hear you."

"Howard Hardoah is now a great criminal. He calls himself Howard Alan Treesong."

Neither Tuty nor Otho Cleadhoe made comment. "Go on."

"I have tracked him across the Oikumene. He is wary. He must be lured and baited with great care. I have failed twice, but now I have the bait to lure him again. Here your help would be useful."

Gersen paused. Otho said, "Go on."

"I don't want to continue unless you feel able to help me. There will be danger."

"You need not worry for us," said Otho. "Tell us what you have in mind."

"You will help?"

"Tell us what you have in mind."

"I want to bring him here, take him out into the jungle and kill him."

Tuty said in an angry voice: "There is nothing for us to do! You will confront him, you will kill him! It is for Nymphotis that he must pay!"

"No matter," said Otho in a heavy voice. "We will help."

Chapter 16

From *The Book of Dreams*:

Gentle and gracious is Blue Rhune Fader, yet when moan the winds of war, Rhune's sword drinks as deep as any. When the land is quiet, then Rhune wanders the flowered fields and sings songs of music.

Not so Loris Hohenger, the feroce, whose color is the reddest of the reds! His ardor needs always a strong control; his truculence balances on a hair. Only the paladins know his tolerance and his true affection. All others, when in his company, walk as if on eggshell. His lusts are intractable; he plunders fair ladies of their treasure, usually to their delight, but occasionally to their distress, as with golden-haired Melissa, who had vowed her virginity to the glory of Sancta Sanctissima. Zada Memar, of fabulous beauty, excited him past all control, but she gave herself to Immir. And Loris was first to hold

high his sword in praise! Gallop forward along your
mad and reckless murst[1], oh Loris, on and ever on!

Arriving in Pontefract, Gersen rode by taxicab to Tara
Square, where he alighted. Around him, on all sides, order
and rectitude: narrow old buildings, pallid folk in formal
garments, pansies and wallflowers in raised beds; mist, overcast, dank winds and smells; all placid, customary and reas-
suring . . . At a public telephone, Gersen called the *Extant*
offices and was connected to Maxel Rackrose, who was serving as interim Managing Editor.

Rackrose gave Gersen a greeting at once cordial and cautious. He reported that, in general, all went well with *Extant*,
credit for which he ascribed to himself.

"I'm glad to hear all is going well," said Gersen. "I suppose I'd better check in with my secretary."

"Your secretary?" Rackrose's voice sounded puzzled. "Who
is that?"

Gersen's heart sank. "Alice Wroke. The red-headed girl.
Isn't she at *Extant* any more?"

"Oh yes, I remember," said Rackrose. "Yes indeed. Alice
Wroke. Girl, sport-model, red-headed. She's gone."

"Gone where?"

"I haven't a notion . . . I'll look in the book . . . You're
in luck. She's left a letter addressed to you."

"I'll be right there."

The envelope was inscribed:
To be given into the hand of Henry Lucas only.
The letter read:

Dear Henry Lucas:
  I discover that I am not really interested in jour-
nalism. Therefore I have resigned my position with
Extant. I am staying at Gladen's Hotel, Port
Wheary, which is south along the coast.
                                        Alice Wroke

Gersen telephoned Gladen's Hotel at Port Wheary. Miss
Wroke was not in but was expected back in an hour or so.

[1] The meaning of this word, like others in *The Book of Dreams*, can
only be conjectured. (Must: urgency? With *verst*: in Old Russia, a
league? Farfetched, but who knows?)

At a rental station Gersen hired an air-car. He flew south along the coastline, following the wavering white line created by wallows of gray water crashing up and over the rocks; across St. Kilda's Bay, over Cape May and Point Kittery. He passed Hannah's Head just as Vega shone through a rent in the clouds to illuminate the white houses of Port Wheary across Polwheel Bay.

Gersen landed at the public plat, walked along the waterfront to Gladen's Hotel.

In the lounge by the fireplace he found Alice Wroke. She turned her head, saw him and started to rise.

Gersen crossed the room. He took her hands, pulled her to her feet, kissed her face, then put his arms around her.

"Henry, stop!" cried Alice Wroke. She gave an excited laugh. "You're smothering me!"

Gersen relaxed his grip. "You needn't call me Henry any more. Henry is just a mailing address. This is me."

Alice drew back and looked him up and down. "Does this version have a name?"

"It's called Kirth Gersen and it's less of a gentleman than Henry Lucas."

Alice inspected him again. "I enjoyed Henry Lucas, even though he was arrogant and hateful. What of you-know-who?"

"He's still alive. There's a lot to tell. Will it keep until I've had a bath and changed my clothes?"

"I'll call Mrs. Gladen and she'll give you a room. She's very respectable, so don't do anything to shock her."

Gersen and Alice dined by the light of candles in the corner of the verandah. "Now," said Alice, "tell me your adventures."

"I went to Howard's school reunion at Gladbetook on Moudervelt. Howard played jokes and danced the hornpipe. He criticized the performance of a musician in the orchestra. The musician shot him in the backside and the party ended."

"And where were you?"

"I was the musician."

"Ah! It's all clear now. What else happened?"

"I found Howard's *Book of Dreams*, which he lost twenty-five years ago. I'm sure that he wants it back." Gersen pushed the old red notebook across the table. "There it is."

Alice bent her head over the book. The candlelight burnished her hair and cast shadows along her slanted cheeks. Gersen sat watching her. Here sit I, he thought, across the table from miraculous Alice Wroke . . .

Alice turned pages. She came to the end and closed the book. After a few moments she said: "Almost always he is Immir. But I've met Jeha Rais and Mewness and Spangleway, and I've had a glimpse or two of Rhune Fader, who paid me no heed. I'm happy that Loris Hohenger was otherwise occupied."

Gersen put the book back in his pocket. Alice mused: "Zada Memar—I wonder what happened to her."

"She came to Gladbetook from offplanet. While on a school picnic she drowned in Persimmon Lake."

"Poor Zada Memar. I wonder . . ."

Gersen shook his head. "Not I."

Alice looked at him, her eyes dark in the candlelight. "What do you mean?"

"I don't wonder at all."

In *Cosmopolis* appeared an article accompanied by several illustrations. The heading read:

HOWARD ALAN TREESONG ATTENDS
25TH ANNIVERSARY SCHOOL REUNION
A Party No One Will Forget

Even Criminals Show Sentiment
The Greater the Criminal, the Greater the Sentiment

—by our local correspondent,
Gladbetook, Maunish,
Moudervelt, Van Kaathe's Star

(Editorial note: Maunish is one of 1,562 independent principalities comprising the political estates of Moudervelt. Its landscape includes prairies, riverlands, farms and forests, supporting nearly a million persons. Howard Alan Treesong was born on a farm near the village Gladbetook.)

Twenty-five years ago a shy brown-haired boy known as Howard Hardoah attended the district lyceum at Gladbetook. That boy is now the preeminent criminal of the Oikumene and Beyond, and is reckoned as one of the notorious "Demon Princes." His name, Howard Alan Treesong, strikes terror into a multitude of hearts, and his exploits have riveted the attention of everyone. But Howard Alan Treesong still remembers old times, and with no lack of nostalgia. At the recent reunion of his class he made a dramatic appearance, evoking from his old school chums what best can be described as mixed emotions.

The event will never be forgotten, and, if only in this regard, must be considered a great success. Early in the evening Howard Hardoah (as he was known at school) became convivial and roamed from table to table telling anecdotes and recalling old incidents, sometimes to the discomfort of his audience.

As the evening progressed, Mr. Hardoah's spirits soared to ever higher levels of fun and audacity. He played merry tunes on the fiddle; he danced several gavottes, a hornpipe and a twitchery. Mr. Hardoah's revelries knew no limits and totally captivated the group. He ordained ingenious pranks and charades to celebrate old episodes; these were dutifully performed by his now-nervous classmates, to whom his ultimate intentions were never quite clear. He sat Mr. Maddo Strubbins on a block of ice; he tattooed Mr. Bloy Sadalfloury; and he arranged to escort Mrs. Suby ver Ahe with her two charming daughters, Mirl and Maud, on a long cruise through the outer worlds.

The festivities were interrupted by a gang of marauders who shot Mr. Hardoah in the buttocks and caused such consternation that the party came to an end. Mr. Hardoah departed in pain. The wound will surely curtail his dancing for some time to come. Mr. Hardoah expressed outrage that in a presumably well-ordered community such crass acts of violence could take place. He hopes to return to the next reunion, providing that it could be termi-

nated less abruptly, inasmuch as he had staged only
a few of his ingenious frivolities.

In the next issue of *Cosmopolis*:

HOWARD ALAN TREESONG
His Memorabilia and Boyhood

(Editor's note: A recent article relating to the notorious Howard Alan Treesong evoked much comment. The following communication, so we hope,
may also be of interest to our readers.)

To the Editors of *Cosmopolis*:

I read your recent article about the school reunion
at Gladbetook with great interest, inasmuch as my
son Nymphotis was a school chum of young
Howard Hardoah. It is strange how life works out.
The two boys were inseparable, and Nimpy, as we
called him, often spoke of Howard's talents and
skills, and his dearest possession was a little book of
fancies, *The Book of Dreams*, which Howard gave
to him.

Our little lad died in a swimming accident shortly
before we left Maunish and we still have *The Book
of Dreams* to remind us of the old days on the
prairie. We find it hard to imagine Howard Hardoah, so shy and careful, becoming the person you
describe, but in our lifetime we have known many
surprising events; more so, I believe, than most
people, since we have traveled from place to place,
and even now hardly know where we will die. We
think often of our poor little Nimpy. If he had
lived, perhaps now he might also be a person of
consequence.

Please do not include my name and address, as I
cannot cope with correspondence at this time.

Respectfully,
Tuty C.

(Full name and address withheld by request.)

Into the *Cosmopolis* office came a spare and saturnine man of indeterminate age, wearing a neat black suit cut in the local style: pinched at the shoulders and flaring at the hips. He moved with the quiet deftness of a cat. His eyes were black, his face was hollow-cheeked and narrow. Dense black hair grew to a widow's peak, then coved back over his temples and down past his ears. He went to the reception desk, looking alertly to both sides as he did so, as if from long habit. The clerk asked: "Sir, how may we oblige you?"

"I'd like a few words with the gentleman who wrote about Mr. Howard Treesong a few weeks ago."

"Oh, that would be Henry Lucas. I believe he's in his office. May I ask your name, sir?"

"Schahar."

"And the nature of your business, Mr. Schahar?"

"Well, miss, it's somewhat complicated. I'd prefer to explain it once only to Mr. Lucas."

"Just as you like, sir. I'll ask if Mr. Lucas can see you now."

The girl spoke into a mesh and received a response. She looked back to Schahar. "Will you have a seat, sir? He'll see you in five minutes."

Schahar sat quietly, his black eyes flicking here and there around the room.

A musical tone sounded. The receptionist said: "Mr. Schahar, if you please."

She conducted Schahar along a hall and ushered him into a room with pale green walls and a lavender rug. Behind a kidney-shaped table lounged a stylishly pallid man with a languid face framed by glossy dark ringlets. His clothes were a confection of superb elegance; his manner, like his expression, was languid and just short of supercilious. He spoke in a toneless voice. "Sir, I am Henry Lucas. Please seat yourself. I don't think I know you. Mr. Schahar, I believe."

"That is correct, sir." Schahar spoke easily in a neutral voice. "You are a busy man and I will not take too much of your time. I am a writer, like yourself, though certainly neither as competent nor as successful."

Gersen, noting Schahar's strong shoulders, long sinewy arms, heavy hands with long strong fingers, controlled a smile of grim amusement. Schahar exuded a psychic aura of lethal expertise, of stabbings and strangulation, of terror and pain. Schahar had been present at the school reunion, standing at the entrance with the short thick man. Gersen recalled an event of months before when Lamar Medrano of Wild Isle had met Emmaus Schahar at Starport, New Concept. She had departed the Diomedes Hotel with him and had never been seen again.

"Tush," said Gersen. "I am not a writer; I am a journalist. What is your particular field?"

"General affairs. Facts and personalities. I have recently become interested in Howard Alan Treesong and his amazing career. Unfortunately, facts are hard to come by."

"I have found it so," said Gersen.

"The article on the school reunion—you wrote that, I believe?"

"Our local correspondent submitted ten pages of very excited prose, which I cobbled together as best I could. For information about Treesong, Maunish would seem the place to go."

"I may well take your advice. What of this woman and her *Book of Dreams*?"

Gersen gave an uninterested shrug. "I haven't looked into it. The letter is around here somewhere. I seem to have been designated the Treesong expert." Gersen opened a drawer, withdrew a sheet of paper, glanced at it. Schahar leaned forward.

"An old exercise book or something similar," said Gersen. "Probably nothing remarkable."

Schahar held out his hand. "May I see?"

Gersen looked up as if in surprise and seemed to hesitate. He frowned down at the letter. "Sorry, I think I'd better not. The woman doesn't want to be identified. I can't say that I blame her, with so many cranks and crackpots running loose." Gersen replaced the letter in the drawer.

Schahar drew back, smiling a faint smile. "I'd like to collect any and all information available on this particular subject. My main interest is Howard Treesong's early life—his formative period, so to speak. I am anxious especially to examine such trifles as *The Book of Dreams*." Schahar paused, but Gersen responded only with a noncommittal nod.

Schahar went on, speaking with a persuasive urgency: "Suppose I undertook to approach this woman in the capacity of a writer submitting to *Cosmopolis*, would you then allow me her address?"

"Your efforts would far exceed your profit, that's my opin-

ion. Why not visit Gladbetook on Moudervelt and make inquiries of his old acquaintances? That would seem more
fertile scope for research."

"Again, that is excellent advice, sir." Schahar rose to his
feet, paused a moment and seemed to sway slightly forward.

Languidly Gersen also arose. "I have an appointment elsewhere; otherwise I'd be happy to discuss the matter with you
at greater length. I wish you success."

"Thank you, Mr. Lucas." Schahar left the room.

Gersen waited. An instrument to the side of his desk
sounded a tone. Gersen smiled. He arranged a telltale to the
drawer of his table, then turned a key in the antique lock.
Clapping a triple-tier Aloysian hat on his head, he departed
the room, strolled down the corridor past a pair of unoccu-
pied offices. Behind one of the doors stood Schahar, so the
signal-tone had informed Gersen.

Gersen walked at a leisurely rate around the block, then
returned. He went directly to his office. Standing to the side,
he slid open the door.

No explosion, no hiss of projectile.

Gersen entered the room. The telltale at the drawer had
been disarranged. The lock showed no evidence of tampering;
Schahar was a skillful operator. Gersen opened the drawer.
The letter remained as he had left it; Schahar had been satisfied with the name and address.

Gersen went to the telephone and called Alice. "It's happened."

"Who came?"

"A man called Schahar. I'm going directly to the spaceport."

Alice's voice was neutral. "Take care of yourself."

"Of course."

Gersen threw the hat toward a chair, changed from his
tight-shouldered suit into spaceman's ordinary and left the
Cosmopolis office—perhaps for the last time.

A cab took him to the spaceport and out the access avenue
to the *Fantamic Flitterwing*. It had been cleaned, washed,
polished, overhauled, inspected and provisioned. The ports
had been scraped clean of space dust. The linen had been
renewed, the tanks were full of water, the bins loaded with
food. The support systems had been recharged; the energy
cells were replete.

The *Fantamic Flitterwing* was ready for space.

Gersen climbed aboard, closed the port, stepped into the saloon. His nose detected the faintest of perfumes. He looked to right and left.

Nothing extraordinary.

He took three strides to the stateroom: empty. He threw open the door to the head. "Out with you."

Wearing mouse-gray shorts and a black tunic, Alice marched forth. "So there you are," said Gersen.

"So it would appear," said Alice.

"I half expected this." Gersen pointed to the port. "Off the ship with you."

"Absolutely not. I've decided never to let you out of my sight again. You might not come back." She stepped close to him and looked up into his face. "Don't you want me aboard?"

"Oh, I'm sure I'd find you useful. Still, it's dangerous."

"I know."

"Well, I can't waste time arguing. Now that you're here . . ."

Alice gave a triumphant laugh. "I knew you'd see it my way."

Chapter 17

Bethune Preserve hung in space full in the light of Corvus 892. Gersen eased the *Flitterwing* close up beside one of the orbiting stations. No pilot was immediately available; he was ordered to stand by.

Alice grumbled about the formalities. "I don't intend to molest their animals! I told them so but I don't think they believe me."

"Howard will be even more vexed. He can't simply show up in his battle cruiser and throw his weight around."

"Perhaps he'll arrive as a tourist. Perhaps he won't dare to come at all."

"I can't see him sending Schahar down for his precious *Book of Dreams*. In any event you'll have to stay in Tanaquil, out of the way; if he catches one glimpse of you, we're in trouble."

Alice put on a submissive face. "Whatever you say. Still, you yourself said I don't look like Alice when I'm dressed as a boy, with my hair covered."

"We'd better cut off your hair and dye the stubble black."

"That's not necessary. I'd be a funny-looking sight. You'd laugh at me; I'd be angry and there would go our romance."

Gersen put his arms around her. "That's a chance we can't take."

"Of course not . . . What are you doing? Stop! You've chased me around the ship twice today already!"

"There's nothing else to do. You bring it on yourself, really."

"Aren't you afraid I'll wear out? . . . No? Oh well . . ."

The pilot presently arrived and took the vessel down to Tanaquil, despite Gersen's request to put down at the Blue Forest Camp airport.

"Sorry," said the pilot. "That's not regulation."

It occurred to Gersen that every third word the pilot spoke was "regulation." The pilot went on: "We can't make it convenient, you know. Everyone would be tracking about, picking flowers, teasing the monkeys. Tourists must go about their visits with decorum and respect. Personally I'd keep the blighters out altogether."

"Then there'd be no one to inflict your regulations on and you'd be out of a job."

The pilot turned Gersen a blue-eyed stare. He decided Gersen had intended a joke and laughed. "I'd make out one way or another. I'm not just a flight attendant, you know. In fact, I'm a fourth-level type and reckoned an expert on the pathology of the segmented melantid-worm."

Alice asked, "In that case why are you here piloting and not out taking care of sick worms?"

"There aren't that many worms. They hide deep in the mud where they are hard to catch. Then, like as not, they are quite well. I may qualify for a second specialty. In the meantime, I do our regulation stint with the company . . . Here we are at the terminal. Leave all weapons and contraband aboard your vessel. Now, if you'll alight I'll seal the doors."

Gersen and Alice, each carrying a small travel bag, alighted, underwent further examination and search and were finally issued clearances.

At a wicket marked: OFFICIAL AND LIMITED COMMERCIAL TRANSIT, Gersen attempted to book passage to Blue Forest Camp aboard the Station Service Flyer. The clerk refused to listen to him and pushed back his money. "You'll have to apply to the designated authorities; we're very keen here on orderly methods."

"Out of curiosity, when is the next departure for Blue Forest Camp?"

"Two departures today, sir, middle afternoon and shortly after, by the left- and right-hand routes."

By open-sided omnibus Gersen and Alice rode into town under tall jacarandas and drupes, pursued by hysterical tree creatures.

At the Halcyon Vista Tourist Service Gersen found a new clerk in attendance: a self-important young woman with narrow eyes and supercilious nostrils. She instantly declared Gersen's request impossible and tried to sell him tickets on Tourist Schedule Route C. Gersen used persistence and reasoned argument; after ten minutes of grim research into travel regulations the woman could find no stipulations expressly supporting her position and grudgingly issued a pair of passage vouchers.

The spaceport omnibus had gone out of service for the day. Gersen located the town's only taxi, and the two returned to the spaceport, arriving only ten minutes prior to the early flight.

Two hours later the flyer dropped down upon the jungle compound north of Blue Forest Camp. The door opened; into the cabin came a waft reeking of the swamp.

Gersen and Alice alighted; the flyer departed into the south, and they stood alone in the jungle clearing.

"The middle of nowhere," said Gersen. "This way to the village."

From the Corporation Circuit Hotel Gersen telephoned Tuty Cleadhoe at the Commissary. "I'm back again. All is going according to plan. Have you had word yet from, let us say, anyone else?"

"Nothing yet." Tuty's voice was harsh. "We await him with hope and anxiety. You have the book?"

"I'll bring what I have to your house, in say, half an hour."

Tuty made a peevish *tsk*ing sound. "We have regulations here. I can't leave my work on an instant's whim! . . . Well, if I must, I must. I'll make an excuse."

Gersen told Alice, "Mrs. Cleadhoe has strong views; in fact, she's obstinate and suspicious." He examined her critically. "You'd better wear something drab and inconspicuous."

Alice looked down at herself. She wore gray spaceman's breeches, black ankle-boots, a dark green shirt. "What could be more drab and inconspicuous than this?"

"Well, pull that hat down over your hair and try to look like a boy."

"Mrs. Cleadhoe might well be more suspicious than ever."

"I'm also thinking of Howard Treesong," said Gersen. "If he sees red hair he'll think 'Alice.' It would be better if you stayed here at the hotel."

"We've been through this before."

"Stay in the shadows. Talk in a low gruff voice."

"I'll do my best."

From his carrying case Gersen took various bits and pieces and stowed them about his person. Alice watched without comment. Gersen finally said, "These are weapons, all involving poison. Take this and be very careful with it." He gave her a bit of glass tube four inches long. "If someone you don't like comes close, aim the tube toward his face and blow into this end. Then, move as far away as possible."

Alice soberly tucked the tube in the chest pocket of her shirt.

They left the hotel and walked around to Tuty Cleadhoe's cottage. She had been watching; the door opened as they approached.

Tuty's heavy face clouded with surprise at the sight of Alice. "Who is this? And what?"

"Her name is Alice Wroke. She is my colleague."

"Hmmf. Well, it's none of my business. Come in."

The room had changed from Gersen's previous visit in a single particular: Nimpy's marmel no longer stood wistfully on the dais.

Tuty gave a grim nod. "Nimpy is gone for the while. Now then, where is the book?"

Gersen gave her a red notebook inscribed: *The Book of Dreams*. Tuty glanced through the pages. She looked up in annoyance. "There's nothing here!"

"Naturally not. Do you think I'd risk the real book so easily? It is a facsimile—bait, so to speak."

Tuty said grimly, "It is enough. You need do nothing more. Otho and I have formed our plans. Nothing is left to chance. You should go back to Tanaquil and wait. When the work is done you will be notified."

Gersen laughed. "You may have formed plans but so has Howard. He is a professional."

"I have no doubt. How would you deal with him?"

"Sooner or later he'll show himself here. When he does, I will kill him."

Tuty stood, arms akimbo, hands on her sturdy hips. "Indeed, indeed. How will you do this without weapons?"

"I could ask you the same."

"I have a gun, a Model J projac. It will blow the head off a thrombodaxus."

"Will you allow me the use of this gun?"

"Certainly not! Regulation strictly forbids it. Nor would Otho approve . . . How long before Howard comes?"

"I don't know. I came as fast as possible. I suspect that he will do the same. There won't be much time between us."

Alice pointed out the window. "No time at all . . . Look."

Along the street came Schahar, and behind him a short, thick man with heavy shoulders and a near-neckless head.

"Those are two of Howard's men," said Gersen. "Do you still think you can cope with them?"

"Certainly. Here he comes! Into the back room with you. And not a sound!" She hustled them into the back parlor and pulled the door shut. Light through a side window shone on a photograph of young Nimpy, in a silver frame, resting on a nearby library table.

Gersen tried the door, which refused to move. He cursed under his breath. "The old fool has locked us in!"

Alice looked at the window. "It's small. But I could squeeze through."

"The door isn't all that solid. We can break through any time we like."

"Shh. Listen."

From the front room came sounds of conversation.

"You are Tuty Cleadhoe?" This was Schahar's voice.

"What of it? Who are you? No one I know."

"Mrs. Cleadhoe, I am traveling secretary—"

"Go to the hotel. I don't want strangers about. I'm not alone; I have a great gun ready for intruders. Be off with you."

"—for a noble and important gentleman, who wants to speak with you, I'm sure to your profit."

"An important gentleman? I know no one like that. What's his name? And if he's so noble why doesn't he come here himself instead of sending you?"

"Like yourself, Mrs. Cleadhoe, he doesn't care to deal with

unpredictable people. He is also nervous and timid. Guns alarm him, so please—"

"Be off with you and your affronts! And be quick, before I nervously and timidly blast off your leg! I am old and alone, but I take no abuse from bald-headed tourists!"

"Excuse me, Mrs. Cleadhoe. I'm sorry to offend you. Please don't flourish your gun so freely. One question: are you the 'Tuty C.' who recently wrote to *Cosmopolis* magazine?"

"What of it? Why should I not write as I wish? What harm have I done?"

"No harm whatever. You brought good luck to yourself as you will see, if you put away your gun and compose yourself; then I will ask my principal to join us."

"And then it'd be two against one? Ha ha. No chance of that. Send in this noble timid gentleman and don't come back. The gun? I'll put it by, unless it wants use."

"I'm sure you'll find no cause for alarm, Mrs. Cleadhoe, and every reason for satisfaction."

"I can't imagine why or how."

No response from Schahar, who evidently had departed. Gersen put his shoulder against the door, which creaked and groaned. At once a loud rap sounded on the panel. "You two stay quiet! You are not to interfere with our plans! Not a sound now; someone's at the door."

Gersen muttered under his breath. Alice said, "Shh. Listen. I think it's Howard."

They heard the sound of the outer door opening and Tuty's voice: "Sir, and who are you?"

"Mrs. Cleadhoe, you don't recognize me?"

"No. Why should I? What do you want?"

"I'll refresh your memory. You wrote to a magazine about old times in Gladbetook and a certain chum of your Nymphotis."

"You're not Howard Hardoah? But I see it now! How you have grown! As a boy you seemed so frail! Well, think of that! I must telephone Otho! A pity he can't be here."

Inside the back room Gersen, clenching his teeth in frustration, put his hand to the door latch. Alice pulled him back. "Don't be foolish! Tuty would shoot you without a second thought! She know's what she's after."

"So do I. It's not this."

"Shh! Be reasonable."

Gersen again put his ear to the door.

"—a marvel how the years go by!—seems so long ago and far away! But how you've changed, so handsome and fine you've become! But come in, do, and I'll pour us a drop of something . . . Here's some good old fructance. Or would you like tea and perhaps a bite of cake?"

"That's very good of you, Mrs. Cleadhoe. I'll take a drop of fructance . . . That's more than enough."

"Have some of these little cakes. I can't imagine how you found me here, or why . . . But of course. My letter to the magazine."

"Of course! It brought back old memories, things I hadn't thought of in years. Like the little book you mentioned."

"Oh dear yes! That funny little red book! What a fanciful lad you were, so full of dreams and glamours! *The Book of Dreams*—that's how you named your book!"

"True! I remember distinctly. I'm anxious to see it again."

"And you certainly will. I'll find it in a moment, but you must join me in my meal. I was just about to cook up some hotchpotch Gladbetook-style, and a dish of lessamy. I hope you haven't lost your taste for home cooking?"

"Worse, far worse! I've taken a stomach ailment and I'm restricted as to what I eat. But don't let me interfere. Cook up your own dinner and meanwhile I'll glance through my old red book."

"Let me think now, what have I done with it? . . . Of course, it's at the station, where Otho does his crafting. He works such long hours, it's a pity and disgrace! But there are so few qualified nowadays, and Otho is at it night and day. He'll be so pleased to see you! Surely you can spend the week here with me until he comes out of the jungle! He'd never forgive me if I let you go."

"A week? Oh, Mrs. Cleadhoe, I truly can't spare so much time!"

"Now then, I have a nice spare room, and I'm sure you need the rest. And then you'll be able to see Mr. Cleadhoe. I'll have him bring your book when he comes. We'll have such good gossips over old times."

"It sounds delightful, Mrs. Cleadhoe, but I can't spare so much time. Still, I'd like to see Mr. Cleadhoe. Where is the out-station?"

"It's away through the jungle, a good hour's ride on the railcar. Tourists naturally aren't allowed anywhere near."

"Really? Why not?"

"They bother the beasts, or give them unwholesome food. Some of these beasts are under experiment; we keep them close under observation and provide their food. Mr. Cleadhoe does things just so."

"A pity he can't come in from the station tonight. Why not call him on the telephone?"

"Oh no. He'd never hear of it. The connections are wrong, in any event."

"How so?"

"By afternoon there's a feed train that tends for sick animals. It goes out to the station and returns by morning; that's routine and won't be changed. Sometimes I drive it out and stay the night when the regular driver wants time to himself. He always reimburses me for my lost time at the Commissary."

A pause, then came Treesong's voice, light and easy: "Why not drive us out tonight? It would be a great experience for us. Of course I'd reimburse your expenses."

"And who do you mean by 'us'?"

"You, me, Umps and Schahar. We'd all like to see the station."

"Not possible. Tourists aren't allowed at the station; that's a strict regulation. One person besides the driver can crouch in the back cab and not be seen, but not three."

"Couldn't they ride elsewhere?"

"Among the slops and swill? Your friends would not like it! It's against all regulation!"

Another pause. Then: "Would fifty SVU cover your expenses at the Commissary?"

"Of course. They don't overpay us, that's a sad truth. Still, we don't complain. Our cottage comes without rent and I get a nice discount at the Commissary. Look in tomorrow and if there's anything you fancy, I can get it at a good price. If you don't care to go out to the station without your friends, why not just stay the week? Otho would be distressed to miss you."

"Actually, Mrs. Cleadhoe, time presses me hard. Here's fifty SVU. We'll go out this afternoon."

"Well, there's not much time for arrangements. I'll have to telephone here and there like a wild woman. And perhaps I should have something for Joseph to close his mouth. He's the regular driver. That way we're on the safe side. Can you manage another twenty?"

"Yes, I think so."

"That should suffice. Now then, take your friends back to the hotel, then meet me with your overnight kit at the terminal; it's just a hundred yards along the road. In half an hour, no later—and don't approach until I signal, in case Superintendent Kennifer is strolling about . . . Oh, and I must call Mr. Cleadhoe to tell him we're on our way, and to air the extra room. If it's jungle you want, it's all there at the station. Perhaps tonight we'll see a lucifer or a scorposaur. Hurry then, be off with you. In half an hour, at the terminal."

The door closed. Tuty Cleadhoe approached the back parlor. "You two in there—did you hear?"

Gersen threw his shoulder against the door; it burst open. Tuty Cleadhoe stood back holding the blaster in both hands, her squat body braced and her face creased in a grin. "Stand back there! Make a move and I'll blow you up! I don't care a whit about you! Live or die! So stand back!"

Gersen spoke with dignity. "I thought that we were in this business together."

"So we are. You brought Howard here; I'm taking him out to Mr. Cleadhoe and we shall see. Now sit down yonder, as I must make my arrangements." She jerked the gun. Alice pulled Gersen to a couch and the two seated themselves.

Tuty nodded and went to the telephone. She made several calls, then turned back to Gersen and Alice. "Now then—as for you—"

"Mrs. Cleadhoe, listen to me. Don't take Howard Treesong for granted. He is clever and dangerous."

Tuty swung her heavy arm. "Bah. I know him well. He was a haunted little milksop who bullied girls and little boys and finally destroyed my Nimpy. He hasn't changed. Cleadhoe and I, ha, ha, we're glad to see him. Now up with you, and remember, you're nothing to me whatever." She herded them into the kitchen and opened a door. "Into the cellar, quick-time."

Alice took Gersen's arm and dragged him through the door, down a steep stairs and into a concrete-walled space smelling of strange molds, old paper and condiments.

The door shut; the bolt jarred home. Gersen and Alice were left in the darkness.

Gersen climbed back up the stairs and listened at the door.

Tuty had not moved. Gersen could picture her standing four-square, gun at the ready, balefully watching the door. A half-minute passed; the joists creeked as Tuty moved away.

Gersen groped around the head of the stairs, hoping to find a light switch, without success. He thrust on the door, which creaked, but withstood the relatively slight force he was able to apply from his unbalanced position.

Gersen groped through the darkness. Floor joists above, otherwise nothing substantial. He descended the ladder. Alice's voice came muffled through the darkness. "There doesn't seem to be much down here. I don't feel any other doors. Just cases full of old junk."

"What I want is a plank or a length of timber," said Gersen.

"There's nothing but the cases, and some boxes and old rugs."

Gersen explored the cases. "Let's unload these things. If I can stack them on the landing so that I can somehow get my back to the door and my feet against the joists . . ."

Ten minutes later Gersen clambered up the rickety construction. "Don't stand below. This is quite precarious . . . Ah." Lying back, he put his shoulders to the door, kicked up and found a joist with his feet. He straightened his legs, thrusting with his thigh muscles. The door burst open and Gersen tumbled backwards into Tuty Cleadhoe's kitchen.

He picked himself up, helped Alice up the stairs, then paused to sort through Tuty Cleadhoe's cutlery. He selected two heavy knives which he tucked into his belt, and hefted a cleaver.

Alice found a cloth bag. "Put it in this. I'll carry it."

They went to the front door, looked up and down the street. Seeing no one, they stepped out into the droning afternoon.

Keeping to the shadows the two set off toward the railcar terminal: a cluster of dilapidated structures a hundred yards ahead.

"Tuty will be angry if things go wrong," Alice remarked. "She is a vehement woman."

"She's a conniving old harridan," said Gersen. "Slowly now. We don't want to be seen."

A heavy fetor assaulted their noses, a smell sour, ripe, rich and rank. Looking through the foliage they discovered the origin of the odor. By a hopper stood a portly, white-haired man with heavy-lidded eyes and a placid expression. He controlled the flow of pink-gray pulp sliding from the hopper into a vat on a railcar. He worked a lever; the flow ceased. A small locomotive backed close and coupled to the vat. Under the locomotive's observation cupola sat Tuty, peering over her shoulder and manipulating the throttle.

The man at the hopper waved his arm, turned away and walked into a workshop. Tuty pulled back the throttle; the locomotive and vat-car moved ahead. Howard Treesong raised himself and settled into the goods compartment behind Tuty. From behind a bush came two men: Schahar and Umps. They ran behind the vat-car, swung themselves up to the small rear platform. The cars rolled around a curve and out of sight.

Gersen went to the workshop. The portly man looked up and gave a peremptory jerk of the thumb. "Sir, no public allowed here."

"I'm not the public," said Gersen. "I'm a friend of Mrs. Cleadhoe."

"You've missed her. She's just taken feed out to the station, along with her nephew."

"We're in the same party. It seems we've arrived a bit too late. Is there another locomotive which could make the trip?"

Joseph pointed to a rusty old mechanism, dented and bent, supported on blocks and bereft of wheels. "There's old Number Seventeen, down for repair. One of these days I'll put on new drive wheels, when time and money come together."

"How far is the out-station?"

"It's a good seventy miles by the track. Shorter air-wise, but there's not a flyer in town. Quite illegal, for reasons of ecology and frightening of the beasts."

"Seventy miles. Ten hours at a steady run."

"Ho ho!" chortled Joseph. "You'd run maybe a mile before an eye would push up from the mud, then a messenger arm sixty feet long, ending in grab-hooks, and away you'd go through the air, over to the mud and down; and then what happens, who knows? Devil a soul has come back to tell!"

Alice pointed across the shop. "What's that thing?"

"That's the track inspector's go-cart. It won't pull freight, but she'll go lickety-split where the track is level."

Gersen walked around the contraption: a platform on four wheels with a pair of cane seats under a hemispherical visor splotched with the juices of smashed insects. The controls were starkly simple: a pair of handles, two toggles and a dial. "It's not beautiful, but it rolls along fine," said Joseph with modest pride. "I built it myself."

Gersen produced a crisp certificate, which he handed to Joseph. "I would like to use the go-cart. Mr. Cleadhoe will be anxious to see us. Is it ready to go?"

Joseph inspected the certificate. "It's not covered by regulation. In fact—"

"There'll be another twenty for you tomorrow when we return. The Cleadhoes wouldn't like to miss us, and that's more important than regulation."

"You don't work for the Corporation! Nothing is more important than regulation."

"Except life and money."

"True. Well, I hereby forbid you to use the cart. The black handle is throttle, the red handle is brake. The toggle controls switches in the track. The first fork to the left goes north to the observation post at Salmi Swamp. The second fork goes right and down to the breeding wallows of the red apes. The third fork switches off through the feeding meadow and back around to the station: so it's right, left, then either way. Now I'm going home, and I'm not looking back. Still, remember, you've been warned off the premises."

Joseph turned and marched from the shop. Gersen climbed aboard the go-cart. He pushed the black lever; the cart rolled forward. Alice quickly jumped up beside him. Gersen advanced the throttle; the cart rolled away from the station and into the jungle.

Chapter 18

From *Life*, Volume II, by Unspiek, Baron Bodissey:

"Intelligence" demands the most strict of definitions, since the word is easily and often abused. Intelligence rates the quality of Gaean man's competence at altering environment to suit his convenience, or, more generally, the solution of problems. The corollaries to the idea are several. Among them: In the absence of problems, intelligence cannot be measured. A creature with a large, complicated brain is not necessarily intelligent. Raw abstract intelligence is a meaningless concept. Secondly, intelligence is a quality peculiar to Gaean man. Certain alien races use different mechanisms and processes optimally to rearrange their environment. These attributes occasionally resemble human intelligence, and, on the basis of results achieved, the effective organs seem to serve analogous purposes. These similitudes almost always are deceptive and of superficial application. For the lack of a more precise and universal term the temptation to use the word "intelligence" incorrectly is well-nigh irresistible, but can be countenanced only when the word is set off by quotes, viz: my own monograph (which I include in the appendix to Volume Eight of this slight and by no means comprehensive series). Students seriously interested in these matters may well wish to consult the monograph: *A Comparison of Mathematical Processes as Employed by Six "Intelligent" Alien Races.*

The vehicle had been built of odds and ends, scraps and makeshifts. The right-hand stringer was a length of tungsten fiber pipe, while the left-hand stringer was hacked from jungle hardwood. A slab of magnesium hexafoam provided support for the seats, these originally a sofa with orange and blue cushions. The hemispheric windscreen was a reclaimed skylight; the wheels were a stock commissary item, for the repair of wheelbarrows, carts and the like, with a flange welded around the inner circumference. Despite all, the vehicle ran smoothly and quietly, and Blue Forest Camp was left behind.

For the first few miles the track led through a floral tunnel of a hundred colors, permeated by shafts and sifts of afternoon light. Drooping fronds, dead black on top transmitted ruby-red light; other fronds showed gradations of blue, green, yellow. Stalks of black and white tubing moved back and forth, thrusting their round black fronds this way and that for maximum impingement of sunlight. In open places moths floated on many-layered wisps of gossamer, black and crimson and lemon-yellow. Other flying things, golden blurs, darted past in a hiss of air.

The jungle became broken. The tracks led across clearings and meadows dappled with ponds, each with its resident water bull: great mottled creatures with horns and shovel-snouts, which they used to enlarge their ponds. A trestle built of concrete posts and timber laterals took the track across a series of bogs crusted over with pale-blue scum, or alternately a carpet of angry orange stalks supporting spherical spore pods.

Beyond the bogs the ground rose to become a savannah. Rodent-like creatures in carapaces armed with prongs and barbs grazed the turf in bands of twenty or thirty. Often these were attended by ten-foot balt-apes: white-skinned creatures splotched with black fur. Sinuous black printhenes skulked through the meadows on splayed legs. These were voracious, cunning and capable of prodigious feats of savagery; still they avoided the vile-smelling balt-apes.

The track led up a slope and ran across a plain of coarse black and green grass clumped with thorn tree. Bands of spindly ruminants wandered the open areas, nervously alert for printhenes or packs of scalawags: ravening, pounding, yelping creatures half-lizard, half-dog. A dozen kinds of ruminants moved across the savannah, the largest an armored monster twenty feet tall supported on a dozen short legs. In the hazy northern distance a pair of apelike saurians thirty feet tall overlooked the landscape with an eerie semblance of brooding intelligence. A mile to the south a flock of birdlike bipeds fifteen feet tall, scarlet-crested, flaunting bright blue tails, ran after a bewildered myrieapod and hacked it to pieces with beaks and spurs.

The tracks led directly across the plain, diving at half-mile intervals under animal pass-throughs. The electric guards were now paralleled by a second electric fence fifty feet to either side of the track.

The sun hung low in the sky, sweeping the landscape with a halcyon unreal illumination, and the creatures of the land, rather than horrid reality, seemed more the subjects of an imaginary, if macabre, bestiary.

The tracks stretched clear and empty; the feed train had passed from view. Gersen pulled the throttle open; the cart lurched forward at great velocity, jumping, bounding and shivering to irregularities in the track. Gersen reluctantly reduced speed. "I don't want to take this thing into a ditch. It's too heavy to carry out and it's too far to walk."

Mile after mile, and still no sign of the feed train. To right and left spread the savannah. Four double-headed browsers watched from sensors at the ridge of their humps.

A mile ahead the track plunged into a dark forest; at the edge of the shade sunlight glinted for an instant on the housing of the locomotive.

"We're gaining," said Gersen.

"And what do we do when we catch up?" asked Alice.

"We won't catch up." Gersen estimated the distance ahead. "We're only a few minutes behind. Still, I'd like to be a bit closer. Howard won't be able to explain Schahar and Umps; there might be trouble right away, unless he's a very smooth talker."

At the edge of the forest, the tracks wound back and forth to avoid outcrops of rock. Gersen reduced speed, accelerating when the tracks stretched empty ahead.

A post beside the track supported a white triangle; almost at once the track switched, one fork leading to the north, the other continuing directly east—the direction the feed train had taken, by the evidence of the open points.

A mile along the track another fork led to the south; as before the feed train had proceeded east. Gersen became even more vigilant; the feed train could not be far ahead. As before he increased speed along straightaways, cautiously slowing and peering around curves.

Another white triangle appeared beside the track. "The third fork," said Alice. "Station to the right, feed lot to the left."

Gersen braked the cart to a halt. "The feed train has gone left. See the switch points? We'd better follow."

For half a mile the tracks led north through a forest. Gaps in the foliage revealed yet another savannah stretching away to the east. The tracks curved east and slanted down upon the savannah.

Alice pointed. "There's the feed train!"

Gersen braked the cart to a halt. The feed train passed over an unloading device, in an area unprotected by the electric fence. Tuty stopped the locomotive, uncoupled the vat-car and proceeded. A valve in the bottom of the feed car opened, discharging the pulp into a trough.

On the back of the car Schahar and Umps rose to their feet, to stare in dismay after the departing locomotive. Then they turned to examine the creatures which from all directions converged on the feeding trough.

A twenty-foot balt-ape, with head half-bear, half-insect, lurched forward at a shambling trot. Schahar and Umps jumped down and ran toward a tree. The ape caught Umps and lifted him by the leg into the air. Umps kicked out in a frenzy and drove his heel into the creature's proboscis. It threw Umps to the ground, jumped up and down on his torso, pounded the body with its fists. Then it turned away and looked toward Schahar, now perched in the lower branches of the tree, where he attracted the attention of a spider-like reptile which inhabited the upper branches. It dropped a long gray arm which it swung toward Schahar, who yelled in alarm, drew a knife and hacked. When the spider-reptile descended by swift acrobatic swings, Schahar jumped to the ground, dodged to escape the balt-ape, which then pulled at the spider-reptile's tentacle. The spider-reptile jumped from the tree, wrapped itself around the balt-ape's head, flourished high its sting and thrust it home. The balt-ape keened in pain, tore at the tentacles with monstrous arms. The tentacles clutched tighter; the sting struck again. The ape banged the spider-reptile into the tree trunk, again and again, reducing it to pulp, and finally tore it loose. The ape staggered away, gave a convulsive bound and fell into a heap. A band of scavengers, attracted by the outcries, loped forward. Noticing Schahar, they circled him, yelling, jumping, biting, and Schahar presently was pulled down to disappear under a seethe of animals.

Gersen spoke in a rueful voice. "Do you think Tuty knew that those two were riding behind her?"

"I don't care to guess."

The train with Tuty and Howard Treesong had disappeared into the jungle at the far side of the meadow. The feed car now blocked the track. "We've got to go back to the fork," said Gersen. He pulled on levers and toggles. "Where is reverse gear?"

He searched in vain. The throttle controlled forward motion; the brake brought the car to a stop. Gersen jumped to the ground and tried to lift one end of the cart, without success; it carried ballast to hold it to the tracks. He tried to push the cart, but the slope defeated him.

"This is absurd," said Gersen. "There must be a way to go backwards . . . If I had a length of timber I could pry the car off the tracks. But I'm afraid to go into the forest."

"It's getting dark," said Alice. "The sun is going down."

Gersen went to the edge of the track bed and looked into the forest—high, low, right and left. "I don't see anything . . . Here I go."

"Wait," said Alice. "What is this little gadget here?"

Gersen returned to the cart. At the center of the platform a handle turned a worm gear. "Alice, you are an intelligent girl. That is a jack, which lifts the cart high enough so that we can swivel it around, end for end."

Alice said modestly, "I thought that perhaps I might be helpful, or even indispensable."

Five minutes later they returned the way they had come, to

the third switch, and now they turned east, and drove at full speed through the twilight.

A mile, two miles, five miles . . . The forest abruptly became a soggy moor. Ahead the sunset glimmered on a wide loop of river. The track led across a bridge of metal bars, evidently electrified to inhibit the creatures of the bog.

Inside the compound the track led past a commissary store, a dispensary and a row of six small cottages. A few yards farther stood the laboratory, which overlooked the swamp and, beyond, Gorgon River.

The track branched into a siding. Gersen coasted up behind the locomotive and stopped. For a moment the two sat listening.

Silence.

At Blue Forest Camp Howard Treesong said in a voice of jovial camaraderie: "The passenger compartment? Nonsense, I'll ride up forward with you!"

"A pity, but it can't be done," said Tuty. "Suppose Superintendent Kennifer should happen by? You sit in the back and crouch till we're in the jungle. Then relax and enjoy the ride. Watch for marshmallow moths and water flowers."

Treesong climbed into the compartment behind the driver's cupola and made himself inconspicuous. The train moved away from the terminal. If, from the corner of her wide-set eyes, Tuty had noticed Schahar and Umps as they clambered aboard the swill car, she gave no sign.

Through jungle, across savannah, in and out of the dark forest, rolled the feed train. At the third switch, Tuty swung north and out upon the feed meadow, which was rarely used except when biologists intended experiments. But tonight Tuty had decided to feed the animals. Almost without halting the train she detached the feed car. Howard Treesong jumped to his feet in the back compartment and stared out the rear window. Tuty Cleadhoe never so much as looked over her shoulder. Howard Treesong, shoulders sagging and ashen of face, sank once more into his seat.

The train trundled into the station, rolled across the compound and halted beside the laboratory.

Tuty climbed to the ground, grunting and wheezing. Howard Treesong alighted from the passenger compartment and stood looking around the compound.

Tuty called out in a brassy voice: "So then, Howard! How did you find our lovely countryside?"

"It's not at all like dear old Gladbetook. Still, it's quite picturesque."

"True. Well then, let's find if Mr. Cleadhoe is expecting us with a nice supper. I do hope he's put out his pets. He's a wonder with animals, is Mr. Cleadhoe. Come along, Howard, the night bugs will be after us in another minute."

Tuty led the way to the laboratory. She slid back the door. "Otho, we're here! Make sure Ditsy is out. Howard won't care to be annoyed by any of your charmers. Otho? Are you about?"

A gruff voice said: "Tush, woman, of course I'm about. Come in . . . So this is young Howard Hardoah."

"Isn't he changed? You'd never recognize him!"

"That's a fact." Otho Cleadhoe stepped forward on long thin legs, standing six inches taller than Howard Treesong. Cleadhoe's great head was bald on top, harsh and craggy, with an untidy tonsure of gray hair, a stained gray beard and eyes in deep lavender sockets. He fixed Howard Treesong with a long stare of impersonal appraisal. Howard ignored the inspection and looked around the room. "And this is your laboratory? I'm told that you're now an important scientist."

"Ha, not altogether. I'm still a practitioner of my old trade, but now both my subjects and my methods are different. Come along, I'll show you some of my work while Mrs. Cleadhoe puts out our soup."

Tuty called out in a voice of brassy jocularity: "Ten minutes, then, and no more! You've all evening to show off your trophies!"

"Ten minutes, my dear. Come, Howard . . . Through here, and watch your head. These arches weren't built for tall men. Let me take your hat."

"I'll wear it, if I may," said Treesong. "I am very sensitive to draughts."

"A pity . . . Well then, along this route we take Tanaquil dignitaries who come to learn how we spend the public money. I might add that they never leave dissatisfied. This is the Chamber of Astinches."

Howard Treesong inspected the room with his eyes heavy-lidded. Otho Cleadhoe, if he noticed Treesong's unenthusiastic manner, paid no heed. "These are all varieties of astinche, the Bethune andromorphs, a local evolutionary development.

The genus is especially rich on Shanar and in this particular neighborhood. They vary in size up to the thirty-foot giant you see there." He indicated an alcove. "I processed the creature almost single-handed, with trifling help from my staff. I worked in an atmosphere of argon, under germicidal conditions. I skinned the beast, marmelized the soft tissues, reinforced the skeletal frame and refitted the pelt."

"Remarkable," said Treesong. "A fine piece of work."

"They are amazing creatures, agile for their size. We often see them capering across the distance . . . These others over here are its cousins, or so we believe. Do you know, there are still mysteries regarding these creatures? How they breed, how they develop, how they order their body chemistry? All mysteries! But I won't bore you with technical details. As you see, they come in every size, every color. 'Intelligence'? Who knows? Some are clever, some—"

A blur of motion, a cry of annoyance from Howard Treesong, as down from one of the alcoves jumped a creature eight feet tall with thin arms and legs, to snatch Treesong's hat and bound from the room.

Otho Cleadhoe laughed a croak of indulgent amusement. "Clever: yes. Mischievous: yes. Intelligent? Who knows? That is Ditsy, who is full of tricks. I'm afraid your hat is gone. I'll have to replace it."

Howard Treesong ran to the door and peered through. "What's got into the beast? It put my hat in the fire!"

"It's a pity, for certain. I can't apologize enough. Ditsy, outside! What can you mean, acting in such a way? He's destroyed your fine hat. If your head becomes cold, please say so. Tuty can provide a hood, or a shawl."

"No great matter."

"Ditsy must be punished, and I will see to it. The creature is attracted to bright colors and makes a mischief with guests. Perhaps I should have warned you."

"No matter. I have a dozen hats."

"None other so splendid, I'll warrant! Well, it's a pity . . . Through here now. We leave the Chamber of Astinches for the Hall of Swamp-Walkers."

Howard Treesong showed only a cursory interest in the twenty purple and black creatures with their odd cloaks of woven vegetation. "A very representative collection," said Otho Cleadhoe. "They are found only along the Gorgon

River . . . Now to the Den of Horrors, as I call my workshop. It never fails to impress."

Cleadhoe led the now bored and languid Howard Treesong into a room illuminated by a high glass cupola. A central platform supported a massive red and black creature with six legs and a ferocious head.

"An awesome beast," said Treesong.

"Quite so. And an awesome project—the largest of my experience. Yonder is my office—a dismal sort of place, but the Corporation won't spare me anything better. Your little book is there and we'll pick it up presently."

"Why not now?" suggested Treesong. "Since it's close at hand?"

"As you like. It's on my desk, if you care to fetch it. Now then, I wonder! Do you think that here and there the hide tends to sag across the haunches?"

Howard Treesong had gone to the side chamber. On the desk lay a small red volume inscribed *The Book of Dreams*. Treesong stepped forward; the door closed behind him. Out in the workshop Otho Cleadhoe turned a valve, waited fifteen seconds, then turned it off. Tuty Cleadhoe looked into the workshop. "The soup is ready. Do you care to eat?"

"I'll be busy," said Cleadhoe. "I don't care to eat."

Chapter 19

Navarth sat drinking wine with an aged acquaintance who bemoaned the brevity of existence. "I have left to me at the most ten years of life!"

"That is sheer pessimism," declared Navarth. "Think optimistically, rather, of the ten hundred billion years of death that await you!"

—from *Chronicles of Navarth*, by Carol Lewis

Navarth despised latter-day poetry, save only those verses composed by himself. "These are faded times. Wisdom and innocence once were allied, and noble songs were sung. I recall a couplet, by no means sublime—quaint, rather—succinct, yet reverberating a thousand meanings:

A farting horse will never tire.
A farting man's the man to hire.

Where is the like today?

—from *Chronicles of Navarth* by Carol Lewis

Gersen and Alice went quickly through the dark to the laboratory. The night was warm, clear and dark, illuminated by thousands of lambent stars. From the swamp and the jungle came sounds: a far strident howl and, uncomfortably near, a grunting bellow of rage.

Light shone from a window; Gersen and Alice watched Tuty Cleadhoe moving around in the kitchen. She sliced bread, sausage and ramp; she stirred the contents of a kettle and set out implements at a table.

Gersen muttered: "For two? Who won't be taking supper?"

"She seems quite placid," whispered Alice. "Perhaps we can just knock on the door and ask if we're in time for supper."

"That's as good a plan as any." Gersen tried the door latch, then knocked. In the kitchen Tuty stiffened, then darted to a sideboard, tucked a weapon into her pocket. She went to a communicator, spoke, heard a few guttural words, then turned, marched to the front door and threw it open, her hand close to her gun.

"Hello, Mrs. Cleadhoe," said Gersen. "Are we too late for the party?"

Tuty Cleadhoe stared grimly from one to the other. "Why did you not stay where I left you? Are you impervious to reason? Can you not understand when your presence is unwanted?"

"All this to the side, Mrs. Cleadhoe, you failed to honor our agreement."

Tuty Cleadhoe showed a small quick smile. "Perhaps I did; what then? You'd have done the same to me, had you fixed on it." She looked over her shoulder. "Come in then. Wrangle with Mr. Cleadhoe if you like."

She led them into the kitchen. Otho Cleadhoe stood at the sink, carefully washing his hands. He swung around and surveyed Gersen and Alice from the depths of his lavender eyesockets. "Visitors, eh? Tonight I'm busy or I'd show you around."

"That's not why we're here. Where is Howard Treesong?"

Cleadhoe jerked his thumb. "Back yonder. He's safe. And now I'll want my supper. Will you eat?"

"Sit down," said Tuty, with automatic if graceless hospitality. "There's enough for all."

"Eat," said Cleadhoe in a cavernous bass voice. "We will

talk of Howard Hardoah. Did you know he killed our Nymphotis?"

Gersen and Alice seated themselves at the table. "He's killed many people," said Gersen.

"What would you have done with him? Killed him in return?"

"Yes."

Cleadhoe nodded ponderously. "Well, you shall have your chance. I took him into a still room and turned gas on him. He'll be awake in about six hours."

"So you haven't killed him?"

"Oh no." Cleadhoe's smile broke a pink gap through the beard. "Life is awareness and Howard Hardoah should become more broadly aware. Perhaps in time he will repent his crimes."

"Possibly so," said Gersen. "Still, you have not kept good faith with us."

Cleadhoe glanced at him uncomprehendingly, then resumed his chewing. "Perhaps in our emotion we acted less than politely. But postpone your annoyance. You shall take part in the ultimate judgment."

Tuty cried out: "And don't forget, we guarded you from harm! Howard brought two of his murderers with him. Ha, but they will murder no more!"

Otho Cleadhoe smiled approvingly, as if Tuty had been describing the recipe for her soup. He said, "Howard is crafty! Imagine this: he carried a weapon in his hat! I instructed Ditsy to snatch away the hat and destroy it. As Mrs. Cleadhoe says, we have done our share in the work."

Neither Gersen nor Alice had any comment to offer.

"In about six hours Howard will recover his faculties," said Cleadhoe. "In the meantime, you may rest, or sleep, or examine the collections, or you may sit comfortably, drink tea, or brandy, and tell us of the harms you have suffered from Howard Hardoah."

Gersen looked at Alice. "What of you?"

"I can't sleep. Mr. and Mrs. Cleadhoe might like to hear of the school reunion at Gladbetook."

"Aye, that we would indeed."

At midnight Otho Cleadhoe left the kitchen. Twenty minutes later he returned. "Howard is returning to consciousness. If you like, you can come."

The group filed through the laboratory, and along a corridor. Cleadhoe halted beside a door. "Listen! He speaks."

Through a mesh came the sounds of a colloquy.

First came Howard Treesong's voice, clear and strong, but puzzled and fretful: "—an impasse, like a wall; I can neither advance nor retire, nor yet sidle away . . . The sunrise is here. We are lost in the jungle. Take care, let none stray aside. Paladins? Who hears my voice?"

The responses came quickly; the voices almost seemed to overlap, as if several spoke together.

"Mewness stands by your side." This, a calm, clear voice, precise and without passion.

"Spangleway here, among the apes."

"Rhune Fader the Blue, and Hohenger and Black Jeha Rais: all are here."

A thin, cool voice spoke. "Eia Panice is here."

"And Immir?"

"I am here till the end."

"Immir, you are steadfast, like all the rest. Now, to set a wise strategy. Jeha Rais, you are grave."

The deep voice of Jeha Rais, the black paladin sounded: "I am grave and more than grave. After these mighty years did you not recognize him?"

Immir: (troubled)
> He called himself Cleadhoe of Dandelion Farm.

Jeha Rais:
> He is the Dree.

A few seconds of silence.

Immir: (Softly)
> Then we are in desperate condition.

Rhune Fader:
> We have known desperate times before. Remember the course at Ilkhad? It was enough to daunt the Iron Giant, yet we won through.

Spangleway:
> I recall the ambush in Massilia Old Town. A dreadful hour!

Immir:
> Brothers, let us fix our thoughts on this moment only.

Jeha Rais:
> The Dree is a brute of malevolence. To shift his

force we need counterforce. Can we offer wealth?
Immir:
 I will open our treasury. He can own Sybaris, for
all of me.
Mewness:
 It will not tempt the Dree.
Loris Hohenger:
 Offer a dozen maidens, each more beautiful than
the last. Let them wear gowns of sheer diaphane
and regard him with gazes neither gay nor grave, as
if they asked, "Who is this marvel? Who is this
demigod?"
Immir: (laughing sadly)
 Good Hohenger, the concept moves you! I sus-
pect that you would throw your brother paladins
into Lake Chill to take part in such a parade.
Mewness:
 Not the Dree.
Spangleway:
 Wealth, beauty—what is left?
Rhune Fader:
 If only we had Valkaris's Cup and eternal youth!
Immir: (In a mutter)
 Complications, complexities. I sense a devilish
plot.
Rhune Fader:
 Silence all! Someone stands outside the door!

Cleadhoe spoke in a whisper: "He is half-awake; he talks
as if he were dreaming . . ." He slid back the door. "Enter."
 Half the room was bare and dim; the other half had been
planted and worked to simulate a jungle glade. Light slanted
down through a hundred sorts of foliage. On gnarled tendrils
hung flowers, bug-catchers and spore pods. A stream passed
through rocks, forming a small pool, which drained through
dark-red reeds into an unseen outlet. Beside the pool, in an
armchair, sat Howard Alan Treesong, nude except for a short
skirt around his hips. His hands rested on the arms of the
chair; his legs, which were stark and glossy white, rested on
the turf. His head had been shaved bald. Across the pool on
a bank of turf reclined the marmel of Nymphotis. In the
bushes moved a half-dozen small astinches, with faces formed
of mottled red and blue cartilage, crests like small black hats

and glossy black pelts. The presence of Howard Treesong interested them; they watched and listened with respectful attention.

The colloquy had ended; Howard's eyes glinted under half-closed lids; his breathing seemed normal.

Cleadhoe spoke to Gersen and Alice. "This originally was a display cage for the little astinches. They are called 'puppet mandarins,' and are strange little creatures. Don't go too close; there is a mesh of invisible pin-rays which will sting you. It seemed a fine place to maintain Howard."

"You have marmelized his legs."

"Quite so. He is immobile, and he must gaze at Nymphotis whom he murdered. This is our judgment upon him. Whatever additional punishment you or Alice Wroke wish to apply, I shall not object. It is your right."

Gersen asked, "How long will he live like this?"

Cleadhoe shook his head. "That is hard to predict. His natural functions continue but he is immovably anchored. His hair, incidentally, concealed a mesh of circuitry. There are no implants or internal weapons; I have made sure of this!"

Treesong's eyes were open. He looked down at his legs, moved his hands, felt the cool material which now composed the sheathing of his upper thighs.

Cleadhoe spoke: "Howard Alan Treesong, we, from among all your numberless victims, are now working retribution upon you."

Tuty cried out in a rich contralto: "There he is, our son Nymphotis, and there sit you, Howard Hardoah, his murderer. Reflect upon your evil deed."

Howard Treesong spoke in an even voice: "I have been well and truly trapped. And who are these other two? Alice Wroke? What brings you here among these zealots?"

"I am one of them. Do you not remember what you asked of me, to save the life of my father? When you already had taken his life?"

"My dear Alice, when one deals in high policy, one sometimes overlooks nice details. Your father's death and your services were both elements in a larger design. And you, sir? Your semblance is disturbingly familiar."

"It should be. You have met me several times. Both at Voymont and at Gladbetook I had the pleasure of shooting you, unfortunately not to serious effect. You also know me as Henry Lucas, of *Extant*. I am responsible for enticing you here through your *Book of Dreams*. But let me take your memory even farther back. Do you recall the raid on Mount Pleasant?"

"I remember the episode, yes. It was a remarkable exercise."

"I saw you for the first time on that occasion, and I have devoted my life to arranging this confrontation."

"Indeed? You are a fanatic."

"You have the faculty for creating fanatics."

Howard Treesong made an easy gesture. "So now I am at your mercy. How will you deal with me?"

Gersen laughed sourly. "What more could I do to you?"

"Well—there is always torture. Or you might take pleasure in killing me."

"I have destroyed you as a man. That is enough."

Howard Alan Treesong's head drooped. "My life has run its course. I intended to rule the human universe. I would have been first Emperor of the Gaean Worlds. I almost did so. Now I am tired. I cannot move and I will not live long ... Leave me now. I prefer to be alone."

Gersen turned and, taking Alice's arm, left the room. The Cleadhoes followed. The door closed. Almost at once the colloquy began:

Immir:

Now all is known. The Dree has done a terrible deed. Oh my paladins, what now? What say you, Jeha Rais?

Rais:

The time has come.

Immir::

How so? Green Mewness, why do you turn away?

Mewness:

There are long roads yet to be traveled and many an inn where I would take refuge.

Immir:

Why do you all look this way and that? Are we not all brothers and paladins? Jeha Rais, make for us a great strategy, to move these marmel legs.

Spangleway:

Immir, I bid you farewell.

Rais:

Farewell, Immir. The time has come.

Immir:

Loris Hohenger, are you deserting me too?

Hohenger:

I must be away, to far places and new battles.

Immir:

And sweet Blue Fader, what of you? And you,
Eia Panice?

Panice:

I will do my brotherly best for you. Paladins,
turn back! A single deed remains to be done. Farewell, noble Immir! And now ...

In the corridor the four heard a thud, a splash. Cleadhoe
ran to the door, threw it aside. The great chair had toppled;
Howard Alan Treesong lay in a grotesque heap, face down in
the pool.

Cleadhoe turned, his nostrils flaring, his eyes a-glitter. He
made a wild gesticulation. "The chair was solidly fixed! He
could not have toppled it alone!"

Gersen turned away. "Whatever has happened, it is enough
for me." He took Alice's arm. "Let's go somewhere else."

Chapter 20

In the *Flitterwing* and traveling space, Alice picked up *The Book of Dreams,* then at once put it down again. "What will you do with it?"

"I don't know . . . Give it to *Cosmopolis,* I suppose."

"Why not just put it out into space?"

"I can't do that."

Alice put her hands on his shoulder. "And now, what of you?"

"What of me, how?"

"You're so quiet and subdued! You worry me. Are you well?"

"Quite well. Deflated, perhaps. I have been deserted by my enemies. Treesong is dead. The affair is over. I am done."

DAW BOOKS

Presenting JACK VANCE in DAW editions:

Presenting C. J. CHERRYH

☐ **SERPENT'S REACH.** Two races lived in harmony in a quarantined constellation—until one person broke the truce!
(#UE1554—$2.25)

☐ **FIRES OF AZEROTH.** Armageddon at the last gate of three worlds.
(#UJ1466—$1.95)

☐ **GATE OF IVREL.** "Never since reading *Lord of the Rings* have I been so caught up in any tale . . ."—Andre Norton.
(#UE1615—$1.75)

☐ **HUNTER OF WORLDS.** Triple fetters of the mind served to keep their human prey in bondage to this city-sized starship.
(#UE1559—$2.25)

☐ **BROTHERS OF EARTH:** This in-depth novel of an alien world and a human who had to adjust or die was a Science Fiction Book Club Selection.
(#UJ1470—$1.95)

☐ **THE FADED SUN: KESRITH.** Universal praise for this novel of the last members of humanity's warrior-enemies . . . and the Earthman who was fated to save them.
(#UE1600—$2.25)

☐ **THE FADED SUN: SHON'JIR.** Across the untracked stars to the forgotten world of the Mri go the last of that warrior race and the man who had bertayed humanity.
(#UJ1453—$1.95)

☐ **THE FADED SUN: KUTATH.** The final and dramatic conclusion of this bestselling trilogy—with three worlds in militant confrontation.
(#UE1516—$2.25)

☐ **HESTIA.** A single engineer faces the terrors and problems of an endangered colony planet.
(#UJ1488—$1.95)

To order these titles,

use coupon on the

last page of this book.

DAW BOOKS

Outstanding science fiction and fantasy

- [ ] IRONCASTLE by Philip Jose Farmer & J. Rosny.
  (#UJ1545—$1.95)
- [ ] TACTICS OF MISTAKE by Gordon R. Dickson.
  (#UJ1534—$1.95)
- [ ] ROGUE SHIP by A. E. van Vogt.   (#UJ1536—$1.95)
- [ ] THE GARMENTS OF CAEAN by Barrington Bayley.
  (#UJ1519—$1.95)
- [ ] THE BRIGHT COMPANION by Edward Llewellyn.
  (#UE1511—$1.75)
- [ ] STAR HUNTERS by Jo Clayton.   (#UE1550—$1.75)
- [ ] LOST WORLDS by Lin Carter.   (#UJ1556—$1.95)
- [ ] STAR WINDS by Barrington J. Bayley.   (#UE1384—$1.75)
- [ ] THE SPINNER by Doris Piserchia.   (#UJ1548—$1.95)
- [ ] A WIZARD IN BEDLAM by Christopher Stasheff.
  (#UJ1551—$1.95)
- [ ] ANCIENT, MY ENEMY by Gordon R. Dickson.
  (#UE1552—$1.75)
- [ ] OPTIMAN by Brian M. Stableford.   (#UJ1571—$1.95)
- [ ] VOLKHAVAAR by Tanith Lee.   (#UE1539—$1.75)
- [ ] THE GREEN GODS by Henneberg & Cherryh.
  (#UE1538—$1.75)
- [ ] LOST: FIFTY SUNS by A. E. van Vogt.   (#UE1491—$1.75)
- [ ] THE MAN WITH A THOUSAND NAMES by A. E. van Vogt.
  (#UE1502—$1.75)
- [ ] THE DOUGLAS CONVOLUTION by Edward Llewellyn.
  (#UE1495—$1.75)
- [ ] THE AVENGERS OF CARRIG by John Brunner.
  (#UE1509—$1.75)
- [ ] THE SECOND WAR OF THE WORLDS by George H. Smith.
  (#UE1512—$1.75)

To order these titles,

use coupon on the

last page of this book.

DRAY PRESCOT

The great novels of Kregen, world of Antares

Fully illustrated

If you wish to order these titles,

please use coupon on the

last page of this book.